You Can Hear the Ice Cracking

You Can Hear the Ice Cracking

a Novel

Robert Lefever

Book 1: Precious

c 2015

Published by RL Books, a trading name of Doctor Robert
Limited, 58a Old Brompton Road, South Kensington,
London SW7 3DY, UK
Registered number 7852730

First Published in 2015

10 9 8 7 6 5 4 3 2 1

Text Dr Robert Lefever 2015

A CIP catalogue record for this book is available
from the British Library.

ISBN: 978-1-871013-96-2 (cased)
978-1-871013-95-5 (tpb)

Cover design by Paul Maley
Typeset in 10.25/14pt Versailles by Falcon Oast Graphic Art Ltd.

Acknowledgements

Gisela Stuart, in a conversation, inadvertently gave me the title. Ian Gregory, in another, set me on a fertile path. Esther Freud enthused me with her own writing, her guidance and encouragement.

Doctors advised me. Professor Oscar D'Agnone, Dr Oliver Foster, Mr John Grindle, Dr Jonathan Boreham, Dr Charles Alessi, Dr Anu Jain, Dr David Lomax and Dr Sam Barclay were generous with their time and expertise.

My brother Andrew, a lawyer, corrected me and advised me.

Friends guided me. Dan Donovan, Jonathan Prime, Titus Searle, Gail Thompson, John Graham and Robert Batt gently pushed me back into line.

Errors that persist are mine and mine alone.

Paul Maley's genius for illustration and Pouya Hosseinpour – and his remarkable gang at Nocturnal Cloud – helped to turn my literary dreaming into physical reality.

To all these lovely people I owe a huge debt of gratitude.

To my wife, Pat, I owe my life and my inspiration and my particular thanks for her patient editing skills.

Disclaimer

You Can Hear the Ice Cracking is a work of fiction. All characters and events portrayed in this book come solely from the imagination of the author. Any resemblance to real people, living or dead, or to any actual happenings in the past or present, are entirely coincidental.

to Simon and Diana
Graeme and Avril
Jeffrey and Aline

with love

Part 1

If the state takes over ultimate
health care responsibility from the
individual . . .

'If you listen carefully, you can hear the ice cracking . . . underneath your society and everything you stand for. – The whole facade's falling through.'

'You mean "edifice".'

'You bloody pedant! You know exactly what I mean . . . You were just the same when I was at school. – Always correcting my fucking "mistakes".'

'Phoebe, dear Phoebe . . . They didn't teach you to speak like that at school. Your father and I chose a good place for you. – We paid a lot of money for your education. – But you seem determined to throw it all away.'

'I'm ashamed of it – and ashamed of you.'

'So much is apparent.'

'I'm glad of just one thing . . . Being a doctor . . . in due course . . . umm . . . my kind of doctor – not like you and your type – means I can help people who really need help. I won't be a pathetic parasite like you . . . Aaaargh! You make me so angry.'

'Nobody makes you angry, Phoebe. You choose to be angry. The problem is your weird values . . . Change your values and you won't be angry.'

'You always have a clever clever answer for everything . . . Haven't you?'

'No I don't . . . I've simply no idea how to get through to you how much I love you – and respect your independent mind. – But I so disagree with your ideas.'

'You don't even know my ideas. – You don't understand my world at all. – You're still stuck in the '60s . . . and the sad thing is you do remember them.'

'Hang on, hang on . . . We're not that old. That was my parents' generation. Your father and I were born in the 60s – not that you ever acknowledge our birthdays – but we grew up in the 70s and 80s. We weren't into drug-fuelled empty-headed idealism . . . That'd lost its attraction – for most of us – by our time.'

'Forget it, Mum . . . just forget it. I don't want to go down your Memory Lane. I've had enough of your stories about how hard you and Dad worked to put me through school . . . I wish you hadn't. I'm stuck with this posh accent – I'll change it . . . if I can. – And I feel guilty about being "privileged". – It revolts me.'

'Your mind comes from our genes, our payment of your school fees – and our reading with you before you ever went to school . . . We set you off in the right direction.'

'Right direction? Right? – You fucking fascist!'

'Phoebe, dear Phoebe. Do please try to vary your use of the Queen's English. Give us a little something for our money.'

'We'll get rid of the Queen – and all that crap.'

'Yes, yes . . . umm . . . and replace her with what?'

'Real people having real power.'

'We've got that already. – My patients pay me if I give a good service and they don't if I don't.'

'Poor people have no choice.'

'Now it's you who's stuck in a time warp. – Thanks to Marx and your friends we have our Welfare State . . . which doesn't work.'

'Don't forget it was our Welfare State that paid for your training . . . and then you – you – turned your back on it to feather your own nest.'

Part 1

'Do you hate me for earning my own living? And paying my own way? I don't like paying my taxes to a wasteful state . . . I develop clinical ideas to benefit everyone.'

'Private practice is evil. As a doctor, you should feel that in your bones.'

'What I see is this . . . For all its good intentions – and the absolutely vast amount of money shovelled into it – the NHS and our whole Welfare State, as I said, simply doesn't work.'

'Well you would say that, wouldn't you? . . . You were educated – for free – by the state . . . Now you repay that generosity by making profits from the sick.'

* * *

'Father, I'm a bit short at the moment. Could I touch you for a couple of quid?'

'You haven't paid back the £2,000 I lent you last month, James. How much is "a couple of quid" this time?'

'Well, if we roll in the two grand from last time, I could do with five altogether.'

'What on earth have you been spending it on? You live rent free in the top flat of our investment property. That's rental income we don't get – as we do from all the other flats.'

'Yes I know, I know . . . You tell me every time.'

'There wouldn't be an "every time" if you paid your own way and kept your spending in check . . . Surely commodity brokering pays you well enough? That's why you went into that shady line of business – for the "filthy lucre", as your sister calls it. Wasn't it?'

'Please leave Phoebe out of it, father. Why d'you drag her into every conversation we have? I'm my own man.'

'I wish you were.'

'Ouch! That's a bit rough when I'm doing my best to be independent.'

'Yes, I suppose it was a bit of an Aunt Emma, as we say in croquet.'

'What's that?'

'Being more concerned with preventing your opponent from making progress than focusing on your own game . . . And I apologise for mentioning Phoebe . . . Go on then . . . I'm busy now – I really haven't got time to discuss things. – I'm working on a case with a great deal of money involved . . . umm . . . Here's your cheque . . . umm . . . Do try to sort yourself out and be just a bit more responsible, James. You're still young at 21 – but you've got to grow up some time.'

'Yes, father. Thank you, father.'

* * *

'Christ, Nate, you really can thrust for Jamaica! I doubt my mother, even with all her experience of gynaecology – and knowing how women function – ever got it like that.'

'She must'a goddit sum taeme, man – or ther'd be no Phoebe an' Jimmie.'

'S'pose not – but I don't like to think about it. – Sex should be banned in old people.'

'You wone say dat when yore her age.'

'I'll never be her age. I'll jump before then.'

'Ya jumped pretty gud jus' na.'

'I mean I'll jump off a cliff before I get too old to have it away.'

'Nah, man, dat's never gonna happen. 'Twad be a waste of gud pussy.'

* * *

14

'Roddy?'

'Hmm?

'Wake up! I'm talking to you.'

'Sorry, Lizzie my love. You know I tend to fall asleep as soon as I sit down after a meal – even after lunch at the Garrick.'

'What d'you mean "even"? . . . Are your lawyer and doctor friends better conversationalists than your wife?'

'I didn't mean it that way. I meant . . . umm . . . Hmm. – And the Garrick's got actors, of course, and singers and politicians and diplomats and journalists and all sorts of interesting people from all walks of life.'

'But no women . . .'

'Well, umm . . . not yet.'

'Not ever, if you and your cronies in the snug have your misogynistic way.'

'Ha! You sound just like Phoebe.'

'Glory! That's a fate worse than death . . . I had the full treatment from her at lunchtime today – on the evils of private practice. She popped in to see me in Harley Street. I was surprised she didn't come in disguise.'

'Why so?'

'Come on, Roddy. Wake up, will you? – Harley Street, idiot. The Mecca of private medicine.'

'It certainly looked like Mecca last time I was there.'

'That's as maybe. It's good honest toil – and we bring in foreign exchange from all over the world, the same as you do at the commercial bar when you're fighting international cases.'

'Yes, yes . . . umm . . . Is this what you woke me up for? – To tell me what I already know? You're like a judge spelling things out to a jury so there won't be confusion . . . resulting in troublesome appeals.'

'That's exactly what I do feel like sometimes – without meaning to be like that – when I'm talking with Phoebe. She's so rigid in her attitudes . . . If I had horns and a tail, she'd think the costume department hadn't gone far enough.'

'Think yourself lucky. I had James, getting another three grand out of me. He knows full well – from my clerk – when I'm busy. So he times his appearances perfectly to catch me off guard . . . And what did Phoebe come to see you for – apart from giving you the statutory political lecture?'

'The next three months' rent. – What else would you imagine?'

'Is that really what you woke me up to tell me?'

'Well, yes . . . She's working hard for her finals – so that's something to be grateful for – but I have to say I'm not thrilled with that "lover" of hers – or "partner" as she insists on calling him – and we seem to be keeping him in house and home as well as her . . . I don't know what to do for the best.'

'The same as for James, I imagine . . . We've got the same two functions as all parents – to love and to pay.'

* * *

'My name is Precious Ellington. Yeah, I guess it's a funky name for a guy . . . As they say in the jazz world I come from, "funky" means it has an earthy, blues-based quality like a rough diamond . . . It's the name my mother – a single mother – gave me . . . People tell me it's a woman's name but I answer to it with pride and with love for her, God rest her soul . . .

'I was born and raised in Harlem, New York. Our home was just near the Cotton Club. – That's where Duke Ellington made his name with his band . . . I'm no relation . . . I wish I were. – He's one of the great African Americans. He said, "Music is how I live, why I live and how I'll be remembered". He was right . . . Well healthcare is how I live, why I live and how I hope to be remembered . . .

16

Part 1

'I studied Medicine at Columbia University in Harlem and I did my clinical training in 168th Street Medical School and the Milstein building nearby. It's part of the Presbyterian Hospital in downtown New York, where I also trained. That's a not-for-profit 2,478 bed hospital – one of the largest and most comprehensive hospitals in the United States . . .

'I'm now on the staff of the Public Health faculty in Columbia – so I'm here to learn as well as teach . . .

'As you all know, we in the United States have recently set up a public health insurance system, known as ObamaCare. You in the UK have had a national health treatment service – the NHS – for over 60 years. You students were born into a state system of healthcare. You know – from the inside – how it works . . .

'I'm here to give a course of lectures and seminars on health-care systems, looking at ideas that've been tried and tested throughout the world. But I recognise that I'm in a country where socialised medicine took root many decades ago. I feel a great sense of privilege to be here with you . . .

'In the coming semesters – Aaargh! . . . I believe you say, "terms" . . . I'll have a lot to learn from you as we discuss the most significant medical challenge of all . . . how we get healthcare to the people who need it most of all and who can least afford to pay for it.'

Phoebe was entranced . . . I like this guy . . . I like him a lot . . .

'So what d'you believe happens when the state takes over – from the individual – the ultimate responsibility for healthcare? D'you have any ideas on that? – Not dreamy pie-in-the-sky ideas but the real nitty gritty . . .

Silence.

'. . . Come on. There must be over 200 of you here . . . Someone must have some idea . . .

17

Silence.

'Yes . . . It's difficult being put on the spot . . . Isn't it? – We take so much for granted . . . and we're so used to complaining when things go wrong. – We get out of the habit of starting with a blank sheet of paper and writing down our ideas . . .

'We get so tied up with the process that we forget to look at the outcome and see that it inevitably follows from the ideas that we had at the start . . .

'We imagine that any failure in a state healthcare system must come from a lack of sufficient funding. Or a failure in administration. – But, if the ideas are inadequate, then the funding will be inadequate and the administration will be inadequate . . .

Shuffles.

'Let me put it to you – on the issue of funding – that it's possible to run a state healthcare system on any budget whatever . . .

Mumbles.

'. . . provided we define what we're *not* going to do . . .

More mumbles.

'. . . For example, in a relatively primitive society our first priority might be to separate the water supply from the drainage . . . We might want to build hospitals but, if we did, our good work would be undone by the lack of commitment to basic issues of public health . . .

Silence except for a few shuffles.

'. . . Public health measures tend to be the Cinderella services. – Nobody pays any attention to them. – But they're absolutely vital . . . The major clinical advances in the twentieth century didn't come from the development of anaesthesia and consequent improvement in surgical techniques . . . Or from the discovery of antibiotics, which enabled us to cure deadly infections . . . They came from clean water, effective drainage, immunisation programmes, clean air, central heating and health and safety measures at home and at work . . .

More shuffles.

'That's right. The points I've just made are not comfortable – particularly for the cream of medical students, in their last year before qualification as doctors . . . Your minds will tend to be focussed on the miracles of modern science and the exciting prospects for the future . . .

Silence.

'But you'll ignore issues of public health at your patients' peril . . .

Lots of shuffles and mutterings.

'I put it to you again that it's possible to fund a state health-care system on any budget whatever – provided we define what we can't afford to offer . . . We might want to give universal access to MRI scans for patients with headaches. – That's an admirable goal on its own in isolation. – But maybe it's not so admirable for the entire community if it means we can't afford to treat breast cancer . . .

Mutterings.

'. . . All I'm asking you today is to consider my basic question, rather than get caught up with specifics. – My point is that no healthcare system anywhere in the world has an infinite budget . . . Politicians and doctors, and other health-care professionals, have to make choices. Then we have to explain them to journalists and the public . . . Then we have to duck when unpleasant things are thrown at us . . .

Nervous laughter.

'Yes, that's right. These issues are very uncomfortable and very unpopular – but we can't avoid them . . . even though most politicians in the UK and Europe will tell you that they'd never get elected on a promise to give people less of something – a treatment or a service that they're used to getting . . . or hope to get in the future . . . People always want *more* . . .

Nervous laughter again.

'. . . But for you and me there's no place to hide. We're in the front line. We're the ones who have to say, "Yes we can". – Have you heard that statement anywhere before? – Or, with a greater awareness of reality, "No we can't".'

Three students got up and walked out.

'Aha . . . Only three . . . That's very good . . .

Nervous laughter yet again.

'. . . Today, in considering specific issues of public health, I've looked at very real benefits that come as a result of the state taking over ultimate responsibility from the individual. In two weeks time – in the lecture after next – we'll look at some of the disadvantages . . .

'Ladies and gentlemen, I look forward to working with you.'

oOo

'I find it difficult, my love, to see where we've gone wrong.'

'I don't know that we have, Lizzie. We're well established professionally and, I must say, living in central London is what life's all about . . . The children'll sort themselves out eventually and we're all healthy – so far, thank God.'

'Who?'

'Umm, whoever . . . and we have a lot of fun . . . We've worked hard all our lives, starting from nothing – both of us – but we're very privileged now.'

'Yes, that's exactly my point. We're treated as toffs even when we're not.'

'Who by?'

'*Guardian* readers.'

'Who gives a damn about them? – or people who believe *The Independent* really is independent? or that the BBC gives a balanced view?'

'I do.'

'Why?'

'Because there's a lot of them and they're getting progressively more power.'

'No they aren't . . . They're simply making more noise . . . Even a Labour government, with or without the execrable LibDems in tow, would come to grief eventually.'

'Why?'

'Because they'll suffer the same fate as socialists everywhere. – They'll run out of other people's money . . . They always do, the socialists.'

'But they'll bring us down in the process – with their mansion tax every year and their inheritance tax before we're even dead.'

'You're worried about the wrong things . . . The City of London is what drives our economy. Kill that – with a financial transaction tax, as the Europhiles want – and we're in big trouble.'

'That's only money.'

'What d'you mean "only money"? Try living without it.'

'I have – we both have, as you know only too well – and I don't want to go there again.'

'Nor do I – but the business cycles and political cycles go round and round . . .'

'Until they stop.'

'What's frightened you all of a sudden – Islamic State?'

'Well, yes, among other things. The home-grown Islamists do worry me . . . They don't share our values. They believe in the literal translation of the word "Islam" – to submit . . . I got that worry from my Arab patients, the moderate ones. They're really frightened by it . . . So are the Jews. – They tell me they see antisemitism – disguised currently as support for Palestinians – on the rise everywhere.'

'You've been reading too much of your *Daily Mail*.'

'And you've been reading too much of your *Financial Times*. – But what worries me most is the article I pointed out to you in *The Sunday Times*.'

'About Generation Z?'

'Well, Generation Y really. The Zeds are too young to have any real power yet . . . But, with the influence of social media, the whole country – the whole world – is changing very rapidly.'

'You're worried about Facebook and Twitter?'

'Yes I am – and the newer ones . . . umm . . . and the Chinese are worried about them too. – But even Phoebe says some of them are now old hat.'

'The Chinese?'

'Ha! That'll be the day! – No, I mean Facebook and Twitter . . . Social media, including the newer ones you and I don't even know about, have vast influence – not always for the good . . . Hmm . . . thinking about the Chinese, I must say they do worry me – and the Russians, and the North Koreans and the Iranians – and all the invidious groups like Al Qaida and now Islamic State.'

'I can understand that – but we've got the Americans.'

'Don't you be so sure about that . . . President Obama isn't on side, the Republicans are all over the place, with the Libertarian wing becoming increasingly isolationist . . . and the Spanish are coming.'

'Huh?'

'Within a generation there'll be more Spanish speakers than English speakers in the USA . . . What'll happen then?'

'Nothing. – All countries change their demographics all the time – but nothing much really changes.'

'You really don't see it, do you?'

'What?'

Part 1

'The changes that are happening now are reaching a tipping point . . . This time there'll be no swinging back.'

'Lizzie, dear Lizzie, you really have been reading too much of your *Daily Mail* . . . Come back into the real world.'

'I am in the real world – Phoebe's world, James' world. That's what worries me.'

'Good God! What's up with them?'

'You just don't see it, do you? Right under your own nose and in your own family.'

'See what?'

'That, as I said, the world is changing rapidly – and it won't change back.'

'Through Phoebe and James? – They're just normal rebellious children, finding their own voices.'

'Their own vices, more like.'

'Just because Phoebe's got a work-shy Rastafarian boyfriend and James is at a bit of a loose end . . .'

'It's far more than that, Roddy . . . We're losing the battle for ideas – in our family, in our country, in Western society and internationally.'

'You really have got yourself into a state, haven't you?'

'And you don't see what's happening . . . Phoebe and James are representative of their generation. Everywhere . . . Phoebe's impatient. She wants change right now and she's determined to get it. – She'll find the power. – James has checked himself out . . . He's the opposite of Phoebe . . . He lives from one day to the next – probably on drugs. – Cocaine would be my guess . . . That'll be where his money's going . . . Up his nose.'

'Oh.'

'Yes, "Oh" . . . We need to have a serious talk about all this.'

'I thought we just did.'

* * *

'Today's topic is a simple one – but very easily missed . . . Any thinker who allows himself – or herself – to be the property of someone else ceases to think . . .

'I use the word "property" in a broad sense – not merely physical, financial or social but intellectual . . . If we accept that an employer, state or private, has the right to dictate what we should think, we really are in Orwell's "1984" and "thought crime" is a reality . . .

Mumbles.

'. . . W. Edwards Deming was an American engineer, statistician, professor, author, lecturer, and management consultant . . .

Whistles.

'. . . He was born in 1900. He trained initially as an electrical engineer and later he specialised in mathematical physics. He helped to develop sampling techniques that are still used today. And he set out three principles for any successful enterprise . . . One: Sell only top quality products and services. Two: There should be no fear in the workplace. Three: Get employees to monitor their own work . . .

'Ladies and gentlemen, I ask you this . . . If these principles apply in the private sector, why should they not also apply in the state sector? . . .

A few drummings of heels on the floor.

'. . . I shall take each of Deming's challenges in turn. – One. Why should we expect any lesser quality service from a state enterprise than we do from a private one? . . . State services are not free. They cost a great deal of money to the taxpayer. This should be understood and respected . . .'

'Soak the rich!'

'. . . Ahem . . . On the important exhortation that has just

24

been made – and thank you for your contribution to the debate, although it would probably be best to make it in a seminar . . .

Louder drummings on the floor.

'. . . I should remind you that the top 1% of taxpayers contribute 29.8% of state revenue from this source. Increasing it – as we've seen in recent years in France – risks driving these high earners and major contributors away . . .'

'Good riddance! Bring back the guillotine!'

Laughter.

'. . . Indeed, the Islamic State does exactly that – by hand . . .'

Silence.

'. . . To continue my point. – The majority of tax income for the government – for the NHS and pensions and welfare services, which are by far the largest state expense, comes from people who would perhaps not consider themselves to be at all rich. – People in work. – Many people who, in this country, consider themselves to be working class are top rate tax payers . . . And professional people, including many teachers – and certainly many doctors – pay a significant amount of their income back to the state that employs them . . .'

'Financial capital is evil! Profits are the undistributed wages of the workers!'

Mutterings.

'. . . Maybe so – Karl Marx argued that . . . But the numbers work against that idea . . . Redistributing the wealth of the top 5%, the major owners of capital . . .'

'Capitalist scum!'

Mutterings again.

'. . . would make little practical difference to the living standards of the 95% – precisely because there are so many of them . . .'

'What do you know? You're an American.'

Louder mutterings.

'. . . I shall be glad to discuss all these points in the seminars, but I think, Sir, I have given your views a fair hearing and – for the benefit of everyone else here – it would be respectful of you to consider their broader educational needs, as they – rather than you – may see them . . .

Applause.

'. . . On the second point made by Deming – that there should be no fear in the workplace – this should surely apply in the state sector as much as in the private sector . . . Yet the state tends to be ruthless in naming and shaming – rather than assisting – providers whose professional standards have fallen below the optimum . . . And the state is mostly an undiscriminating employer, paying a standard amount regardless of the quality of service given by individuals . . . And further, the state tends to be dismissive – and even brutal – towards those who challenge state ideas and practices . . . The treatment of whistleblowers is a case in point . . .

Silence.

'. . . On the third point made by Deming – that employees should monitor their own work – I might add that if we treat people with respect and dignity, and with appreciation for their enthusiasm and creativity, they will tend to behave with respect and dignity and become more enthusiastic and creative . . .

Silence.

'. . . We have to ask ourselves whether this is what we see in either private or state enterprises . . . Are employees – at any level – trusted? Or are they hounded? . . . When considering this issue, you might like to ponder why it is that many people choose to work in the private sector for less money, and a lot less security of tenure and much smaller pension pots, than they would receive in the state sector . . .'

'Scabs!'

'. . . One advantage of a mixed economy, with state and private sectors operating side by side as in the UK, is that it gives researches like me an opportunity to study the effects of different political philosophies in the same community . . .

Silence.

'. . . Today we have covered a broad sweep of ideas. And we have illustrated the importance of the point I made at the start. – Any thinker who allows himself or herself to be the property of someone else ceases to think . . .

Shuffles.

'. . . Incidentally, just for the record, lecturers are not top rate taxpayers – and I pay British taxes on my British earnings.'

A mock sympathetic 'Aaaaaaah!'

oOo

This Precious Ellington dude has some fascinating ideas . . . He really is "funky" . . . Not like Nate. – Only one idea in Nate's head . . . Well two, including the Ganga . . .

* * *

'What say we go to the nightclub?'

'We went there last night, Jamie. – My head's still spinning . . . and I'm bored with it.'

'We've got to live a bit, Mandi. Life's too short to mount a camel.'

'To what?'

'Mount a camel.'

'What does that mean?'

'I don't know . . . I made it up – but it seems to amuse people.'

'Oh.'

'Not you?'

'Not really.'

'Why not?'

'Well I know you go to that club only because you hope you might bump into Prince Harry. – Dream on, kiddo. – He's moved on . . . No chance with him anyway. He's got friends already and they're all sworn to secrecy – and that's not your strong point when you're off your face, like you were last night . . . You tell everybody everything – even about us – when you're in that state. And you find it very funny . . . I don't and other people don't . . . It's very embarrassing.'

'Tough tits.'

'Is that all you have to say, James?'

'Yes, as a matter of fact it is. Here I am, offering you a night out – an expensive night out in a very smart place – and you're getting at me.'

'Yes I am . . . Any girl would if you tell people about her knickers and how easily you get them off her.'

'That was just a joke.'

'It's not funny – and I'm surprised you even remember it.'

'I don't.'

'Well that's it. I'm going back to the flat to collect my things . . . It's over . . . You're a nice man – most of the time – but you're a coke-head and a piss artist and that says all there is to say about you nowadays.'

'Lah di dah.'

'And what's that supposed to mean?'

'Nothing. I made it up.'

'You need serious help, James.'

'Fuck off will you? I don't need any mothering. I had more than enough at home when I was a kid.'

'You still are.'

'Well just you remember this, Amanda Whatever-your-name-was. There's plenty more where you came from.'

* * *

'How about supper at the Hurlingham tonight?'

'Thank you, my love. That's kind of you – but I'd rather not.'

'Why not?'

'Because the food isn't very good.'

'People don't go to the Hurlingham for the food. It's a club. They go for the sports facilities, the ambiance, the company, the conversation . . .'

'The booze – same as in the Garrick and any other club.'

'Hey! What's all this? Open hunting season on husbands?'

'Oh, sorry my love . . . I'm just worried about the children . . . I sense that something dreadful could happen to them if they go on as they are. – Call it a woman's intuition, if you like.'

'I don't like . . . But there's no point in worrying about it in advance.'

'It makes more sense than worrying about it afterwards – whatever "it" might be.'

'Come on, sweetheart. Settle down, settle down . . . Let's go to the Garrick – if they've got a table – although we can always have a simple after-theatre supper in the side room . . . And I can poke my nose in on me mates in the snug . . . and wonder whose name they're supporting – or not – in the files of sheets on proposed members.'

'Oh, you men! You're so tied up in your pretend world that you don't see the real one.'

'Oh yes we do. – We run it.'

'Roderick Finch, you're a pain in the arse – but I married you for your arse so I won't complain.'

'Supper?'

'Yes. – Thank you.'

'And what comes after?'

'Wait and see.'

'Women!'

*   *   *

'I'm not sure that our relationship is going anywhere very fast, Nate.'

'What ya goin' on baht, man? You was all over me lars' ni'.'

'Well I'm not now. It's time for me to move on.'

'Yu got summwon?'

'N . . . no, of course not. It's just that we're not really compatible. – You and I . . . Damn! – You and me . . . I'm a young girl, studying for my finals and you're a deadbeat Rasta who's taken too much dope to be able to think straight or even get out of bed sometimes . . . unless it's to munch something.'

'T'anks. But ya knows dat when ya met me – and ya din' complain baht me munching ya lars ni' – not at all . . ."Yaaaaah wah wah", she says.'

'I don't want to be reminded about it now . . . That's rude.'

'Ya gon' posh, man.'

'Don't you ever say that about me. It's the worst thing anyone could ever say.'

'Ya gon' posh.'

oOo

'So here we are this week . . . to look at the downside of the state taking over ultimate health care responsibility from the individual. We need to consider first of all whether individuals come to think that they have rights . . .'

A voice from the back: 'Yes they do.'

'Thank you . . . and, if so, whether they can demand a service without acknowledging at the same time that the service is inevitably the product of the life and work and integrity of someone else . . .'

'Of course not! It's the duty of all medical staff to serve.'

A few heels drummed on the floor in support of the heckler.

' . . . Thank you again . . . I'm very happy for you to show in this way when you disagree with a point I'm making . . . umm . . . It's probably not a good thing to throw things . . .

Laughter.

' . . . However, it might be best to leave the discussion to our small group seminars, rather than these formal lectures, which are designed to make general points and stimulate thought rather than give personal opinions . . .

Loud drumming of heels.

' . . . The issue here is not whether healthcare workers are simply doing a job or living out a vocation. It's whether the recipient of care can *demand* a service . . .'

'Yes!'

' . . . Thank you . . . in which case the healthcare worker is not a free agent with choice but a slave – or, at best, a robot programmed by someone else . . .

A few hesitant – possibly confused – drummings.

' . . . Do we acknowledge a difference between men and machines? . . . If so, we are obligated to appreciate what is done by human beings and give respect to each man – and woman – for employing skill in a responsible way . . . with the best interests of the patient at heart . . .

Applause.

' . . . Alternatively, if there's no difference between men and machines, is it reasonable for potential recipients of care – all of us – simply to make demands, irrespective of the effect this may have on the provider? . . .

Silence.

'. . . For each of you – in this final year as a student – you need no reminding that in due course you yourself will be that provider . . . Are you prepared for those demands? And if you're not going to be a front-line provider, would it be reasonable for you – or anyone – to expect others to work under those expectations? . . .

Silence.

'The simple question is this. – Does a healthcare worker have rights as well as responsibilities? . . . I leave it to you to consider the implications of this question. I would suggest that we – every one of us in our society looking at healthcare issues – can answer in any way we wish . . . But we cannot avoid the question.'

Shuffles, mumblings and coughs.

* * *

'James Finch . . . Yes, Sir, that's correct – commodity brokering . . . I'm a senior account executive . . . It means that I work with you, discussing possible investments with you . . . Yes, I *am* young – 21. Stockbrokers tend to be older. Their markets tend to be slower, looking at stocks and shares that change their value over weeks or months, as you're probably aware from your own portfolio . . . Yes, that's absolutely right. I agree with you. We have to have a significant measure of security in our own overall financial position . . . Yes . . . Yes, to protect our families . . . umm . . . My own family investments are in gilts. They give a very stable and secure return – low risk . . . You do?

. . . Yes, I understand. That's very wise, if I may say so . . . Yes, I see . . . Well, "funny money" isn't the term that I myself would use. I prefer to think in terms of "surplus money" – with full awareness of higher risk but, of course, greater opportunity to make some real money . . . Well, the sort of money that we might take many years to accumulate – if ever – in a steady job. Or, more likely, the sort of money that really skilful entrepreneurs earn through sheer hard work . . . Yes, my clients – the more experienced ones – often tell me that . . . Yes indeed. Life's too short . . . Ha! Yes, I hope I've got a day or two left on this planet . . . Ah, I see . . . umm . . . it's really a question of exposure. What's your entire position? What's your "must have" fall-back security? . . . Yes . . . Yes . . . Is that really so? You've never invested in commodities before? . . . Not even in gold – a few Krugerands set aside for when governments cock things up? . . . Yes, they certainly do, don't they? . . . Well gold is a commodity that's generally very stable – but it can alter its value rapidly in times of international crisis . . . Yes, that's absolutely right – and the advantage of Krugerands or diamonds is that they're easily portable – which bricks and mortar aren't . . . We here trade in more general commodities – like cocoa or bananas, rice or cotton. We take a view on world situations – local political events, shortages and surfeits in world supply, acute crises of one kind or another – such as sudden changes in climate that might lead to crop failures – not all that other political stuff – although, of course, our research department does have to keep a very close eye – and take a considered view – on political situations throughout the world . . . Yes, you've got that on the button. We save you the anxiety – and the time – of trying to keep up to speed with everything day after day . . . Yes, that's our job . . . Yes, we have to know where particular cargos are right now so that we can see immediately what the implications are for future commodity prices. Then I telephone you . . . Yes, that's right, I become your personal broker – like the personal bankers I'm told they used to have in the old days in local branches . . . Yes, our research department occupies a whole floor of this building. They're our private resource, our back-up team . . . Yes, we're more select. On this floor we have just a few brokers like me – with personal clients, each of us, and we gradually build up personal relationships with them – at least I do – getting to know your individual likes, dislikes and preferences . . . That's kind of you to say so . . . Well thank you . . . Now then, how would you personally like to take things on from here? . . . Straight away? Well yes – if that's your considered wish . . . Yes indeed, no time like the present . . . Well, right now, I would suggest coffee – there's always a high demand for it, as you know from every high street – but the countries that grow it can be very volatile. That gives us the opportunity – if we're sharp – to get in quickly and get substantial returns before other people catch on . . . Yes, that's fine. I can arrange that. How much do you reckon would be a sensible initial investment? . . . It's your money but I would suggest that you might like to be really cautious to begin with, until we get to know each other and you get a feel for how things work – and maybe an interest in a particular sector of the overall commodity market . . . Yes indeed. I'll take the details and put in the trade . . . Yes that's right. As you will have seen from our website, we charge a fixed percentage on each transaction . . . Not at all – it's my privilege to be doing business with you.'

. . . Ha! Got you, you stupid fucker . . . 'Churn em, burn em', I say . . . Still, that's his problem – but I'll be able to pay off the old man at the end of the month. It isn't every day that I pull off a trade like this one. Well done, James! That'll keep my particular supply line with father open – and I can have some more fun at the nightclub – whatever that idiot Mandi says . . .

* * *

Yes . . . I couldn't tell Nate but I do admit it to myself – I like Precious Ellington a lot. He's really funky. He excites me in every way. Yeeehah! Best of all, I love his confident command of 200 medics . . . Not an easy audience . . . That does something very warm and tingly for me. – And he also makes me think . . .

* * *

Yes . . . What my dear wife said about James possibly taking cocaine does worry me – although I'd never acknowledge it to anyone else. – Some things best kept to meself. – Hope it's just temporary exuberance of youth. The idiot! . . . And I'm an idiot too for trusting him . . .

* * *

Yes . . . It's a woman's instinct – and I'll say it to myself. – Well done Lizzie! . . . But how Roddy missed it, I can't think. – Head in the clouds that man of mine. – But I'm better off with him than with some of the cynics at the commercial bar . . .

oOo

'Doctors who allow themselves to become mere units in state provision of health care, rather than people who are responsible for their own philosophical and mental integrity, are not worth asking the time of day let alone their opinions about clinical or personal problems . . .

Silence.

'. . . Yes, that's quite a bit to take in, isn't it? – Quite a chunk. – Maybe initially it's a bit indigestible . . .

Sounds of someone retching.

Laughter.

'. . . Thank you . . . Thank you . . . umm... While we try to get back on track after that valuable contribution to our special subject for today – you might like to be aware that scientific researchers, like me, tend to be "splitters" or "lumpers" . . . Either we break things down into little bits, so that we can see all the constituent parts and work out how they fit together, or we lump everything together in an attempt to see the big picture and work out how the system works as a whole . . .

Silence.

'. . . Maybe ideally we should be both splitters and lumpers . . . You might like to ask yourselves which camp you're in . . .

'Yours, duckie.'

Laughter.

'. . . Ha! I left myself open to that one . . .

'Oowoowooo!'

Loud laughter.

'. . . Yeah. Yeah . . . So let's look at how medical services are split up into different areas of accountability . . . In the UK – more so than in the USA – we have a structural division between hospitals and family practice. The UK Department of Health lumps them together as its overall area of responsibility. But each division is more or less independent . . . The public health services we were referring to in a previous talk are fully independent . . . There is very little movement of doctors and other staff between these various aspects of the provision of healthcare . . .

Silence.

'. . . For instance, hospital doctors rarely work in the community aside from doing specialist clinics in large health centres . . . And some GPs take on clinical assistantships in hospitals, maybe for one or two sessions a week, but then go back to their offices in the community . . .

'Aaaah, diddums.'

Laughter.

'. . . Yes, that's right. The intention may be to keep their clinical interests alive – but in practice they may become no more than an extra pair of hands in the hospital . . .

More significantly – sadly maybe – some of them may feel they only become "real" doctors when they're working in a hospital . . .

'Yesss!'

'. . . And some of their hospital colleagues might agree with that judgement . . .

General pitying chorus: 'Aaaaaah'.

'. . . And – as I said previously – little, if any, attention is paid to the public health services . . . How many doctors, in hospitals or in family practice, have ever visited a public health laboratory and talked to an epidemiologist? Or seen behind the scenes at the blood transfusion service? . . .'

'I have.'

'. . . Yes – as a student – but from now on you will each tend to become progressively more specialised . . . One friend of mine has spent his entire professional life studying one particular type of blood cell – the basophil. It's very interesting work for him – but he's now a super-specialist, a long way away from the day-to-day experience of family doctors or those who run family planning clinics or school health services . . .'

'What's this got to do with the price of fish?'

Mumbles of semi-agreement.

' . . . The relevance is this. – Splitters, who look only at their own area of special interest, may lose sight of the bigger picture. . . . However, this might be appropriate for those patients who suffer from just one clinical condition . . . And lumpers, who see the broad picture in local or national healthcare strategy, may not understand the perspectives of the foot soldiers. This might be appropriate for patients who have many conditions . . . But in your own clinical perspectives I would encourage you to be both splitters and lumpers . . .'

'Ouch!'

Laughter.

'. . . Thank you . . . Now then, looking more at today's primary topic, we need to ask whether any of us – splitters or lumpers or whatever – retain a sense of balance and clear vision when we allow the state, or any large corporation, to do our thinking for us . . .

Shuffles.

'. . . Are doctors the only people who can make judgements on health issues? . . . Are teachers the only people concerned with education? . . . Are architects the only people who have views on the structure and function of buildings? . . .

Silence.

'. . . And now consider politicians . . . Do we let them run our lives without ever being challenged? – Not just at election times and in parliamentary debates and television interviews but by each and every one of us in our own minds every day? . . .'

'Anarchists of the world unite!'

Hesitant laughter – from the few members of the audience who had not heard that joke before – followed by 'Shhhh!'

'. . . I suggest – as I said at the beginning – that doctors who allow themselves to become mere units in state provision of healthcare, rather than people who are responsible for their own philosophical and mental integrity, are not worth asking the time of day let alone their opinions on clinical or personal problems.'

oOo

This guy's cool. He really makes me think . . . I like that. It's difficult to disagree with him. I'd like to – but he's done his homework. Right then . . . I know . . . I'll do mine. – I'm not going to shout like that imbecile at the back. – That plays into Precious's hands . . . Yeah . . . mmm . . . Wouldn't mind doing that myself – in a different way . . . Ha! Mum always said sex, not just fantasy, is an activity of the mind . . . But how would she know? – Even as a gynaecologist? . . . For Nate it was just body – and I enjoyed that . . . for a time. – But it's not enough . . . Precious is something different. His mind's so clear. I can't wait to find out how he applies it in personal ways . . . First off, I'll play it his way. – I'll brush up on my ideas on healthcare systems. Then I can challenge him every inch of the way . . . Yeah, I like that idea – every inch of the way . . .

* * *

It's hard to know where I've gone wrong in bringing up the children . . . As a woman, they're my responsibility – not Roddy's. – His duty's to bring home the bacon . . . Yup. He's done that . . . I've let him down – and let the children down . . . Maybe I've worked too hard, competing in a man's world . . . Damn it, what else could I have done? – I had nothing. I've worked for everything I've got. – Phoebe's a student so she has to be supported . . . Hmm . . . not to the extent she expects sometimes . . . James? – God, I do hope he's not on drugs. – What's to make of him? . . . Huh . . . What's he making of himself? . . .

* * *

I'm caught, damn it, I'm caught. I'm a professional man – a good one, a hard-working one . . . It's what I do. It's who I am . . . Working as much as I've done to get where I am has left no time for anything else . . . It's all very well – for people with nothing better to do – to call themselves "house husbands". Well, I'm not. I'm a QC – on my way to being a judge – if I can afford the drop in income . . . So what do I do when my son – my only son – goes off the rails? . . . I simply don't know . . . I've had no experience of this sort of thing. Lizzie's the one who always sorts things out. – Women's work . . . umm . . . Maybe I should sit down with James and have a fatherly talk with him. Ha! Good idea . . . maybe . . . But I wouldn't know what to say . . . Ha! Me – a barrister, on me back legs talking to judges, umm . . . persuasively I hope . . . day after day – and I don't know what to say to me own son . . . It's pathetic – really pathetic, me lud . . .

* * *

'Let's start today's talk with a statement many people believe should be uncontentious . . . a state health service should provide equal access to good quality care for all citizens, irrespective of their location, age, gender, economic status, social class and personal beliefs . . .

Drummings on the floor.

' . . . This is a fine principle . . . Our enquiry today focuses on whether this actually happens in the UK, where the NHS has provided universal free access for more than half a century . . .

Part 1

More drummings.

'. . . From your brief experience of secondment to a family practice as part of your training, you'll be familiar with what's called "the postcode lottery" . . . All GP practices now belong to a Clinical Commissioning Group and a local area team, which awards contracts for many services on behalf of their patients. These services include emergency care, community care, planned hospital care, and mental health and learning disability services in their local areas . . . That's the theory . . .

Groans.

'. . . Yes . . . You'll have seen the practice in real life. – It plays catch-up with theory in one national reorganisation after another . . . Each successive government fails to keep the best of what is there already but is determined to do things their own way . . .

More groans.

'. . . And groups in different areas have different priorities. Some services may be readily available in one geographical area but not in others . . . And services in Scotland, Wales and Northern Ireland are largely autonomous. Even within the regions of England there may be significant variations in provision and access. – Yet all are part of the NHS . . .

Less confident drummings.

' . . But now let me draw your attention to some unin-tended consequences of universal provision of healthcare and welfare services . . .

Groans again.

'. . . First . . . Poor areas tend to get the poorest services . . . General practice is the patients' gateway to the NHS. Yet in the poorest areas doctors often have the fewest post-graduate qualifications, the worst premises and the fewest staff. The best-qualified and most enterprising doctors tend to work in areas where there are stable populations . . . whereas areas that have a high turnover of population, like city centres, inevitably have greater difficulties in clinical and administrative management . . .

Silence.

'. . . They also tend to be the least attractive areas for doctors themselves to work and live in. – They want to bring up their own families in nice areas that have attractive local facilities, stable communities, good schools and reliable services – including medical services . . .

Shuffles.

'. . . As a result, the best services tend to be in Oxford and Exeter and the worst in areas like North East London and Toxteth in Liverpool – where the measured basic indices of health and social problems show the greatest need . . .

Silence.

'. . . Second . . . Individuals and families with the greatest number of medical and social problems will tend to drop down the economic strata. They move out of rich areas into poor areas. This results in poor areas getting even greater clinical and social challenges . . .

Silence.

'. . . So how do we deal with these problems – that exist even in a welfare state? . . . Do we force doctors to go where they're most needed? Do we restrict free choice – for the general population – in their place of home and work? Do we abandon the principle of universality and – with positive discrimination – give disproportionately good services in poor areas?

'Yes!'

'Well, Ayn Rand – the Russian/American writer and philosopher – argued that the difference between a welfare state and a totalitarian state is merely a matter of time . . .

'No. No. No.'

Part 1

'. . . I'm merely reporting what she said . . . But you can see why it might be true – despite the best intentions of all concerned . . . Governments tend to take more power when given the chance to do so. – And they tend to put a gloss on their power grabs by tying them into promises of increased welfare services . . .

Uncomfortable shufflings and a few mutterings.

'. . . And what are the unintended consequences of living in a welfare state? – People may assume that the state will care for the less fortunate. But, when presented with evidence that it doesn't do so, they tend to complain that it should . . . And here's the catch . . . They don't feel obliged to take any positive helpful action themselves . . .

Silence.

'. . . Do the rich now go out of their way to help the poor? And the strong to help the weak? – Except when forced to do so through the taxation system or when they're emotionally blackmailed by charity muggers? – Or do they all say the same thing, "The government ought to do something!"? . . . And, as a result, is the state itself responsible for creating this cruel, arid and uncaring society? . . .

More shufflings and mutterings.

'. . . Yes indeed, these are very uncomfortable challenges. They've not been solved anywhere in the world . . .

'Scandinavia!'

'. . . You think so? Well maybe – but isn't that comparable in global terms to saying that the NHS works well in Oxford and Exeter? . . . And in any case the social and economic evidence from Sweden indicates that it benefited in times of free market government and suffered in times of a more controlled economy . . .'

'Shame!'

'Yes maybe. – But why?'

43

oOo

'Earwigo, earwigo, earwigo . . .'
  Thud.
James Finch wasn't going anywhere.

* * *

That's odd . . . Tired for no reason. And me leg feels a bit stiff.
– Crampy . . . Been like that for some time. – Nearly tripped
walking up the stairs to me chambers just now . . . Good job
I wasn't carrying a bunch of files... Always walk up. – Gotta
keep meself fit . . . Huh! Far too busy to take time off to see
anyone about me leg right now . . . Anyway, it's not that bad . . .
Sure it'll get better on its own. – These silly little things usually
do . . .

* * *

Shit! That's all I need right now! – Fucking pregnant – and I
can't tell mum after all she's told me . . . Ha! – the daughter of
a consultant gynaecologist got herself up the duff! . . . Yeah,
I suppose I'll have to see my NHS GP. She doesn't give me
much confidence – always wanting to talk about my illustrious
mother . . . But she's useful for prescriptions . . .

* * *

Ouch! There's that indigestion pain again. It must have been
the stuffed peppers I gave Roddy for supper. And my back's a
bit sore just to the right of the middle there. – Can't think what
I've done to that. – Lifting something probably . . . And why's

Part 1

Roddy dragging his foot? Silly man! . . . Ought to see a doctor
. . . but I know how stubborn he is . . .

*   *   *

Following on from the last talk, some of you have asked me
who Ayn Rand is . . .

'Boooo. Boooo. Boooo!'

'. . . Ah! You know her. – Clearly some of you do – from her
political writing. That's surprising – unless you've just googled
her. – She's better known in the USA and Australia than over
here. – She's the author of the novel *Atlas Shrugged* which
looks at what happens when capitalists . . .

'Boooo. Boooo. Boooo!'

'. . . who – she says – drive the motor of the world, go on
strike. . . And she established the philosophy of Objectivism . . .

Mutterings.

'. . . In opposition to Ayn Rand's beliefs, we should look
at Julian Tudor-Hart's *Inverse Care Law*. This communist GP,
who worked in a mining village in South Wales . . .

Scattered applause.

'. . . said that those who need the most help are least likely
to get it.'

More applause.

'And this is exactly what we saw illustrated in our last talk.
There is no doubt that Dr Tudor-Hart's Law is correct . . .

Even more applause.

' . . . but it appears to be as true in the UK in the NHS as it
is in the USA.

'No. No. No.'

'. . . The evidence would appear to point to Yes, Yes, Yes . . .

'No.'

'. . . As you wish – but bear in mind that I've worked in

both countries so I have some experience of seeing the clinical and social effects of their different political philosophies . . .

Hisssss. Hisssss.

'. . . and you will recall that we mentioned ObamaCare – America's first steps towards universal socialised medicine – in our first talk . . .

Applause and a few whistles followed by some hisses.

'. . .Thank you . . . umm . . . Shall we move on now? . . .

'Get on with it!'

'. . . Thank you . . . We have to ask ourselves whether the state creates a cruel, arid, uncaring society that smothers individual compassion and human charity and creativity – as Ayn Rand believed and as illustrated in Solzhenytsin's novel *Cancer Ward* . . .

'No!'

'. . . Or whether Dr Tudor Hart is right . . . His view is supported by the writer John Berger in his story, *A Fortunate Man: The Story of a Country Doctor* . . .

Scattered applause.

'. . . My point is this . . . No country in the world has the perfect system. To illustrate this, there's another book you might like to read . . .

More groans.

'. . . *The Public-Private Mix for Health,* published by the Nuffield Trust. This looks at different healthcare systems in different counties, with each section written by someone with personal experience of working in that country . . . The conclusion I come to, as a result of reading this report and visiting several of these countries to discuss healthcare ideas, is that doctors anywhere in the world will undermine the local healthcare system and turn it to their own advantage.'

Silence – quickly followed by more applause and whistles, groans, mutters and mumblings.

Part 1

oOo

'Wassgoinon? Wassgoinon?'

'It's all right, Sir. It's all right . . . I'm just checking your blood pressure and pulse.'

'Gerroffme!'

'Just lie still for a moment, please Sir.'

'Gerroffme! – Gerroffme, I said.'

'Calm down, Sir. Calm down, please. Right now. You're perfectly safe.'

'Wherami? Hooru?'

'I'm a staff nurse in the Accident and Emergency Department.'

'Howdigerrere?'

'An ambulance collected you from the pavement outside the station.'

'Don'memberat.'

'You wouldn't remember it, Sir. You were unconscious.'

''Worrappened?'

'It appears you'd been drinking, Sir.'

'Uh . . . Gorragonow.'

'You're not going anywhere, Sir. The doctor's got you on half hourly observations – in case of a head injury.'

'Wassatime?'

'Five-thirty – in the morning.'

'Gorragonow!'

'Just calm down now, please Sir . . . I have to make the observations on you in case you're bleeding internally.'

'Snuthinrongwimme.'

'We don't know that, Sir. – We have to make sure that you're safe.'

'Gorragonow. Gorragonow!'

'Just calm down now, please Sir. You're disturbing the other patients.'

'GORRAGONOW!'

* * *

'Ten days! Whad'ya mean ten days? I can't wait ten days.'

'I'm afraid you'll have to, Miss Finch. All the appointments are fully booked – unless it's an emergency'

'Of course it's a fucking emergency. – I wouldn't come here otherwise. – I'm fucking pregnant.'

'That's not an emergency in medical terms, like a heart attack. – And I should be grateful if you would mind your language.'

'Listen! It's a fucking emergency to me – and I'll speak as I fucking well like.'

'The doctors have instructed me that pregnancy is not an emergency unless there's acute abdominal pain.'

'You're not listening to me . . . It's an emergency because I say it's an emergency. – I'm the fucking patient and this is the National Health Service. – I have my rights.'

'So have all our other patients, Miss Finch. I can't put you in ahead of them . . . You'll have to wait. – The same as they do.'

'I'm not waiting. I'll have you know that my mother's a consultant gynaecologist.'

'Then talk to her.'

'How dare you say that? That's highly offensive, elitist, sexist . . .'

'Call it what you like, I still can't put you in ahead of the queue. – But I apologise if you feel I have been rude to you.'

'You bloody have – and I shall be making a formal complaint.'

'As you wish . . . And, for your pregnancy, here's an

information sheet from the British Pregnancy Advisory Service . . . It's a charity.'

'I know what it is – but it still charges money if I go privately because I can't afford to wait for you to refer me – and I haven't got any money . . . I'm a fucking student. I'm entitled to free care, just like everyone else in the NHS.'

'Yes you are – and so are the other patients here. And they've booked appointments ahead of you.'

*   *   *

Well that's better. Me leg seems to be settling down . . . Just a few days – weeks maybe . . . didn't count . . . Minor inconvenience, that's all – Niggly though. – Can't afford to be away from this case at present . . . Far too important . . . Course I could've asked one of the medicos in the Garrick – but that doesn't do . . . talking shop. Anyway it's no big deal. Obviously pulled a muscle or trod on something awkwardly . . . Hmm . . . Don't remember doing anything like that . . . Odd . . . Ha! Nothing to worry about . . . I'm sure . . .

*   *   *

Yerrow! That really is sore. I never realised that simple indigestion could be quite so troublesome – unless it's a perforation, which this certainly isn't . . . Nothing a bit of Gaviscon won't sort out . . .

*   *   *

'The crucial issue – in our current consideration of health and welfare services in these talks – is whether the state can be relied upon to produce responsible clinical care at the time that it 's needed . . .

'The private sector doesn't!'

'. . . You're absolutely right . . .

Applause.

'. . . The private sector "cherry-picks", as you say in this country. – It chooses what it wants to do. – What it likes most are simple surgical procedures – like varicose veins and hernias – where there's a clear-cut treatment, a mostly predictable outcome and a generally quantifiable cost . . .

Silence.

'. . . But what the private sector likes least are chronic illnesses – like diabetes, which takes more than 5% of the total NHS budget, lung problems such as chronic obstructive pulmonary disease, which – as you probably know – used to be termed chronic bronchitis – and heart disease . . .

Silence.

'. . . Patients who die of acute illnesses are no great challenge to the survival of the private sector. They can be very expensive at times – like in some treatments for cancer or auto-immune problems or leukaemia and other blood disorders – but many of these conditions are time-limited. The patients die. – Not always but often . . .

Silence.

'. . . But chronic illnesses can bankrupt the private medical insurance companies – which is precisely why they do everything they can to avoid providing cover for patients who suffer from them . . . They don't take them on, they look for any opportunity to say that a claim cannot be met because it refers to a pre-existing condition – that was present before the insurance was taken out – and they progressively increase the premiums as a result of previous claims . . . and also with age. They do whatever they can to ensure that patients go bankrupt before they do . . .

'Shame!'

Part 1

'. . . Would I be right in assuming that you mean that you support these actions of the private insurance companies? . . .

'No! No! No!'

'. . . Ah, I thought not . . .

Laughter.

'. . . But the issue we are studying is this. – Does the state system do any better? . . .

'Yes. Yes. Yes.'

'. . . Or does it ration by queue? . . .

Silence.

'. . . And are some of its services worse than useless and even dangerous? . . .

'Better than nothing!'

'. . . Are you sure about that? – May I remind you that – in any healthcare system anywhere in the developed world – three times as many people die as a result of medical error as die in road accidents . . .

Silence.

'. . . Currently the outstanding financial claims against the NHS for medical errors run into billions. In the most recent figures in 2012 it was estimated that the cost of malpractice claims against the NHS runs at £15 billion a year and this figure increases by 9% each year . . .

Silence.

'. . . I return to the question asked at the beginning of this session. – Can the state be relied upon to produce responsible clinical care at the time that it is needed? . . . I leave it to you to consider the issues of postcode lottery, rationing by queue and medical malpractice. To be sure, the private sector has glaring inadequacies – but so does the NHS. Is one worse than the other? And what should be done? . . .

'Eat the rich!'

'Ah! I see someone's been reading PJO'Rourke . . .

'Listening to Motörhead!'

'. . . Oh yes . . . Yes, I remember them. I grew up with that song. My mother used to play it . . . umm . . . Some problems don't go away – and some solutions don't solve them.'

oOo

'Not you again!'

'Whadya mean, "me again"?'

'You were in here last week.'

'Was I?'

'Good God! Don't you even remember? – The ambulance brought you in after a drinking bout.'

'Must be some mistake.'

'We got your name from the driving licence in your wallet. – James Finch – easy to remember.'

'Well you can remember it now . . . I'm in real pain. My head's turning itself inside out. – But I don't want anyone to know.'

'I did warn you . . .'

'What about?'

'Leaving the hospital when you might have a head injury causing internal bleeding.'

'Not after all this time.'

'So much you know, Mr Finch. A slow bleed can cause symptoms lasting several days before it really takes off . . .'

'Nah. You got it wrong . . . umm . . . I was in good shape until this evening when I . . . umm . . .'

'When you what?'

'When I . . . Look, you're not going to tell anyone about this, are you?'

'I have to put everything in the medical records.'

Part 1

'Well that tells everybody, doesn't it? – The police, the social services, the insurance companies – everybody wants a slice of the action these days . . . On medical records. Nothing's confidential any more. – I . . . Shit, that hurts! . . .'

'Just tell me what it is – so I can give you the appropriate tests and give you effective treatment . . .'

'But you mustn't tell anyone . . .'

'Come on. Out with it. I'm busy.'

'Er . . . I've been at the devil's dandruff.'

'The what?'

'The devil's dandruff – cocaine.'

'I've never heard it called that before – and I thought we saw and heard everything in A and E.'

'So what are you going to do, for fuck's sake? . . . They'll catch up with me if I hang around here much longer.'

'Who will?'

'The people who've been following me – trying to find out my secrets – my ways of making millions on a trade . . .'

'We can talk about that later – but right now I'll get the doctor to see you . . . I still think you need further investigation for internal bleeding – an MRI scan – but I can't order that. Only a doctor is allowed to commit that resource.'

'What language are you speaking? "Commit that resource"? – and I'm dying . . .'

* * *

'It belonged to my grandmother. It was her engagement ring. It's my most valuable possession – personally and financially. It's insured for five grand.'

'I'll give you two.'

'But that's not enough for what I need.'

'That's not my problem . . . I'll tell you, young lady, what

53

the problem is. – This sapphire's got a flaw in it. You can see it with a jeweller's lens – right across the middle.'

'I was told it was flawless – other than the minor flaws that all sapphires have.'

'They all say that. That's how they sell them to yer . . . Two grand's the value – and that's my price. Try somewhere else if you like.'

'No, no . . . I need to get this sorted . . . umm . . . I've got the matching pendant.'

'I'll have a look at it – but don't assume it's worth the same . . . Every gemstone's unique . . .'

* * *

Well that case has netted a tidy sum – enough to pay the Garrick subscription – and the nosh and vino for a year – and take a bite out of the fees for the chambers . . . Good job the children are through school. – That's a fixed penalty if ever there was one! One night of passion and then a lifetime of bills! . . . Don't suppose people would ever have children if they knew how expensive they were going to be – mine still round me neck even now . . . Still, so long as me health keeps up . . .

* * *

Yup. There's something particularly satisfying about obs and gobs. Getting out of bed to deliver a baby's a bit of a bore – but nowadays so many of the city high-flyers postpone having their children until well into their thirties. – They all want elective Caesars anyway. – And my trade's a sure-fire bread-winner . . . You can persuade people to give up smoking – but I'll never be out of work . . .

Part 1

*   *   *

'Today's session is the last of the group in which we consider what happens if the state takes over ultimate healthcare responsibility from the individual . . . Let's look at how the state tries to implement its ideas. – You'll see immediately the incongruity of that concept . . . The state is inanimate . . . it cannot *do* anything . . .

Shuffles.

'. . . Let me illustrate this point in a psychodramatic demonstration . . . You all know the saying – and maybe the song – *Money is the root of all evil* . . . Well here's my money clip. I'll drop it here on the floor. Have a look at it there . . . Ask yourself what power it has – by itself . . . Can it actually *do* anything at all? . . .

Silence.

'. . . Now Madam – you here in the front row – might I please ask you to pick it up? . . . Thank you . . . Now, in this lady's hands, the money has power – for evil or for good . . .

Phoebe waved the money clip in the air and then put it in the pocket of her jeans.

Laughter.

'. . . With that analogy in mind, let us consider the concept of "state money". – The state cannot have money . . . Of itself it cannot have – or do – anything . . . State money is private money that has been confiscated – by law – by the people in power. They do this in just the same way that . . . Tell me your name please . . .'

'Phoebe Finch.'

'. . . the same way that Phoebe Finch took my money. State money is the product of legalised theft. We allow it – well most of us do – because we trust that people in power, elected democratically, will use it responsibly for the common good . . .

Guffaws.

'. . . Yes. Some of you disagree that governments spend money responsibly . . . For example, some of you might believe that less money should be spent on the military and more on schools and hospitals . . .

Loud drummings of heels on the floor and a few cheers.

'. . . and some of you will believe the opposite . . .

Silence.

'. . . Well maybe not in this audience – in your age group – but maybe there are some who form a silent minority . . .

Silence.

'. . . and who fear the possible consequences of demonstrating an unpopular belief . . . Rebelling against perceived oppression is easy. We see it all the time in street marches and demonstrations . . . But standing up for our beliefs when they would be likely to be unpopular with our own peer group is more difficult . . .

Silence apart from one pair of drummed heels.

'. . . Ah – an individual . . .

'No I'm not.'

Laughter.

'. . . Well, at least a fan of Monty Python . . .

Laughter.

'. . . In this parliamentary democracy in Britain, the benches on which MPs sit in the House of Commons are separated by two sword lengths. The MPs may shout but they do not fight . . .

'Shame!'

Laughter.

'. . . Correspondingly, governments protect themselves from being attacked by the populace . . . Every law that is passed has penalties – fines or imprisonment – attached. Disobey the law at your peril . . .

Part 1

Silence.

' . . The people in power retain their power by force. The only restraints are the judiciary and the constitutional monarch – who has no power of her own but denies absolute power to anyone else . . .

'Off with her head!'

Laughter.

'. . . Now we can see the relevance of all this to today's consideration of what happens if the state takes over ultimate healthcare responsibility from the individual . . . I put it to you that, just as money has no power until it is in the hands of individuals – or in the pocket of Miss Finch . . .

Laughter.

'. . . the state – of itself – has no power to create or destroy . . . Only the individuals in power can do that – backed up by force in the laws they pass. They apply the force of these laws to other people and – just occasionally – to themselves . . .

A few hesitant laughs.

'. . . So let me leave you with one thought for you to contemplate . . . A true sense of commitment can only be the product of an individual mind and personal philosophy. It can never be instilled by rules, regulations and committees set up by the state.'

oOo

'The results of your MRI scan show no evidence of an intracranial bleed. The blood vessels around your brain are not leaking as a result of trauma.'

'Well that's ok then . . . I've been wasting my time here.'

'That's one way of looking at it, Mr Finch, but there are others.'

'You're going to tell me something "for my own good",

57

aren't you? I get enough of that at home – and sometimes at the office.'

'And sometimes from girlfriends?'

'That's unfair.'

'It's just that if you get the same observations from several different sources, that increases the probability of them being accurate.'

'I live my life my own way – and I have every right to do so. – I'm not a bank robber or a terrorist or anything. I don't steal things or frighten other people.'

'Would you like to discuss that – in terms of general principle?'

'Huh?'

'I think you can be challenged on what you've just said.'

'About stealing and frightening?'

'Yes.'

'That's ridiculous. You're paranoid.'

'Would you like to discuss it?'

'Not really – but go on, if you must.'

'Put it this way. – From the evidence of your two recent visits to this A and E department, I don't think you're fully aware of the effect you have on other people.'

'Of course I am. How d'you think I do my job in the sales team?'

'Very well, I suspect – when you're the master of your own mind.'

'What d'you mean by that?'

'From what we've seen here, you don't function very well after you've drunk too much or snorted cocaine.'

'That's just party time, fer Chrissake.'

'At other people's expense.'

'What yer going on about? I pay my way.'

'As a result of your self-indulgence, you've taken up medical time and used clinical resources – and been a disturbance to other patients. We . . .'

'Listen, mate. I'm not taking any more of this shit . . . Just because you're a doctor, you think you're God. – Well you're not. – You're part of the National Health Service . . . The public owns you . . . Instead of you wasting your very valuable time – God knows you're well enough paid – lecturing me, you should be looking after patients.'

'Indeed I shall . . . Oh, by the way, you might like to look up the meaning of the word "paranoid" and reflect on some of its causes.'

* * *

That spot of bother with me leg . . . Hmm . . . makes me think I'd better check the health insurance. – I know there were some things excluded when we changed from one company to another . . . Yes – when they were offering lower premiums . . . umm . . . Yes . . . That's right – I remember addiction was one – took it off all their policies . . . and inpatient psychiatric care for more than one episode. – No problem there in our family, thank God . . . And what was the other? . . . umm . . . Oh yes. – Something to do with nerves . . . That pain in me back and down me right leg some time ago. – Different from this silly thing . . . Yes – disc – the doctor said then . . . All gone now . . . Can't see that being any great difficulty . . .

* * *

Damn it . . . This indigestion is becoming tiresome – and the pain in my back . . . Gallstones? Liver? Pancreas? DU? . . . I dunno . . . Ouch! That really is sore . . . Really really sore. S'pose I kneel on the floor and put my head on the sofa – that's one position I

haven't tried . . . Nope . . . Lie on my left . . . Nope . . . Right . . .
Hmmm. – This really is becoming very boring . . . Oooh-wah!
That hurts! . . . Well that's enough pain. – I've got some mor-
phia in my case . . . umm . . . No, Lizzie . . . not a good idea . . .
S'pose I've got to ask someone for some help . . . But who?
. . . No general physicians or surgeons nowadays – or very few.
– All so specialist . . . Other people better at ovaries than I am . . .
Hmm, there's a thought – ovaries? Nope can't be. Not up there,
not even secondaries... I hope... Yeeouch! Ooh that was bad!
– And nausea . . . Yaah! . . . Aaah! . . . Whoops! – Run girl, run
. . . Splaaaa! . . . Whoopsplaaa! . . . Whoopsplspl! . . . Aaaaah
. . . Ooh . . . Ooh . . . Ah. Ah. Ah . . . Gosh – lucky to get
here . . . to the loo. – Oh God, pain's still there! Damn it! . . .
This won't do . . . No . . . won't do at all . . . and Roddy's out at
his blessed Garrick. Wretched man – just when I need him. –
Hmm . . . Know where to find him . . . He won't be pleased . . .
dragged out of supper . . . Ha! – or the bar more like . . . or the
snug . . . Best give him a ring . . .

'Ah, Roddy . . . There you are . . . No, nothing's happened,
nobody's died . . . No. It's just me. My tummy's playing up a
bit . . . No, I don't think it's food poisoning. – I haven't eaten
anything out of the ordinary . . . No, I really don't know – and
I s'pose I've got to be sensible and not diagnose myself for
once . . . No, idiot, it's not a gynae thing – it's higher up . . . and
I've been sick . . . No. Not on your silk carpet . . . I got to the
loo in time . . . Yes, indeed . . . No, I think it's more than that
. . . I think I ought to go to see someone . . . No, not tomorrow
– tonight. Yes, I know everybody will've gone home by now
. . . No. Don't you come. – Stay in the club. – I know where
you are . . . I'll go to the Cromwell . . . Oh, come to think of it,
that's no good. – It doesn't have an emergency department . . .
No private hospital does . . . S'pose I've got to trust the NHS
. . . No – not there – Not a good idea at all to go to my own

teaching hospital . . . I'm still known there . . . The junior staff would be too nervous – and hospitals run on their junior staff . . . No, that's not modesty . . . It's reality – just like you being run by your clerk. – No . . . No, Roddy – just my little joke . . . Aaaah! Yeeouch! Here it comes again . . . No. Not an ambulance. Far too much fuss – and it'll . . . Owowowow! . . . will probably take too long . . . No, I'm not dying – you silly man . . . I'll get a cab. There'll be plenty aro . . . Wooo! . . . around – and it's only . . . Wahwah . . . ten . . . Yaaaah! . . . minutes . . . Ooooop . . . Must go . . . Love you . . .'

* * *

'In today's session we'll consider what happens if resources are distributed according to need. Think about this for a moment . . . Will people be more likely to compete to show how well they can do without assistance from the state? Or will they be more likely to compete to prove how their particular need should be given special consideration? . . .

Silence.

'. . . Consider this question in your own case. Do you naturally want services to go first of all to other people or to yourselves? Do you primarily have a commitment to the welfare of other people or a strong sense of personal entitlement? In this particular audience – of future doctors – we might expect to see a high level of altruism . . .

'Give us the money!'

Laughter.

'. . . but let's look at the population at large . . . If resources – scarce resources – are distributed according to need, will people be more likely to compete to establish their need or, alternatively, their capacity to do well on their own account? . . .

Silence.

'. . . Will an individual be more likely to say, "After you . . ." or will he or she demand his or her so-called rights, without any thought that these will come from a common budget and therefore inevitably – in one way or another – be at another person's expense? . . .

Silence.

'. . . And will the corporate body, answerable for its expenditure of public funds, be likely to prove how well it can do? . . . Or will it be more likely to spend its budget up to the hilt – or even over-spend, regardless of the needs of others – so that it can demand the same again or more the following year? . . .

Silence.

'. . . These are difficult questions to which some people have facile answers . . . To judge from the editorial stance of some newspapers, the Welfare State is in dire straights because of greedy bankers bankrupting the country . . .

Hisses. 'Boooo. Boooo.'

'. . . Other newspapers claim that the problems are due to benefits cheats and immigrants taking resources from the genuinely needy . . .

'Boooo. Boooo.'

'So let's look at the figures . . . The UK government estimated in 2012 that total fraud across the whole of the economy amounted to £73 billion for the year. Overpayment of benefits due to fraud were £1.2 billion and tax credit fraud by claimants was £380 million. Therefore the total – of just under £1.6 billion – is just over 1% of the total of £159 billion in overall benefits and tax credits paid . . .

Whistles.

'. . . Public sector fraud, including benefit fraud, is £20.3 billion a year. The majority of this is due to tax fraud . . .

Hisses.

. . . which costs the economy £14 billion annually, or 69% of the £20.3 billion . . . Therefore, in absolute and percentage terms, tax fraud is a much bigger issue than benefit fraud . . .

Hisses.

'. . . The evidence is clear, benefit fraud and tax fraud are very big business . . .

Hisses.

'. . . But now let's look at charitable donations by the general public – even within the Welfare State and excluding financial support given to some charities by government . . . The proportion of people in the UK donating to charitable causes in 2012 was 55%. This equates to 28.4 million adults . . . The typical amount given per donor per year was £120. The estimated total amount given by individuals in 2012 was therefore £9.3 billion . . .

Whistles.

'. . . Putting all these figures together, we can see that the UK is a generous society – even within the Welfare State . . .

Applause.

'. . . but tax fraud and benefit fraud come to more than double the level of charitable donations . . .

Hisses.

'Shame! Shame!'

'. . . Our question today is whether individuals in the UK – at all social levels – are by nature altruistic or mean-spirited and demanding . . . Do we have a generous society or an entitlement culture? Does the Welfare State make the situation in general better or worse? – and lead to individuals becoming more compassionate or less? . . .

Shuffles.

'. . . As I said, these are difficult questions . . . Facile solutions will be no comfort to those of you at the sharp end of medical practice . . . Very soon you'll all be making clinical decisions – with budgetary implications for the NHS – every day with every patient you see . . .

Silence.

'. . . We can blame the government for underfunding . . .

'Yes! Yes! Yes!'

'. . . and we can blame administrators for mismanagement . . .

'Yes! Yes! Yes!'

'. . . but it's patients who make the demands – or not – and you, as doctors . . . as agents of the government in one form or another . . . make the front-line decisions . . .

Silence.

'. . . Welcome to the real world.'

oOo

Part 2

If resources are distributed
according to need . . .

'Thank you for helping me with my lecture, Miss Finch. You added some humour – which keeps people's attention.'

'I was deadly serious.'

'Oh really? What about?'

'Demonstrating that if I had financial resources I would know what to do with them.'

'By keeping them for yourself, even though they're not yours?'

'Yes – if that leads to creating a fairer society.'

'But that would be unfair to those who had created the resource.'

'Not if they had acquired it unjustly.'

'So one injustice counters another?'

'Yes . . . That's legitimate if it's the only way of achieving equality of outcome.'

'So equality of opportunity is not enough?'

'No. People in power – the wrong people – manipulate opportunities so that only their cronies rise to the top of the heap.'

'That's true in any society – if by "crony" you mean "people who share my values" . . . umm . . . Please may I have my money back now?'

'No.'

'Why not?'

'Because you demonstrated that you didn't know how to

use it responsibly – for the benefit of people who have no resources . . . You threw it away.'

'So who decides what is a responsible use of resources?'

'Enlightened people.'

'Enlightenment by force?'

'Yes.'

'Even by the barrel of a gun?'

'Yes – if necessary.'

'Fascinating.'

'What is?'

'You are . . . umm . . . That even in a free society you would use force to impose your ideas.'

'This isn't a free society. It's riddled with inequality. Force may be the only way of changing it.'

'I hope not. – I've always believed that the pen should be mightier than the sword. – My father was killed in Vietnam . . . My mother told me.'

'He was probably on the wrong side.'

'We can talk about that some other time.'

'Good. Here's my mobile number. You can tell me where and when.'

'And my money?'

'I'll give it back to you over a cup of coffee – or a meal . . .'

'. . . Which you will pay for with my money?'

'Yes. That's fair.'

'Not to me it isn't.'

'Yes it is. This whole course of lectures is on ideas. If you're genuinely open-minded, you'll want to hear from those who disagree with you.'

'Fair enough – but to impose that by force isn't my idea of a fair society.'

'If you listen carefully, you can hear the ice cracking underneath your society . . .'

Part 2

'Hmm ... Interesting dilemma. Stay here – Lizzie says she knows where I am – and enjoy m'self. Excellent company. Or go home and be miserable all on me own ... Ah, come to think of it, that's a point. – I wonder if Lizzie secretly wanted me to go to the hospital to be with her. But didn't want to be thought soppy ... Hmm ... Probably not the best thing – soppy – for a powerful woman ... Anyway, I'd get in the way of her manipulating the system. – Not much point in being a consultant if you can't pull rank occasionally when you need to ... Husband in tow would rather queer the pitch ... Decisions. Decisions. – All me life's decisions ... One kind or another ... Still, s'pose I'd miss them if I'd got none to make ...

'I didn't want to be a nuisance ... I'm so sorry.'

'You're not a nuisance at all. It's the young drunks and druggies who cause the trouble – half our work in the evenings like now – and it'll be even more over the Christmas break.'

'What's the other half?'

'Some are genuine emergencies – like you. I'm sure someone like you wouldn't trouble us unnecessarily – but others are people who should've seen a GP but couldn't get an appointment.'

'Or didn't trust them?'

'Well there is that ... umm ... Is that why you came here?'

'No. – I think I've probably got biliary colic.'

'Looked up your symptoms on the net?'

'I didn't need to. I feel fine now – after vomiting in the street

69

. . . So undignified – but it'll come on again, like earlier this evening.'

'Are you a doctor?'

'Yes – a consultant gynaecologist. It's a funny thing being on the receiving end.'

'Don't you worry . . . I'll get my chief to see you straight away.'

'Earwigo earwigo earwigo . . .'

'Oh God . . .'

'Don't worry. – We won't let him be a nuisance to you. He's just a stupid young drunk, singing a football chant – Liverpool, I think – or maybe any team . . . I recognise the song. He was in here last week . . .'

'I fear I recognise the singer.'

* * *

No. This won't do . . . Can't sit here in the bar – with Gielgud and Larry Olivier and the other portraits staring at me . . . Probably disapprovingly . . . while heaven knows what's going on with Lizzie . . . Least I could do is give her a ring . . .

* * *

'You were right. The ultrasound shows a gall bladder full of stones. Of course, as you know, it isn't the big ones – the visible ones on the scan – that cause the trouble. They've probably been there for years, gradually building up. No, it'll be one of the small ones that's gone on the move – out of the gall bag, down the common bile duct, and got itself stuck at the ampulla. The waves of back pressure – and the inflammation in the GB itself – will be causing the colic.'

'Damn it, I've got a full list of minor ops tomorrow.'

'I'm afraid not. – That'll have to go.'

'So what do I do? – Sorry. It's all at the wrong end of the abdomen for me.'

'You stay here.'

'For how long?'

'Well it's up to you really . . . You'll have no choice initially. You have to stay here in the hospital – on a drip with anti-spasmodics, antibiotics and painkillers – until the inflammation settles down . . .'

'How long for?'

'As I said, that's up to you – and the surgeon, of course. It'll take a few days for you to be safe to move around and then you can come back at a later date – that suits you – to have the surgery. Or you can stay in for ten days to let the inflammation settle down completely and have the surgery there and then.'

'Oh . . . But I'm so busy.'

'Not now, you're not.'

'Oh . . . Do you mind if I give my husband a ring?'

'Not a bit. That would be very sensible – to discuss it with him . . . although if he's anything like mine . . .'

'Ha! – Oooh. Ow! – Please don't make me laugh. It's painful!'

'So sorry . . . Thoughtless of me . . . Yes. Do phone him. – You and I know that won't really cause medical equipment to malfunction. Phones just disturb other patients – and the doctors when we need to think. But keep it as brief as you can, please . . .'

'Actually, come to think if it, there's someone I don't want to overhear me – if he's still here. That's the problem with these cubicles, isn't it? Safe and convenient medically but no real privacy . . .'

'Maybe we could put you in a chair and wheel you into the corridor . . . umm . . . Who was it you wanted to avoid?'

'The singer of football chants.'

'Oh yes. – You said you might know him.'

'Yes . . . umm . . . Slightly.'

'Well he can't very easily be a patient of yours!'

'Ha! – Ow! Wow!'

'I'm so sorry. I keep forgetting. – You're so normal between the bouts of colic. – Not like that young man. He's a right pain in the whatsit . . . Obviously not brought up properly.'

oOo

'You don't seem to realise, I should've had better care than I did. I'm off home now – but why didn't the nurse come when I rang for her earlier? The service this clinic – in the private sector, my God – gave me for the termination was pretty crappy. Ha! – Just like a cattle market in fact . . . And I was paying for it myself!'

'Why didn't you have it done on the NHS?'

'I wanted the best service – of course I did – but I was told the local teaching hospital doesn't do terminations except in very late stages of pregnancy when there are medical complications. – And I thought this excuse might have been something to do with one of the gynaecologists being a Roman Catholic.'

'No. It's a clinical decision. Highly specialised staff and equipment might be needed if things look at all dodgy. – And Catholics would be unlikely to be appointed to the staff in the first place – because the other NHS gynaecologists wouldn't want to have to take on all the terminations that Catholics refuse to do.'

'Catholics should be made to do the terminations. They're paid by the NHS. They should do the work that the NHS needs.'

'It comes to the same thing when the patients are referred

72

to somewhere like the British Pregnancy Advisory Service on an NHS contract. The BPAS does the work but the NHS pays the bill.'

'It's not the same thing at all. – And I heard that the service there is even more like being on a production line. Huh! It's all very posh here – single room, silver service meals, flat screen TV, fresh flowers and a phone – but the nurses don't even speak English . . . I deserve better than that. All patients deserve better than that.'

'Then they'd have to pay even more than the fees you've paid to be in this private clinic . . . And if you'd taken post-coital contraception – the morning after pill – within five days after unprotected intercourse, you would simply have had a heavy period and not have had to go anywhere at all.'

'You doctors are all the same – always lecturing us . . . I made a little mistake, that's all – but now I'm having to pay through the nose for it.'

'Well, as I said, you might have been happier in a BPAS Clinic. It's a charity and the fees are subsidised . . . or you can get a totally free NHS referral if you're entitled to it as a resident.'

'That's just the thin end of a private practice wedge being driven into a fully free and comprehensive NHS . . . The ideals of the founding fathers – and mothers – of the NHS are being progressively compromised.'

'Do you have any concerns over the clinical service you received here?'

'No – but I resent having to pay for something that should've been free. I have my rights to be treated where and when I want on the terms that I want and with the understanding that I want – and totally free. That's the pledge of the NHS.'

'I doubt any state service – or charitable service . . . or even a fully private service – could provide that.'

'Well it damn well should. They all should. Healthcare isn't a fucking commodity that can be bought and sold in the marketplace by someone like my bloody broker brother.'

'Well . . . umm . . . let us know if you have any of the symptoms on this information sheet . . . umm . . . Happy Christmas.'

'Happy Christmas? – Celebrating the birth of a baby when I've just had an abortion? – What fucking planet are you on?'

*　*　*

'Oh dear. This really is going to mess things up . . . I can phone the RMO at the Princess Grace and I'll call Alice. They'll sort out tomorrow's list and cancel my appointments – but Christmas will be a real mess . . . Poor Roddy. He likes his familiars. But I'm sure the Garrick will look after him even if it's not open on the day itself . . . Phoebe will probably refuse on some principle or other, same as last year – and then turn up at the last minute to get some free food . . . James – I do so dislike it when people call him 'Jimmy' or 'Jimbo' – would like to see his father . . . Hmm . . . for reasons that are becoming increasingly obvious and concerning. – And now I'm going to be stuck in here . . .

*　*　*

What a right royal palaver! Get a bit merry at Christmas and they read you the riot act! Bloody hell. – What's the NHS for if not to reassure you that you haven't gone just a bit over the top and hurt yourself? . . . But that's a funny thing again. – Wonder how I got there . . .

*　*　*

Part 2

'Ah – There you are . . . umm . . . Where are you exactly? I tried calling you earlier but you were on voicemail . . . Oh – I do hope they're looking after you. Have you got a private room? . . . Oh I see – In that case I'll come down to see you . . . No I'm not in the club. I came home to see you – and found you weren't here . . . Not a bit, not a bit. – You're my woman . . .'

oOo

Yeah, well . . . it's just another form of contraception really. No big deal. I mean . . . having it wasn't very nice – but I'll survive. And no 'retained products of conception' they're referring to – so primly – in the information sheet . . . Why can't they just say, 'bits of baby and proto-placenta' and be done with it? All these euphemisms . . . Mum specialises in them. – They're what she sells – Ha! I bet she never tells her yummy mummies that every coil she fits results in the abortion of a living fertilised ovum every month . . .

*   *   *

Gotta hold it together. – Do m' work and get some dosh from the idiots . . . – 'Churn 'em, burn 'em', I say . . . But, hell, what's Christmas for – if not to have a party or three? Doesn't do any harm . . .

*   *   *

'Dear Lizzie . . . What a performance! How're you feeling?'
   'Not so bad . . . It's kind of you to come to see me . . .'

'What else would I do, you silly moo?'

'Run off with one of the young pupils in your chambers.'

'Hey hey, Lizzie – you know that's not my style . . . Shitting on me own doorstep.'

'Or anyone else's, I should hope.'

'Certainly not . . . umm . . . Has the consultant seen you yet? – I don't want you being seen by one of the juniors. – And anyway what's the point of paying the insurance company all those hefty premiums?'

'Well, actually, I can't fault any of the staff. They've all been very professional.'

'So they should be. – You're one of their kind.'

'No. I've been listening to them – and watching them sometimes – while I've been waiting to see the consultant. She'll be along in a minute. – You'll probably meet her – Miss Thorneycroft. – She must be good to be a consultant in a general subject – general surgery – rather than gynae or paeds or geriatrics or something.'

'You're not so bad yourself, my clever darling. – And I think Phoebe would call that comment of yours 'sexist' – even against your own sex.'

'Gender.'

'Huh?'

'Oh. Sorry . . . umm . . . I know Miss Thorneycroft slightly from meetings at the Royal Society of Medicine . . . I wonder if she's related to the politician from the old days . . . umm – nobody else would have the authority to arrange a private room . . . A consultant I mean. – Not a politician.'

'That's good. I'm glad you've got that sorted.'

'I haven't yet . . . There may not be any vacant private rooms.'

'Well we can't have you going into a public ward.'

'Why ever not? I'm just a patient now . . . Ha! – Ouch, damn it . . .'

'You ok?'

'Of course I'm not, you twit. – Otherwise I wouldn't be here . . . umm . . . As I was saying – or going to say – Imagine me saying 'just' a patient! – We all look the same under the skin.'

'I don't like to think about the gory details . . .'

'They're not so bad. – Routine really. – And Phoebe would approve . . . which reminds me . . . We've got to talk about James sometime.'

'Well not now. – I think this must be Miss Thorneycroft.'

* * *

'Starbucks wasn't your most generous choice of venue and – on principle – I would never choose to come here.'

'Why not?'

'Because they exploit the farmers who produce the beans.'

'Well the chairs are comfortable.'

'That's just marketing.'

'And what's wrong with marketing?'

'It's subliminal coercion.'

'But, from our previous conversation, it would appear that overt coercion is acceptable.'

'Yes – in the process of achieving a fair society.'

'We've been round that loop before . . . umm . . . Please may I have my money back now?'

'Not yet.'

'Why not? – I kept my side of the bargain.'

'Only the first part. You showed up but you haven't yet listened to my ideas . . . And if you really wanted to know my ideas you would've laid out a larger investment – to use your terms – in Ronnie Scott's or somewhere.'

'Ronnie Scott's is a jazz club – I'm a member – I wouldn't hear a thing.'

'Yes you would – if I came up close . . .'

'You don't hang about, do you?'

'Why should I? – You've already shown your commitment by coming here.'

'I wanted my money back.'

'Don't give me that . . . Why would you go out of your way to meet me just to get back a few measly quid?'

'Because it's my money. I earned it – and it represents the time and effort I put into earning it.'

'But you threw it away – and now you've invested even more time and money just to meet me.'

'To get my money back.'

'We've been round that loop before . . .'

oOo

That's sad. No family Christmas this year. I'm stuck in here. Good job there aren't many patients wanting surgery over the holiday – Got the elective Caesars out of the way last week . . . Roddy's got his friends in The Garrick. James won't mind avoiding being asked what he did with the last 'loan' Roddy gave him. And – just for once – I could do without Phoebe declaring World War III . . . And it won't be too bad in here. – The run up to Christmas in hospital can be quite fun – and the general principle for all families at home seems to be to gather round to have a good fight . . .

* * *

'Mingus? You don't know Charlie Mingus – the Duke's bassist?'

'I'm more into heavy metal – but I thought you could give me an education. It's a cool deal here – the low lights, the band, the dance floor . . . just on special occasions like tonight, you told me . . . with tables nearby . . .'

'And the music, for heaven's sake! Ronnie Scott's is a jazz club – not just a cool restaurant.'

'Are you going to be boring?'

'Mingus boring? Where've you been all my life? Charlie Mingus – he's dead now but "The Mingus Big Band" is named after him – played with Duke Ellington, the king of swing . . . Probably the most influential musician last century.'

'I thought that was John Lennon – or Mick Jagger or Elton.'

'Well them too – in their own way – but this is for real . . . I thought that was why you wanted to come here.'

'Yes it is – to learn about your music from you. – I've done rock concerts before but, with your background in Harlem, you're the main man to teach me – all sorts of things.'

'Well, this side of the pond you've had Chris Barber and Ottilie Patterson, Johnny Dankworth and Clio Lane – and nowadays Michael Nyman . . . And on our side of the pond we had Dave Brubek – You must have heard *Take Five*.

'Is that a group?'

'Ha! No, it's a piece written in 5/4 time – dada-Dadi-dadi-dadi-daa Daa-di-Daa Diddleyda-Daa.'

'Hey that's great, dude! Do it again.'

'Nah – you're just winding me up.'

'No I'm not. I really don't know this stuff.'

'And you don't know Nina Simone, Ella Fitzgerald, Louis Armstrong – "Satchmo" – Dizzy Gillespie, Thelonius Monk and that crowd?'

'Nope – and what's "Satchmo"?'

'Ha! "Satchmo" – "Such a mouth" – was the nickname of

You Can Hear the Ice Cracking

Louis Armstrong – the greatest trumpeter who ever lived – apart from Dizzy Gillespie in his way or, more recently, Miles Davis – originally of the MJQ – Modern Jazz Quartet – or Wynton Marsalis . . . He's amazing – just as hot on classical music as on jazz. – He plays both at the Lincoln Center in downtown Manhattan.'

'You'll have to take me there.'

'Hey, whoa! – I haven't got all that much cash. – And this place will use up all I had in my wallet.'

'I'm worth it. I'll show you just where I've been all your life . . .'

* * *

It's a sobering thought, really – Lizzie being in hospital. Never think much about either of us being ill – 'part from coughs and colds, that sort of thing . . . Good job it's only a gall bladder, not cancer or anything . . . Wonder what would happen if I was the one . . . umm . . . If Lizzie had to look after me, we'd both be out of a job. – But that's not going to happen . . .

* * *

'I thought you might be interested in a commodity that I believe has a particularly exciting position in the market at present . . . Yes, you're absolutely right: coffee has done well. It's been a very sound investment for you . . . Thank you. That's kind of you . . . Yes, a significant amount of my work is based on what the markets term "sentiment", an instinctive feel . . . If you're content and secure in the position I took for you in coffee, I suggest we leave well alone . . . Yes, that's true. All commodities and all stocks and shares have some risk. And even houses aren't always safe . . . Yes, too true! – Everything in life has a risk of some kind. – But we have to remind our-selves that commodities have greater risks than gilts – which is why the return on investment tends to be greater . . . No. I'd recommend you to take things a bit easy at present . . . I remember you saying that this was your first venture into commodities . . . Yes, what I'm saying now is that, before ven-turing into uncharted territory, you might perhaps consider a modest increase in your coffee holding . . . I see . . . Yes – it's really a question of relative risk. Some people want low risk and low returns. Others want to play the market with their spare cash and look to enjoy the possibility of a high return as the potential reward for taking an increased risk . . . Well I don't know that I would call it "more fun". After all, this is my profession . . . No. Absolutely not. – I'm not offended in the slightest. – It's just that I have to give considered advice – based on what I learn from our researchers – rather than merely follow a hunch . . . umm . . . Cotton . . . Yes that's right – the political situation isn't what you'd call "stable" in that part of the world at present . . . Yes indeed. That's the risk – and I'm glad you're so well aware of it. You clearly have some knowledge of the area and a sensitivity to the local situation . . . A paddle steamer on the Nile? Yes, I've been on one myself – from Luxor to Aswan . . . Yes, that's right. I need to get some sort of basic *feel* for the countries that produce the commodities I recommend my clients to trade in . . . Yes, that's right. – There certainly are places I would steer clear of – Columbia for one . . . But, y'know, I wouldn't go so far as Sir James Goldsmith . . . Oh, you don't know that one? Ha! – He said he'd never do business in a country that has green in its flag . . . Yes – he certainly did do very well – and it's very sound advice, politically and financially . . . umm . . . These are the criteria our research people have to consider at any one time . . . Yes, of course, if that's really what you want to do at such an early stage in our professional relationship . . . Yes indeed, I also hope that it will be a long one – and prosperous . . . So, if that's the position you believe would be most favourable to your overall portfolio of investments . . . Well that certainly is very reassuring . . . Right then. I'll take down your instructions and set up the trade . . .'

Sucker. – But a great percentage commission for me . . . And he takes all the risk! . . . You've certainly got the gift for this, young James – 'Lucky Jim' every time in this game! . . .

oOo

'You look pretty healthy today, sweetheart.'

'Well I am really.'

'Then what are you doing still in here?'

'Just letting the inflammation die down before I have surgery.'

'Can't you have it now?'

'So that I can come home to look after you?'

'Well . . . umm . . . yes.'

'Roderick Finch you are the absolute end! You're "something else" – as my American patients would say . . . Here I am – on my deathbed – and you want me to come home to look after you!'

'I hope you don't.'

'Don't what? – Come home?'

'Don't die.'

'Of course I won't . . . Nowadays they take out gallbladders through minimally invasive surgery – keyhole surgery.'

'What the butler saw?'

'Roddy, you really are disgraceful – and I love you for it.'

'Well I miss you.'

Part 2

'I'd never've known it from the amount of time you spend in the Garrick or at the Hurlingham.'

'Ouch! – That's a painful thing to say.'

'Don't worry, I didn't really mean it – except that I miss you too at times.'

'Not all the time?'

'No. – You'd get under my feet . . . and you'd sulk for not being in the club.'

'Would I really? Am I that bad? Is it that obvious?'

'You know how to be inscrutable in court but you can't hide anything from me. – I'm your wife, remember?'

'. . . Umm . . .'

'Roddy?'

'Yes, dear.'

'Don't say it like that.'

'Oh . . . Ah – Yes, my love.'

'That's better . . . umm . . . Would you miss me if . . . umm . . . If something er . . .'

'Yes. – Lots and lots and lots – but it won't.'

* * *

'Hey, Precious, you sure can dance!'

'What did you expect? I was raised in the area where swing took root . . . The Cotton Club, where black performers played to a white audience, was over opposite our house. My mother rented some of the musicians a place in our back room – my room.'

'So where did you go?'

'I slept in my mother's bed when I was young . . . but I moved to the sofa when I was older.'

'And from that background you got to Columbia and became a doctor?'

'Yes, why not? – It was my mother's ambition for me and I went along with it . . . I stayed in Harlem. – Most students choose a university far from home to give them a better feel for the big wide world . . . Well another part of the United States anyway . . . I wanted to be close to my mother – to provide for her and support her in some way.'

'But that must've been an immense challenge for you – growing up in those difficult circumstances.'

'No. It was an immense challenge for my mother. – And she taught me the importance of having a hierarchy of values . . . knowing what's really important and what isn't . . . I just did what I was told. – Black people have a great sense of responsibility and pride.'

'I thought Harlem was dangerous – with drugs and guns and things.'

'It is – further south toward downtown at night – but that's also true in London and many cities all over the world . . . It wasn't so dangerous in our area. And there's Morningside Heights just above us. Wonderful views . . . It's really nice nowadays. All of Harlem's getting to be an "in" place.'

'But in your childhood?'

'There was a lot of social investment – good people, smart ideas – not just money and buildings . . . New Yorkers love our city. We don't really have much in common with the rest of the United States. – We're an island off the east coast. We have our own ways of doing things.'

'Show me, show me, show me . . . Maybe you should educate me in lots of ways . . .'

* * *

Part 2

'Dad, I'm sorry I can't pay you back the full five grand just at the moment . . .'

'Oh. – Really, James, this is a bit much. You must get your financial affairs into better order . . . You can't rely on the Bank of Mum and Dad indefinitely.'

'I'm aware of that – and I'm very grateful for the help you've given me during difficult times.'

'Well I hope there won't be too many more of these "difficult times", as you call them.'

'Umm . . . I've brought you a cheque for two. It won't bounce . . . I've left behind what – in my line of business – we term a "prudent reserve". I'd hoped to be able to pay off the full five from my Christmas bonus but trading hasn't been too brisk recently – with all the economic uncertainty that you know about only too well.'

'James, James, I do apologise. – I've completely misjudged you.'

'Not at all, father. I have to admit . . . I haven't been the model of financial rectitude.'

'You certainly seem to have inherited the gift of the gab . . . umm . . . I'll tell your mother. She'll be very pleased – as I am.'

. . . That's good . . . the prodigal son and heir apparent has pulled a surprise . . . Ha! – The Bank of Mum and Dad should be good for a few more loans . . . when needs arise . . .

*   *   *

'It's so kind of you to take care of me, Miss Thorneycroft.'

'Petra please – and I haven't done anything yet.'

'But I have a feeling – right here – that you will.'

'Yes, I expect so . . . umm . . . What's your preference – stay in and get it all over with? or come back at a later date that might be more convenient for you?'

'As in your case – I anticipate – there's no convenient time to be away from work.'

'Oh, I don't know. There's always someone who can cover.'

'In the NHS – but it's not so easy for those of us in the fully private sector . . . We usually have one friend with whom we box and cox for planned holidays but it's more difficult to find appropriate cover when something unexpected – like this – turns up. I was meant to be on call right now.'

'Don't the locum services provide a list of potential deputies?'

'Yes, they can do – but they don't fill me with confidence . . . After all, what would it say about a specialist if he or she is able to swan off at a moment's notice?'

'Maybe those doctors who do regular locum work are glad to have none of the committee work that full-time staff have to do – and none of the hassle of NHS paperwork... computer work... forms to be filled in one way or the other.'

'There's even tighter regulation of private doctors than there is in the NHS . . . There seems to be a basic assumption in officialdom that we wouldn't be in the private sector unless we were charlatans and thieves.'

'Well maybe that's true for the cosmetic surgery people – but I can see that it's obviously not universally true, certainly not in your case.'

'Umm . . . Thank you.'

'I've got very little private practice . . . I have the opportunity to do private work – all teaching hospital consultants do – but I don't want it. I'm keen on my NHS work. I believe in it.'

'Yes . . . I did once . . .'

* * *

'In the next part of this term – you see I'm learning to speak English . . .'

Scattered drummings and one cry of 'Dream on, baby'.

Laughter.

'. . . we'll be covering two questions. – "What happens if resources are distributed according to need?" and "What happens if services are free at the time of need?" . . .

Silence.

'. . . Yes indeed. These questions are rarely asked – if ever. – But they have to be asked if we're to live in reality – which is the challenge I left you with at the end of the last lecture – or whether we'll live in a dream world, as our friend here suggests I do . . .

A few laughs.

'. . . So let's start by considering what happens if resources are distributed according to need . . . To illustrate this point, let's make it personal for you in this lecture room . . . Supposing the university were to decide that your access to lectures, seminars and hospital wards – scarce and valuable clinical resources for you students in your final year – were to be given to you in inverse proportion to your success in examinations. – Those who came top would have the least access and those who came bottom, and who therefore had the greatest educational need, were given the most . . .

Silence.

'. . . Yes – you can see where this is going . . .

'Eugenics!'

'. . . Not so fast, not so fast – but ultimately you may be right . . . In a Google search of Hitler's ideas, you will see that as early as 1925, in Chapter 4 of *Mein Kampf*, he outlined his view that science, specifically the Darwinian natural selection struggle, was the only basis for a successful German national policy. As Hitler interpreted it – with terrifying sincerity and

terrible consequences. – Only the fittest should survive . . .
Silence.

'. . . But let us here today consider the consequences of a policy based on the opposite premise – that the weakest should preferentially be given the greatest access to resources. What would happen then? . . .
Silence.

'. . . I very much understand that this is a hypothetical question. But let me remind you that George Orwell emphasised the importance of ideas – and therefore the particular significance of the words we use in expressing them . . .
Silence.

'. . . Let me ask you this . . . Would you here – faced with prized educational resources being given preferentially to those who had done least well in examinations – compete to establish how well you can do? Or how badly? . . .
Silence.

'. . . Yes . . . Now you can see the relevance of this question to the issue of the distribution of healthcare resources . . . If resources are distributed according to need, it's likely that people – individuals and healthcare authorities and anyone competing for a share of a defined budget – will compete to establish need, rather than the capacity to do well . . .
Silence.

'. . . Furthermore, little attention will be paid to the capacity of the recipients to benefit from the resource. An absolute need may be totally unchanged even after all the resource has been devoured . . .

'Fascist!'

'. . . You think so? Is that your best answer – personal abuse – to a serious question that has to be asked precisely in order to avoid the gas chambers of Hitler or the murderous pogroms of Stalin?'

Part 2

oOo

'How are you doing today, me love?'

'Bored.'

'In a private room?'

'Yes – even in a private room for which the insurance company pays plenty.'

'I'm not surprised when you're usually so busy all the time.'

'I like being busy. Always have done. S'pose that's part of the reason I preferred surgery to medicine.'

'What's the other part?'

'I enjoy the technical side – cutting, separating, finding, clearing, working out the best option, doing it and then sewing up the wound so that it leaves a neat scar and a healthy and contented patient – or two or even more.'

'Two or more?'

'Of course – if I'm delivering babies by Caesarian section.'

'Oh. I forgot about that.'

'Yes – you would. You're a man.'

*   *   *

'Hello, mum. Dad told me you were in here. I hope you're feeling ok.'

'It's very kind of you to come to see me. I thought you might already be swotting up for your finals next May.'

'No . . . You're more important to me than that.'

'Heavens above, little one. What's come over you?'

'Ha! – You haven't called me that since I really was little . . . umm . . . I'd miss you if you weren't around. I'd have no one to shout at.'

89

'You as well! . . . You're such a glum lot – all talking as if I'm on my way into the next world rather than having a bit of routine surgery . . . I'm going to have to put up a notice – like Granny Weatherwax, when she was temporarily leaving her body – and "borrowing" the physical forms of other creatures – usually birds – to go visiting, saying, 'I ain'tn't dead'.

'Who's Granny Weatherwax?'

'A witch – the best witch ever – and a specialist in "headology", thinking things through.'

'Huh?'

'She's a creation of Terry Pratchett in his *Discworld* novels . . . I'm bored out of my cranium in here – I'm reading them through again now.'

'Well I'm b-. Sorry, mum, I nearly used a silly word.'

'Come along Phoebe. What's up? Something's got into you. What is it?'

'I've met a wonderful man. He's lecturing us on ideas in healthcare systems.'

'Don't tell me . . .'

'Well yes . . . Of course he's black – all my boyfriends have been – but this one wants to use his mind rather than blow it . . . Like the last one.'

'I'm going to need all the time I've got in here to get over the shock – even before I've had any surgery.'

*   *   *

'Gosh! You as well. – Phoebe was in here yesterday . . . You remember her, don't you? – Your sister?'

'Ha! Here you are – in a hospital bed – cracking your favourite joke . . . That's pretty bloody marvellous, if you ask me.'

'Oh I don't know. This is the real me – the one you don't see

90

when I'm too busy to think of anything much other than my work.'

'Well you do have to think about it. – You're a doctor.'

'That's generous of you, James. I didn't see enough of you when you were young. It's not easy being a professional woman.'

'It's not all that easy being a professional man.'

'I think it worth mentioning – while we've got some time together, just by ourselves, that it might be a lot easier for you if you drank a bit less. Then you wouldn't finish up in A and E.'

'Who told you that? It's a gross infringement of confidentiality. I'll sue the hospital out of existence.'

'Calm down, calm down. – I was in one of the cubicles when you were singing one of your favourite songs.'

'Which one.'

'Something along the lines of, "Here we go" . . .'

'Oh that one. – Thank God for that.'

'Huh?'

'It could have been a lot worse.'

'The noise level was impressive.'

'It would be. – It's a football chant.'

'So I gathered.'

'Who told you?'

'Everyone in A and E heard it – and the ambulance crew – and the people walking by in the street, I expect.'

'Oh.'

'It's just that I love you, James. – You're my boy. – I don't want you to come to any harm.'

'Well I . . . er . . . don't want you to come to any harm either.'

* * *

Hope Lizzie's going to be ok . . . Can't imagine life without her . . .

* * *

What is it with this place? Why has everybody packed me off to the morgue when I'm still very much alive and kicking? – Well not exactly kicking but not in all that bad a shape . . . I s'pose people associate hospitals with disease and death . . . Does me no harm to see things from the other side – to get my patients' perspective . . .

* * *

'Meanwhile – following on from last week's talk about what happens if resources are given to someone in greatest need – someone else with a lesser objective need is left with no possibility of the benefit that could have been his or hers because the resource has in effect been squandered . . .

Hisssss.

'Yes, I know, I know – This is a very unpopular realisation. Actions have consequences . . . As we discussed previously – and it's worth emphasising – if resources are distributed according to need, it's likely that people – individuals and healthcare authorities and anyone competing for a share of a defined budget – will compete to establish need, rather than the capacity to do well . . .

Silence.

'. . . And, as I said, little attention will be paid to the capacity of the recipients to benefit from the resource. An absolute need may be totally unchanged even after all the resource has been devoured . . .'

'Soak the rich!'

'. . . I had anticipated that there might be calls of this nature again. – So have a look at this UK chart from the Inland Revenue:

Central Government and Local Authority Expenditure

Fiscal Year 2015

Public Pensions	£150 billion⁻
National Health Care	+ £133 billion⁻
State Education	+ £90 billion
Defence	+ £46 billion
Social Security	+ £110 billion
State Protection	+ £30 billion
Transport	+ £20 billion
General Government	+ £14 billion
Other Public Services	+ £86 billion
Public Sector Interest	+ £52 billion
Total Spending	£731 billion

Look where the really big money goes . . . pensions, health, welfare and education. Expenditure on the military is only one tenth of what's spent on those four departments.

Silence.

' . . . And consider this one from the Institute for Fiscal Studies. – This looks at where the money comes from . . . umm . . . Please note that this is for a different time period than the previous chart – which is why the totals differ . . . But I want to draw your attention to the relative percentages of total income obtained from various sources. These haven't differed greatly in recent years.

Table 1. Sources of government revenue, 2012–13 forecasts

Source	Revenue (£bn)	%
Income tax (gross of tax credits)	154.8	26.2
Tax Credits	– 4.2	- 0.7
National Insurance contributions	105.6	17.9
Value added tax	102.0	17.2
Other indirect taxes		
Fuel duties	27.3	4.6
Tobacco duties	9.8	1.7
Alcohol duties	10.6	1.8
Betting and gaming duties	1.7	0.3
Vehicle excise duty	5.9	1.0
Air passenger duty	2.9	0.5
Insurance premium tax	2.9	0.5
Landfill tax	1.3	0.2
Climate change levy	0.8	0.1
Aggregates levy	0.3	0.1
Customs duties	2.9	0.5
Capital taxes		
Capital gains tax	3.8	0.6
Inheritance tax	3.0	0.5
Stamp duty land tax	6.4	1.1
Stamp duty on shares	3.0	0.5
Company taxes		
Corporation tax (less tax credits)	43.9	7.4
Petroleum revenue tax	1.6	0.3
Business rates	26.2	4.4
Bank levy	2.2	0.4
Council tax (net of Council Tax Benefit)	26.3	4.4
Other taxes and royalties	27.9	4.7

Net taxes and N I contributions	568.8	96.2
Interest and dividends	4.6	0.8
Gross operating surplus, rent, other receipts & adjustments	18.2	3.1
Total Current receipts	591.5	100.0

'As I've mentioned previously, the top 1% of income tax payers pay 29.8% of the total . . . Bearing in mind that many poor people pay no income tax at all, it can be argued that anyone who pays income tax is "rich" and these people pay all of this tax . . .

'So they should!'

'. . . But, looking at this the other way round, it means that 71% of all income tax is paid by regular guys in regular jobs – because there's a lot of them . . .

'And women.'

'. . . Yes, women too . . . Sorry. – My insensitivity. – I've just been watching a DVD of the musical, *Guys and Dolls* . . . It was made before the days of political correctness . . .

A few nervous laughs.

'. . . Yes . . . Women constitute a significant proportion of the workforce – especially in the caring professions and often part-time so their jobs may be relatively insecure . . .

Silence.

'. . . And observe this from the chart . . . Income tax and national insurance payments are a percentage of income but value added tax – VAT – is a standard charge, at variable rates but still universally applied, on many goods and services . . . VAT therefore hits poor people hardest . . .'

'Shame!'

'. . . This means that, in terms of the total of all taxes paid, poor people pay a higher proportion of their income in taxes than rich people . . .

Hissss.

'. . . The poorest one fifth of households – who pay any tax at all – pay 38.7% of their income in taxes whereas the richest one fifth pay 34.9% . . .

Hisses again.

'. . . But the crucial issues for us to observe today are that tax revenues are finite for practical purposes – as President Hollande found out in France . . . When he imposed a top rate of tax of 75% many rich people left France, took advantage of the open borders in the European Union and came over here . . .

Mixed hisses and drummings.

'. . . The Laffer curve – named after the economist who described it – demonstrated that there is a level of taxation that produces an optimum level of revenue . . . Any attempt by government to raise more tax will be counter-productive . . . Clearly the advisers to President Hollande didn't know their economics . . . Or they did and – for political reasons – he didn't listen to them . . .

Silence.

'. . . But the optimum level of taxation is surely not merely an economic high point but one that maximises welfare . . . This point – as shown in economic studies – is well below the optimum level for revenue – because it encourages entre-preneurial activity . . . that leads to growth. And, even though the government may have less money to spend, families have more to spend in the way they wish . . .

'Beer!'

'. . . Come on. Come on . . . You can do better than that . . . But you're right . . . People don't always spend their money wisely . . . Why would they if the government – or someone else – is always picking up the tab?

Silence.

Part 2

'. . . So, if state income is finite, it follows that state expenditure also has to be finite. Ultimately debts – government debts and private debts – have to be paid . . .

Groans.

'. . . Sorry about this message from reality . . . It applies not only to governments paying their bills to international lenders, and town halls making sure that council house tenants pay their rents, and banks not lending to unreliable businesses or families – but also to the repayment of student loans . . .

'No. No. No.'

'Shame!'

'. . . Anything other than payment of all these debts is theft . . .

Silence.

'. . . And anything spent in one area – be it on one government department or one individual person – denies that resource to another . . .

Shuffles.

'. . . The important point today is that state expenditure should be apportioned wisely . . .

'Fat chance!'

Laughter.

'. . . and we therefore must consider the capacity of the recipient to benefit . . . Otherwise the money – or another resource – is wasted . . .

Silence.

'. . . I shall be talking more about this next week.'

oOo

'So . . . Tomorrow's your day for the chop.'

'I wouldn't put it quite like that, my love.'

'Well, I mean . . . umm . . . you know . . .'

97

'Heavens, Roddy. – You're more nervous than I am!'

'Well yes. – You're used to this sort of thing . . . You'd be nervous in court.'

'There's no need to be nervous. My gall bladder's gone cold by now. – All the acute inflammation's gone.'

'I hope Miss Thorneycroft – That was her name, wasn't it? – knows her stuff.'

'I've absolutely no doubt about that. – She's very professional and very nice. – And anyway it isn't surgeons who kill people, unless they take out the wrong organ or cut through the aorta or perforate the bowel.'

'You're really making me nervous now . . . umm . . . So who is it who kills patients? – Nurses?'

'No – although I was reading a news story last week about a nurse who murdered several patients in an Intensive Care Unit. – Ha! Call that "intensive care"!'

'Are you winding me up, Lizzie?'

'Oh dear. Poor Roddy . . . Because we're in a medical environment – my comfort zone – I keep forgetting that you're not medical.'

'You're worse than a criminal or dodgy financial dealer in the witness box . . . You're not answering the question I'm putting to you. – Who is it who kills people?'

'Anaesthetists – when the oxygen runs out or the patient inhales vomit or when they get the decimal point in the wrong place and give ten times the correct dose.'

'God alive! This gets worse and worse.'

'No it doesn't – not since the days of Lord Nuffield.'

'I thought he made cars.'

'He did – but he also endowed a professorship of Anaesthesia at Oxford.'

'Why anaesthesia? – of all subjects? . . . Why not eyes or hearts or brains or something?'

'That's exactly what people wondered at the time. They said, "Any fool can give an anaesthetic". And he replied, "That's exactly what worries me." – Or something like that . . . He'd had a bad reaction to the anaesthetic when he had his appendix out.'

'Enough, Lizzie, enough – or I'll tell you what lawyers get up to.'

'I think I know. – I've had two children by one . . . Come on. – Givusakiss . . . One last kiss . . .'

'Aaaargh!'

* * *

'Ah, Phoebe . . . Come to tell me about your new man?'

'He's not mine yet . . . I'd like him to be – but I mustn't rush things. Got to keep some modesty . . .'

'That'll be the day . . .'

'Mum!'

'Yes . . . er . . . That was a bit sharp. Sorry about that.'

'No prob. – I expect you've been saving it up for a long time.'

* * *

'That you, mother? – Hi! – Bit busy at the moment. Just calling to wish you well for tomorrow. – You ok? . . . Great! That's the spirit . . . I'm sure everything will be just fine. – You'll see . . . Me? – Yeah . . . Top form. Always top form . . .'

* * *

'Good morning, Mrs Finch – or would you prefer me to call you by your first name or some other name?'

'Mrs Finch is fine.'

'I am Dr Wilhelm Schmidt, your anaesthetist.'

'There must be some mistake. – My anaesthetist – who's worked with me for many years – is Joan Prendle.'

'I'll be giving you the anaesthetic for your operation.'

'Ha! I quite forgot . . . I've been totally engrossed in a book I've been reading. – Do you know any Terry Pratchett?'

'Is that a new drug?'

'Ah . . . umm . . . yes, I think it probably is.'

'I'm not familiar with it. – I'm a locum.'

*   *   *

'We need to ask ourselves what happens in practice – to individuals and to healthcare systems – when no consideration is given to the capacity of the recipient of any resource to benefit from it . . . Does individual care become more compassionate or less? Does a doctor or other healthcare worker become more thoughtful or less? Does a healthcare system become more efficient and effective or less? . . .

'D'oh.'

Laughter.

'. . . Yes, we can joke about it. Life's too short to be deadly serious all the time . . . But we do have to be deadly serious some of the time – and in considering the answers to these questions, this is one of those times . . .

Silence.

'. . . Consider the position of a hypothetical builder . . .

'How does he build a hypothesis?'

Loud laughter.

'. . . Ok. ok. – I walked into that one with my eyes wide shut . . . umm . . . He's self-employed. He works hard and he pays his taxes. He supports his family and he also contributes to the care of his elderly parents . . . As he's a young man, he very rarely goes to see a doctor – except for sports injuries or accidents at work – a significant risk in his trade. – He's no trouble and no significant expense to the healthcare system . . . Then he develops a simple medical problem – an inguinal hernia. – Because of it, he can't lift any weights – something he does all the time in his work – without the risk of making it significantly worse . . .

'Ouch!'

A few laughs.

'. . . Settle down, settle down please . . . He goes to his GP – and has to wait ten days for an appointment. Ten days with no work and therefore no income, no capacity to support his family or care for his elderly relatives . . . Because other people – with coughs and colds, minor injuries, bellyaches from eating or drinking too much and some people with genuinely significant clinical problems – are all in the line ahead of him. What does he do? . . .

'Get on the job with his missus!'

Laughter.

'. . . Yes. I see I'll have to avoid asking this audience rhetorical questions. – But d'you think it might be possible to have fewer interruptions? . . .

Drummings.

'. . . The resource that should have been his – after all, he's paid for it over the years in his taxes – has been squandered. A fair chunk of the doctor's time has been taken up with treating some conditions that would've got better on their own and others that wouldn't get better whatever was done . . .

'And paperwork.'

Shhhhh.

'No, that's only partially true. There's paperwork – or computer work – in any profession and doctors – obviously

I hope – have to keep comprehensive records . . . umm . . . When I was referring to intractable problems, I was thinking of housing problems and benefits claims and all sorts of things that take up the scarce resource of a doctor's time. – You'll have seen this in your own visits to GP practices, particularly those in poor areas, during that part of your clinical training. – And there may be little or nothing to show for the expenditure of this resource – other than a full book of appointments . . .

Silence.

'. . . Let me be clear on this . . . I'm not saying that social issues – such as housing conditions and benefits claims – are not important. But I am saying that in a welfare state they can take up an inordinate amount of expensive medical time . . . So can the minor – or the intractable – medical conditions that fill up the appointments book and keep our builder stuck at home . . .

'Aaaaah.'

'. . . His clinical problem is straightforward – but it hasn't even been assessed yet . . . And the delay will be even greater when he's referred to a hospital specialist. – That could take months . . .

'Employ more doctors.'

'Build more hospitals.'

'. . . Yes. That's what the British Medical Association – the doctors' trade union – says . . . And in our last session we saw that the money to do that would have to come from some-where – but where? . . . Aaargh! Sorry – don't answer that . . . These rhetorical questions will be the death of me . . .

'Poor dear.'

Laughter.

'. . . Doctors' time is valuable . . .

'Precious!'

Laughter.

Part 2

'. . . Thank you, thank you . . . But the patients' time is also valuable – and this deserves to be taken into account . . . And a further consideration is that the vast majority of patients are very considerate. – They don't make a big fuss . . . Sometimes they make too little fuss – so that an important opportunity for early diagnosis is missed . . . These issues have to be considered – and resolved – in every individual medical practice. They will not be resolved by government . . .

'Why not?'

'. . . Because we would need a government inspector – or controller – in every medical practice in the land. That would certainly bring about Ayn Rand's prediction that the difference between a welfare state and a totalitarian state is merely a matter of time . . .

Hisses and boos.

' . . . And this reaction – from some of you – illustrates another difficulty that springs from failure to consider the capacity of recipients to benefit from valuable resources . . . You will find that scientific assessment of benefit sometimes takes second place to the repetitive, mindless, arrogant hollerings of political pressure groups . . .

Cries of 'Whoop! Whoop! Whoop!', 'No! No! No!', 'Shame!'

'. . . Ha! I may overstate my case – but I believe it has just been made for me by some of you.'

'Boo. Boo. Boo.'

oOo

Dear God – if you do exist – Please look after my Lizzie . . . She's a good girl – and I don't know what I'd do without her . . .

*   *   *

You Can Hear the Ice Cracking

I've never felt like this about a man before . . . I always screwed first and then wondered who he was . . . Precious is different – a real gentleman, I reckon. God knows I gave him the green light – and he took me out and gave me a fabulous evening . . . Jesus, he's a mover! . . . But why didn't he take me back to his place? . . . Oh please, please let him like me . . . I hope he hasn't got anyone 'Stateside'. – Funny word . . . Side of what? – I'd love him to be side of me . . . I'll clean up my act – and my language – for a chance to go to New York with him . . . Yup. That's the way to get him . . . And what was that saying? . . . based on blood groups proving that many children are not their father's . . . Oh yes . . . Women marry for security but breed for brains . . . And he's got both . . .

*　*　*

I wonder what mum meant by, 'a lot easier for you if you drank a bit less' . . . I don't drink much – not really . . .

*　*　*

'There you are, Mrs Finch, all done now . . . Just squeeze my hand . . . That's right . . . Good, good . . . Wide awake now . . .'
　'Nngoo.'

*　*　*

'. . . Suppose you have an acute headache and a chronic back-ache . . .
　Groans.
　'. . . The headache is potentially more serious because you don't know what might be causing it all of a sudden . . .

Part 2

'New Year's Eve parties!'

Laughter.

'. . . You've had the backache for ages so you'd like to get rid of it at some time in the future but you're not too worried about it right now. You'd probably consider the headache to be more important today than the backache . . . Your doctor examines you carefully and decides that the headache isn't clinically significant. You're given medication – or physiotherapy to your neck – and the headache resolves . . . At that point your attention switches to the backache . . .

'Aaaaargh!'

'. . . Ha! These sessions wouldn't be the same without the sound effects. American students are supine by comparison. I'd miss your contributions – well, maybe not all of them . . .

'Aaaaaah'

'Thank you . . . The point I'm making is that our perceived needs change from moment to moment. We tolerate some things for a long time. Others we want fixed right away . . . Now let's bring in a free and comprehensive healthcare system . . . Perhaps – from that precise moment – we decide we want the headache investigated with an MRI scan. – We're very sophisticated patients . . .

Nervous laughter.

'. . . and we want the backache sorted out at the same time . . . The principle behind this is that if services are free at the time of need, perceived needs become relative rather than absolute. Meeting a need does not satisfy . . . It merely shifts attention to another need . . .

Shuffles.

'. . . In this respect it's interesting to note that Nye Bevan, the Minister of Health in the Attlee Labour government . . .

Drummings.

... that brought in the NHS and all the apparatus of the Welfare State ...

More drummings.

'... believed that as people received treatment they would become healthier and the NHS costs would go down ...

A few laughs.

'... Yes. He could hardly have been more wrong. He overlooked three factors ... The first is that healthier people live longer. – They stop smoking and avoid a heart attack. – But they go on to get diabetes or arthritis or cancer or some other illness ... Now, as you know, many of these conditions are treatable or manageable nowadays – but they're very expensive – all together – because so many people get them ...

Silence.

'... The second factor that was not forseen when the NHS was born is also a consequence of people living longer ... Their welfare costs, especially their pensions and eventually the cost of their care in nursing homes, increase ... This becomes a significant social and economic problem when young people in work have to support increasing numbers of elderly people in the population ...

Shuffles.

'... The coalition government is looking to increase the retirement age ...

Hissss.

'... That's right. Young people like you tend not to like that idea ...

Silence.

'... The third factor is that medical advances – new ways of investigating and treating illnesses – are often exceedingly expensive ... In the UK, NICE – the National Institute for Health and Care Excellence – exists to determine which new treatments are effective and affordable ...

'Shame!'

'. . . Possibly . . . That's what the tabloid newspapers say when they highlight a particular case of treatment that's been denied to an individual sufferer . . . They say "It's wicked to deny care" and then they say, "It's only money" . . .

Shuffles.

'. . . As you yourselves know only too well, some people have progressive incurable neurological conditions . . . Amyotrophic Lateral Sclerosis – ALS – the most common of the five types of motor neuron disease – is a case in point. Its progress cannot currently be reversed or slowed down significantly. The average survival time from onset to death is three or four years. The disease causes gradual loss of function – as a result of deterioration in some areas of the brain . . .

Silence.

'. . . In the later stages, the patient will be totally dependent and will need full nursing care . . . It might be compassionate – and perhaps also make fearful economic sense to the patients themselves when they consider what they want to bequeath to others – to consider voluntary euthanasia, as some of the sufferers do . . . at Dignitas in Switzerland.

Hissss.

'. . . So how about voluntary euthanasia for those people who are not ill but fear their productive and sentient lives are over? . . .

Hisses again.

'. . . or compulsory euthanasia as an instrument of government social and economic policy? . . .

'Boo. Boo. Boo.'

'. . . Mass murder of its own citizens has been government policy in totalitarian states throughout history . . .

Silence.

'. . . It still is . . .

Silence.

'. . . but whereas governments may deliberately kill millions of people in wars against other countries – and, as I say, sometimes in their own – ALS is responsible for only 2 deaths per 100,000 people per year . . . It's a fearful death – but it's not an economic catastrophe for a healthcare system . . . By contrast, type two – usually elderly onset – diabetes, which affects millions of people, most definitely is an economic disaster. – This is what Aneurin Bevan didn't anticipate . . .

Silence.

'. . . This is why it's so important to recognise that – in large populations as well as in individuals – perceived needs become relative rather than absolute. – The clinical needs of a population change as its demographic structure changes . . . An ageing population – as in the UK nowadays – has different needs from the population in Nye Bevan's time. – Meeting one need at one time in history does not satisfy . . . It merely shifts attention to another need . . .

Shuffles.

'As a result, the plain economic and social truth – like it or not and despite all the worthy intentions of the NHS and the Welfare State in general – is that individuals and governments have to make hard economic and social choices . . . I'm not saying what these choices should be . . . I'm just pointing out that when budgets are limited, as they always are in any society other than fairyland – and worthy though it may be for services to be free at the time of need – we simply can't give all the people everything they want all the time.'

oOo

'Oh Lizzie, dearest Lizzie. I'm so glad you came through.'
  'Came through what?'

'The operation, silly.'

'Oh that.'

'You're quite remarkable. You have major surgery and you just shrug it off.'

'A laparoscopic chole isn't major these days.'

'It was major enough for us – well for me anyway – wondering how you'd do.'

'Dearest Roddy, you are lovely – but nobody dies from this sort of op, unless they're in the hands of complete idiots. – And Petra Thorneycroft's no fool . . . Anyway, they wouldn't dare kill one of their own colleagues.'

'Why ever not? I'd gladly bump off one or two of mine.'

'Oop! Ow!'

'Oh . . . Sorry . . .

* * *

'My life's changing, mum. Seeing you in hospital – as a patient – has really wised me up. Previously I've always seen you as a doctor – a helper, a provider.'

'I still am.'

'But you might not have been.'

'That's interesting.'

'What is?'

'You were thinking about negative possibilities that hadn't occurred to me . . . As a final year medical student – I do hope this and other things in your life haven't got in the way of your studies – you know that the statistical chance of anything going wrong was very small.'

'I *think* the numbers but I *feel* the possibilities . . . Suddenly being reminded – by one thing or another – that we're all human, made me look at the "what ifs?".'

'That's a very healthy approach for a future doctor . . . You have an excellent mind – which you may not always have used in the best ways for yourself and others – and you've been very well trained.'

'But you're thinking academically even now.'

'No I'm not . . . I love you and I want the best for you.'

'I love you too, even though I haven't always shown it.'

'Well, we'll let that go.'

'No we won't . . . umm . . . I won't . . . umm . . . You're still thinking about what sort of a doctor I'll be. I'm wondering what sort of human being I am – and how events can suddenly change my take on that.'

'As a woman, that's always true – biologically and culturally.'

'I was thinking more generally and socially . . . If you'd died, dad's life would change dramatically. So would mine – in having to look after him – or at least think about him, which I don't do very much at present.'

'That's just a function of your age. The young are always egocentric.'

'That's not true. – We're highly idealistic.'

'Yes. Maybe too much so at times. – Men sometimes never grow out of that . . . They're focussed on their careers and on changing the world.'

'You're a career woman.'

'But also a wife and mother.'

'A very good one.'

'Heavens, Phoebe. What's got into you?'

'I looked in the mirror – and into a crystal ball.'

'What did you see?'

'That I don't much like myself as I am. – And hopefully I've got better possibilities.'

'Is it that new man of yours?'

'I'm a bit stuck there at present. I've got no more hold over him.'

'I don't know what hold you had before . . . But have more confidence in yourself . . . softly softly. Let him come to you.'

'I don't know how to do "softly softly".'

'I think I'm aware of that.'

'Yup . . . umm . . . Sorry mum.'

'No matter.'

'Well I'm beginning to see that it does matter to me . . . I really am growing up all of a sudden.'

'Gosh, he really has had an effect on you . . .'

'Yes he has – and we haven't even done anything yet.'

'Perhaps that's why.'

'Why what?'

'Why you're thinking rather than rushing ahead.'

'Yes, I've always done that . . . umm . . . rushed ahead.'

'You don't have to tell me! – But what else is on your mind? Are you worried about finals? – and what kind of doctor you'll be?'

'Not really . . . and I still don't know what specialty I want to work in . . . General practice, I guess. – I'm more interested in people than diseases . . . umm . . . I'll be my kind of doctor.'

'Yes, I'm sure you will – and a very good one, a thoughtful one.'

'Thanks – and right now I'm thinking about you.'

'Me?'

'Yes you – and me.'

'In what way?'

'Umm . . . Wondering what tricks fate could play on us.'

'Huh?'

'What would've happened – to all of us – if you hadn't come round from the anaesthetic – if you'd died or been left as a vegetable.'

'You're cheerful today.'

'Well it's what Precious has being saying . . . umm . . . That's his name. – You won't laugh will you?'

'Certainly not – I'm an obstetrician. People call their children all sorts of things. – His mother must have loved him very much.'

'So do I . . . I think.'

'Ha! Fancy me telling you about this! – Dear Phoebe – It's not about "think".'

'Yeah – I do know that – but we've gone off the point . . . I was thinking about what Precious was saying on scientific assessment of benefit taking second place to shouting by political pressure groups – or something like that – and about taking into account the capacity of recipients – of any resource – to benefit . . . umm . . . Supposing you were a vegetable – God forbid! . . .'

'God?'

'Whatever . . . umm . . . It might have been . . .'

'Better if I'd died?'

'Yes, I guess . . .'

'Is he American?'

'Yes. – How did you know?'

'You've used that expression twice. – We English don't say, "I guess".'

'Well I guess I'm taking on his way of speaking – as well as his ideas . . .'

'Well I'm certainly not dead . . . I'm very much alive – and I'm very glad to have had such a lovely conversation with you.'

'Yes . . . umm . . . Thanks, mum . . . Love you.'

'Love you too.'

* * *

112

Part 2

'James Finch here . . . umm . . . Yes – I am listening to you . . . Yes . . . Yes . . . Well that's the way it is with all commodities. – Some go up, some go down . . . We can't account for things like Islamic State turning up out of nowhere . . . So the price goes up... and then the Egyptian army cracking down so the supply of cotton is more secure – and the price goes down again... Yes, you'd think Al Qaida were bad enough – and on the retreat with all the drones coming down on them . . . That's true – but there'll always be a market for cotton . . . No? . . . Well it might possibly be the best time to stay in cotton – bucking the trend of the woolies . . . umm . . . sheep – people who merely follow the flock . . . Yes . . . er . . . No. – I fully understand you. It really has taken a beating . . . There might be a better position – steadier in some ways – in rice . . . No? . . . Well I fully understand that. Maybe on another occas—'

. . . Oh. He's gone. No probs. – It was good while it lasted . . . And there'll be another mug along in a minute . . .

* * *

I do hope my Lizzie'll be ok, coming out of hospital so soon. I know these laparoscopic dodahs are meant to be safe – and I know the insurance company has its tariffs on specialists' fees and room costs . . . Yup – They'll be putting on the pressure . . . But just one day after the op seems a bit quick. – Whatever happened to convalescence? Still, my hunch . . . umm . . . certainty – is Lizzie won't mind . . .

* * *

'In an earlier talk I mentioned to you the book *The Public-Private Mix for Health*, published by the Nuffield Trust. As you will recall, it looks at a range of models of healthcare systems throughout the world . . . The book – an explorer's account rather than a political tract – makes no conclusion on which model is best or worst. . . To do that – to give no viewpoint in the subjects of healthcare or education – takes courage . . .

Silence.

'. . . These are emotive subjects. Strong views may be held for reasons of "feel" or "belief" rather than be supported by evidence . . . As an example, may I ask you to reflect on the opening ceremony of the 2012 Olympic Games in London. Danny Boyle, the distinguished film director of *Slumdog Millionaire* . . .

'My goodness.'

Hisses.

'. . . put on a magnificent show. One scene can only be described as homage to the NHS – the holy grail of socialised medicine . . .

Drummings.

'. . . To a UK audience that would seem reasonable. – People over here are fiercely proud and protective of the NHS . . .

More drummings.

'. . . But imagine the reaction in any one of the countries featured in the book I mentioned . . . If they thought the NHS was the hottest ticket in town they'd have copied it by now – but they haven't . . .'

'Shame!'

'. . . They wouldn't agree with that judgement . . .

'Shame!'

'. . . Thank you. I think you've made your point – and you're also making mine by giving us an emotional rather than rational contribution . . . Comparative studies on outcomes for treatment of cancer, diabetes and heart disease in European countries show that the NHS does not do very well . . .

'Tory cuts!'

114

'. . . Again I believe that you are making my point – very effectively. – The evidence is in outcome studies . . . on per capita expenditure on healthcare and welfare services in each country. In some outcome studies the NHS comes out well . . .

Applause.

'. . . The Institute of Commonwealth studies show that the NHS comes out near the top of the pile . . .

More applause.

'. . . but this may be influenced by the low expectations of many patients . . .

Silence.

'. . . and in terms of hard outcome figures, the NHS does not come out at all well – either in clinical outcome or in value for money . . . You can see all this for yourselves by googling the web – but let me give you one example . . . To quote from a 2013 report in the Conservative newspaper, the *Daily Telegraph* . . .

Hisses.

'. . . "Survival rates for almost all common cancers are worse in Britain than the European average. A recent study of more than 29 countries compared five-year survival for stomach, colon, rectal, lung, melanoma skin, breast, ovarian, prostate, and kidney cancers as well as the blood cancer non-Hodgkin's lymphoma. It found that only for skin cancer was survival in this country better than the EU average . . .

'. . . Ciaran Devane, when he was chief executive of the cancer patient charity Macmillan Cancer Support, said: "This is truly depressing. One in two of us will get cancer in our lifetime so this is a big deal and has to be a wake-up call for the NHS." . . .

Silence.

'. . . Then you can google for yourselves a study conducted by the Economic and Social Research Council's Centre for Population Change (CPC) in 2012 . . . This found that the UK had below average levels of welfare spending among developed nations, with many European countries outranking us . . .

Hisses.

'You're not one of us! – You're an American.'

'. . . As I've said before, as a UK resident I pay UK income tax. I also pay American income tax because I'm an American citizen . . . President Benjamin Franklin said that in this world nothing can be said to be certain, except death and taxes . . .

Silence.

'. . . To quote – selectively – from the CPC report, "While the UK was found to have larger than average social assistance schemes, including housing and family benefits, as well as unemployment assistance, several other nations offered better benefits in other areas." . . ..

Hisses.

'. . . The Organisation for Economic Co-operation and Development (OECD) report, dating from 2007 – and up-dated in 2012 – shows that the UK is ranked significantly *below* many other European nations – including France, Germany and Italy – in terms of the money spent on welfare . . .

Hisses.

'. . . And it also says that if we focus purely on money given out by the state, the UK slips even further down the rankings . . .

'Boo. Boo. Boo.'

'. . . To continue my selective quotes from this report, "Eurostat, the official statistics outlet of the European Union, would seem to support the view that the British benefit payments are no more generous than most of Europe . . . Looking at total social expenditure, the UK ranks just above the EU average, but again below France, Germany, Italy and the Eurozone mean – in terms of spending per inhabitant . . .

Silence.

'. . . But it goes on to say, "However, this includes both public and private spending on welfare – including private pensions and health spending . . . So if we focus purely on that portion of spending administered by central government, the UK gets bumped straight to the top of Europe's league table for benefits spending . . .

Applause.

'. . . The report continues, "Thus the relative 'generosity' of the UK's benefits system in comparison to other European countries can be measured in a number of different ways . . . With this in mind, the UK can rank anywhere from top to below average in a European league table of benefits" . . .

Silence.

'. . . Mark Twain, the American writer, attributed to the British Prime Minister Benjamin Disraeli the well-known saying, "There are three kinds of lies . . . lies, damned lies, and statistics" . . .

Laughter.

'. . . It would appear, ladies and gentlemen, that we can believe anything we want to believe. And we can find – from somewhere or other – statistics to support our views . . .

Silence

'. . . There is, however, one very practical consideration from real life in the UK Welfare State at times . . . Instead of the individual patient not being able to afford treatment, the state runs out of money so that either the individual cannot get treatment at all or, alternatively, the treatment that he or she can get may not be worth having.'

'Tory cuts!'

oOo

Where's the work? The punters? They can't all have wised up over Christmas . . . Spent all their money maybe . . . Huh! . . . I work hard following up leads – and get nowhere. Nothing to show for it. – And when I do get a good run, a great chunk of it goes in tax to pay for skivers who can't be fucked to get out of bed . . . Yeah, as father says, the City pays for everyone else . . . People who work for the state – millions of them – get their feather-bedded pensions . . . We have to make our bread while we can. No security. 'No such thing as a free lunch?' – Ha! That's a laugh! God knows how many people's lunches I've paid for . . . Makes me wonder . . . What it'd be like getting a regular job – or a vocation, like mum or Phebes . . . Problem is – sales is the only thing I know . . . And what about my rights? The bloody government – well the LibDem tossers – talk all the time about rights. And entitlements… What about mine? What do I get back for all the hard graft I put in? Street lights and policemen doing paperwork . . . and doctors who think nothing nowadays of going on strike. They're not worth asking their opinion . . . Mum can't do that. – She's got no more security than I have. – It's no good us demanding our rights. We haven't got any. Only the scroungers, immigrants, asylum-seekers and benefits cheats have rights . . . Ha! . . . That's something . . . S'pose I can't live off the parents – in the flat – indefinitely . . . Mother being ill was a bit of a wake-up call. – And what if something happened to father? . . .

* * *

'Precious? . . . It's me – Phoebe . . . I'm being cheeky phoning you on your mobile when I . . . Oh, that's kind of you . . . I

118

won't take advantage of you – not like last time – and you've been very kind to me already . . . Oh thank you . . . Yes, you got me thinking about rights and responsibilities . . . Are you sure? I thought you'd tell me to bring it up in a seminar . . . Well, I remember the elective I did in general practice . . . Four weeks in a health centre. Then I did another two in a private practice my mother arranged for me to visit . . . Yes, I thought it would be interesting to see what I absolutely loathe – to visit a doctor who obviously has no interest in getting healthcare to the people who need it most and can least afford to pay for it . . . umm . . . I don't know really . . . After seeing her at work, I don't think she's a real private doctor . . . No, she doesn't work for the NHS at all. She used to but she doesn't now . . . She said she has her own ideas but couldn't implement them in the NHS . . . because that's the way it works. – Doctors have to do what the Department of Health and the Care Quality Control people tell them to do. Even in the private sector . . . Well, as you may well know if you've heard them beefing about it, they have to monitor their patients for specific conditions – and monitor all their prescriptions and hospital referrals – all to protect patients, so they say . . . Yes . . . That's what she said – so I can understand her point about not wanting to be a mere number in someone else's plans . . . She has a mind of her own – a good mind and a kind heart . . . But what really surprised me was her patients. – They were ordinary people, some toffs but lots who seemed just to want to be listened to and examined properly . . . No, in the health centre the patients were rarely asked to take any clothes off. – It was just one prescription or sickness certificate after another . . . No, they saw fewer real patients – people who really did have something wrong – in a day than the private doctor did . . . Umm . . . Long consulting hours . . . Yes. Sure she charged them – although there were some she didn't . . . No, I don't know

119

why not. – And the doctors in the health centre were always taking time off . . . How could they practice responsible clinical medicine if they hadn't even examined the patients properly? . . . They have district nurses and health visitors and social workers and chiropodists and all sorts of people – but that's all social, not really medical . . . And they make a lot of money nowadays – the doctors . . . but, as I said, I don't think the private doctor I saw was a real private doctor. – They can't all be like her. – She was kind and thorough and . . . umm . . . human . . . No, that must also be true – but, talking to other students who did a GP elective in health centres, they saw the same as I did. – Who would ever want to work on a production line like that? . . . No wonder so many GPs want to take early retirement . . . Yes, maybe. – But what happened to the enthusiasm those doctors had when they were students? . . . And what happened to the ideals that made them want to be doctors in the first place? . . . The things I wanted to talk through with you – if it's at all possible – follow on from your early lectures . . . things like do patients have rights over the lives of medical staff? and do the staff have rights over their own lives? . . . and also should there be more mobility of doctors between hospital and general practice . . . Yes . . . Yes . . . I see . . . Well what happened over here was that the last government sent in a hospital doctor to advise on restructuring general practice – the bloody nerve! – What would he know? He was just a Labour party hack, doing the government's bidding . . . Yes – and that's what the private GP found so unacceptable . . . umm . . . Sorry, Precious. – Yes, it was rather a mouthful . . . Oh . . . That would be very nice of you . . . Thank you . . . Ha! You remembered – not Starbucks . . . No, not Pret either – it had some form of tie-up with McDonalds . . . ok, Byron it is . . . umm . . . Precious? . . . Would you let me pay this time? – out of my own money rather than yours? . . .

Part 2

*   *   *

'Welcome to the Garrick, James. We'll go upstairs to the members bar so I can introduce you to a few of my friends. – You never know when you might want to become a member. Then they could sign the front of your sheet – in the snug down there . . . Yes, there . . . indicating they've met you and spent time with you. Signatures on the back, simply recommending you on reputation, don't count so much.'

'Thank you, father.'

'Here we are . . . Gosh, that's tiring – just climbing the stairs . . . and struggling with that silly foot of mine. Really odd . . . umm . . . Let's just get our drinks and then pop into the library. – It's a small sitting room really. – It'll give us a chance to have a quiet chat . . . if no one else is in there.'

'Thank you, father. – Mine's a tomato juice, if that's ok.'

'Nothing in it?'

'Nope – on the wagon.'

'Any pressure from your mother? or anyone?'

'Not a bit . . . I just thought I'd prove to myself that I can do it.'

'. . . Good . . . Good . . . There we are. – Take one of the armchairs. People often fall asleep in them after lunch but we should be ok now – unless someone wants to watch the telly . . . for a race or something.'

'Thank you, father.'

'Anyway, I wanted to follow up on you giving me the cheque. That showed me a new James . . . Well done.'

'Thank you, father.'

'I thought it might be helpful – particularly in this environment – if I spoke to you a bit about how the world works . . . Jeremy Paxman, in his book *The English* concludes that the most influential part of the country is the men's clubs.

He's probably right – along with the livery companies, of course. – You'll know all about them from your contacts in the City.'

'Yes, father.'

'What I want to get across to you is that the enemy of individualism – of people who want to get on in life through their own efforts – is the state. There's no shortage of funds in the state system . . . For anything . . . There's vast amounts of money – for schools, hospitals, the legal system. Everything. – And the administration is pretty sound, by and large . . . It's the ideas that are wrong . . . People don't do things out of the kindness of their hearts nowadays. – Bankers certainly don't . . . Never did. – And, without banks doing their bit for England, the whole system grinds to a halt . . . as we saw in the credit crunch . . . Dreadful business.'

'Yes, father.'

'Politicians promise everything to voters or they don't get elected . . . But that's not the real world . . . Money makes the world go round. – That's what it said in the song. – And it's right . . . More than one Chancellor of the Exchequer has been brought to his knees by the money men . . . You can't buck the market.'

'No, father.'

'The problem is universal access. – You can't give everything to everybody and expect to stay solvent.'

'No, father.'

'Umm . . . Fancy some red-legged partridge? – It's very good here. It's been an excellent season and it's on today . . . umm . . . Good to have a chat with you, James.'

*   *   *

I wonder why Precious didn't take his chance. He felt very

close – a natural fit – when we were dancing. He's certainly not gay, that's for sure . . . Maybe he's got someone . . . He's not wearing a ring. – Hmm . . . Come on girl, get a grip, you can do better than this . . . umm . . . Ah! I know . . . I'm getting things in the wrong order. – Yes. Mum told me that. – Yes, wrong for him and . . . umm . . . for the first time in my life, wrong for me. – I'll have to attract him through my mind . . . Hmm . . . Such as it is . . . He's a thinker . . . umm . . . Not just with my body . . . Yup, that's what Mum's been telling me all these years. – Sex is an activity of the mind . . . All imagination and creativity . . . not porn and erotica or procreation and duty . . .

* * *

'Roddy?'

'Yes, my love?'

'Umm . . . You won't think me silly?'

'I always think you're silly.'

'No – I'm being serious . . .'

'Really serious?'

'Yes.'

'Oh.'

'Is that all you're going to say?'

'Umm . . . No . . . Tell me . . .'

'I think I'm losing my mind.'

'You? – Never!'

'You haven't heard what I'm going to say . . .'

'Oh . . . umm . . . Sorry . . . What is it?'

'It seems bizarre now I'm home. – I'd have thought I'd have remembered it immediately.'

'What?'

'You promise you won't laugh at me – or go all legal on me?'

'Legal? What on earth for? What've you done? . . . I expect trouble from the children – but not from you.'

'No, no. – It's nothing like that . . .'

'Gosh, Lizzie, I can see you're really upset . . . umm . . . frightened even. – That's not like you . . . Here, let's sit on the sofa, side by side like we do when we do the puzzles . . .'

'It is a puzzle . . .'

'What is, sweetheart?'

'Umm . . . You know I had a nightmare last night?'

'I could hardly forget! – You screamed your head off – and kicked me in the back . . . umm . . . rather that than if I'd been facing you.'

'Don't joke about it, love . . . I was terrified . . .'

'Oh . . . umm . . . Sorry. – Still it's only a dream.'

'Well that's the whole thing about it . . . I think it was reality.'

'What was?'

'My dream . . . umm . . . I . . . er . . . I don't think it was a dream. – I think it was a memory.'

'What of? – Childhood stuff again?'

'No, that's gone – although this reminded me of what it was like . . . umm . . . being trapped and not being able to tell anyone . . .'

'Heavens, Lizzie . . . Here, cuddle up close. Put your head on my shoulder and let me hold you . . .'

'Not too tight! Not too tight! Not too tight!'

'Sweetheart . . . Poppet . . . What on earth's it all about? . . . Tell me . . .Tell me, my love . . .'

'You won't be angry? – umm – with anyone?'

'Of course I won't . . . Here, let me just stoke your hair . . .'

'Don't do that! Don't do that! Don't hold my head!'

'Sorry, sorry, sorry . . . Sweet Lizzie – This isn't like you . . . It isn't like you at all . . . What is it, dearest? What is it?'

' . . . I'm not absolutely clear – and I don't know why it wasn't obvious to me, one way or the other, before now – why I didn't remember it straight away. I . . . er . . . Don't be angry, Roddy . . . I . . . I woke up during the operation.'

'God! Oh God. – You poor love . . . er . . . Why didn't you tell them?'

'I couldn't. I was totally conscious and I wasn't in any pain – at least he'd got that drug right. – I just had a feeling of pressure . . . in my tummy . . . But I couldn't say a word or blink an eye or anything.'

'Why not? Why didn't you scream like last night?'

'I couldn't. I wanted to – but I couldn't move a muscle, not even to breathe on my own . . . I was intubated. – You know, when they put a tube down your throat and join you up to the machine. They use a drug to paralyse you – Curare – or something like that . . . The Amazon natives use it on the tips of their arrows so that they paralyse their prey even if they don't kill it with the arrow . . . They use more modern techniques nowadays.'

'I should hope so . . . Don't tell me, sweetheart. Don't tell me . . . No wonder you had such a nightmare. You're terrifying me now – just thinking about it . . . But how d'you know you were conscious? What proof have you got?'

'There you are, Roddy. I thought you'd go all legal on me. Please don't be angry . . . umm . . . It still isn't all clear – and I still don't know why not.'

'Okay, no legal – but why d'you think you were awake?'

'The anaesthetist was German.'

'So?'

'He was joking with his English student . . . about football.'

oOo

Part 3

If services are free at the
time of need . . .

'Welcome back . . . As you are aware, in this, your final year, there's no time for a break for Christmas. – This prepares you for your real life as future doctors. – Illness doesn't take a day off. Every day at this time of year has to be covered by one doctor or another in every ward and every practice . . .

Silence.

'. . . As I see it, my function as your course lecturer is to challenge you, unsettle you and support you in thinking for yourselves rather than following the party line . . .

Silence.

'. . . I want to encourage you to be individuals rather than mere units in someone else's grand design. After all, your patients – for those of you who will become front-line clinicians – will see themselves as individuals rather than mere numbers . . .

Shuffles.

'. . . Today I'll look at a further issue in people's emotional commitment to a welfare state . . . The proponents of such a system point to a few people who've been dramatically helped "at no cost" . . .

Drummings.

'. . . They need to be careful when they define precisely what they mean by the phrase "at no cost". As students, paying your own tuition fees . . .

'Hissss. Hissss. Hissss.'

'. . . you know only too well that money doesn't come from the money tree . . . In part it may come from the Bank of Mom and Dad. – But in state healthcare and welfare systems it comes from . . .? – You tell me . . .

'The government!'

'. . . I'm afraid not . . . It's *distributed* by the government – after huge administration costs – but it *comes* from taxpayers . . .

Silence.

'. . . As I've mentioned before, it's taken from them by force – under threat of fines or imprisonment . . .

Drumming.

'. . . Yes. You choose to drum your heels on the floor in appreciation of the rule of force . . . Governments can behave in this way but individuals must not . . .

'It's in a good cause!'

'. . . Tyrants down the ages and in all systems other than free market capitalism . . .

'Boo. Boo. Boo.'

'. . . have used that same justification for their actions. – But does free market capitalism help those people who are most in need? . . .

'No! No! No!'

'. . . Which country do you think embodies free market capitalism? . . .

'America!'

. . . The "Tea Party" Republicans disagree . . .

'Hissss. Hissss. Hissss.'

'Fascists!'

'. . . For some socialists every political philosophy they disagree with is "fascist" . . .

'Yes!'

'. . . I wonder whether Hong Kong – a highly successful

and largely egalitarian society, before mainland China took it over, was "fascist" in your definition . . .

Silence.

'. . . Incidentally – as PJO'Rourke points out – Hong Kong is just a rock with no natural resources but it had one of the highest per-capita incomes in the world . . . Tanzania has vast natural resources of all kinds – and lives off hand-outs . . . and tourism . . . It's a zoo for American tourists . . .

'Boo. Boo. Boo.'

'. . . You can boo my political incorrectness if you like – but that doesn't alter the facts . . .

Silence.

'. . . Maybe – when you call out, "Fascist!" – you're thinking not only of Nazi Germany and apartheid South Africa but also America under George W Bush . . .

'Yes!'

'. . . and the UK during the industrial revolution and before the Welfare State . . .

'Yes!'

'. . . and especially under Margaret Thatcher . . .

'Yes! Yes! Yes!'

'. . . Again, we need to look at the evidence . . . In the UK many of the great schools and hospitals were built as privately-funded charitable institutions. At the origin of the Welfare State, many of these hospitals were nationalised. The government determined the level of compensation to be given to the original benefactors . . . If any . . .

'Quite right!'

'. . . Ah, here we are again. The state can commit acts of violence and theft but individuals must not . . . What sort of morality is that? What example to young people? What basis for a truly compassionate society? . . .

Silence.

'. . . And what has happened to those schools and hospitals when run by the state? Did the quality of teaching and clinical care improve? . . .

Silence.

'. . . Last week we saw the effect on healthcare. Well, the international figures for numeracy and literacy rates – and educational achievements – show that the UK is slipping down the league table while the Far East is dramatically on the rise . . .

Shuffles.

'Nationalise all schools and hospitals!'

'Abolish all privilege!'

'. . . Incidentally, you might wish to ask yourselves whether the UK state schools and hospitals have become fiefdoms of power for a new ruling class . . .

'Smash the class system!'

'. . . Altogether?' . . .

'Yes!'

'. . . What about the – in effect – self-selecting meritocracy of taxpayer-funded quangos – the quasi-non-governmental organisations that advise and advise and advise – and keep the Great and the Good well fed on a perpetual merry-go-round of privilege? . . . Should they be abolished too? Or is their privilege acceptable simply because they don't work in the private sector? . . .

Silence.

'. . . And should all residual private schools, that provide charitable support to individual pupils and managerial and technical support to many schools in the state system, be abolished? . . .

'Yes!'

'. . . Ah . . . I note that you're not all convinced about that . . . Maybe some of you are already looking ahead to what you'll do for your own children . . .

Silence.

'. . . In the country of my birth there is certainly racial discrimination, particularly in some areas – I've experienced it myself – but there's no class system . . .

'Money, money, money!'

'. . . Yes, you're right. – A great deal of money goes into charitable donations. The Internal Revenue Service makes generous allowance for charitable donation. The result is that many hospitals, schools and universities have very significant endowments . . . These are further supplemented by personal legacies and by donations from corporations, including the pharmaceutical industry . . .

'Hissss. Hissss. Hissss.'

'That's an interesting reaction – when we consider that many professorships and research programmes – in this university and many others in the UK – are supported by Big Pharma . . .

'Shame!'

'. . . You'll be too young – So am I – to recall that the Soviet Union nationalised private industry and did not allow advertising . . .

Some drummings.

'. . . and the end result, as Solzhenitzin illustrated in *Cancer Ward*, was that they had poor clinical facilities and no new drugs . . .

Silence.

'. . . As I was saying, charitable donations in the USA provide very generous support to clinical and educational establishments, from which they're able to provide financially assisted places . . .

Silence.

'. . . The UK Inland Revenue is similarly flexible . . .

'Tax avoidance!'

'. . . Yes. That's a common attitude – in many newspapers and members of the general public . . .

Drumming.

'. . . Even so, as you will recall from an earlier talk – Oh. That reminds me . . . In addition to e-mailing you summaries of my notes each week, I'll provide you at the end of the course with a summary of all the major points I make . . . Now then . . . Back to where we were . . .

Coughs.

'. . . Please bear in mind that these figures I'm giving you now – for personal charitable donations in the UK – are on top of the provision by government from tax revenue . . . In the Welfare State – 55% of adults, 28.4 million people in 2012 donated £9.3 billion. Imagine how generous they would be if there were no Welfare State . . .

'Lady Bountiful!'

'. . . I'm sorry? . . .

'Patronising toffs!'

'Not dependable!'

'. . . Ah I see . . . "Charity" has become a dirty word . . .

'Yes!'

'. . . As you wish . . . But now I want to add another point that applies to America today. – There's significant social mobility . . . In a "can do" society, people strive to improve themselves and their social and economic situation . . .

Silence.

'. . . If an industry dies, the unemployed move on to another area – and also new industries move in . . . The USA certainly does have areas of poverty, particularly where there are significant numbers of immigrants. – And a lot of people persist in wanting to come to the USA – but poor people don't necessarily stay poor for very long . . .

'Rubbish!'

Part 3

'. . . A survey by the USA Census Bureau showed that poverty is primarily a temporary condition . . . While 29% of the nation's population was in poverty for at least two months between the start of 2004 and the end of 2006, only 3% were poor during the entire period . . .

Silence.

'. . . But in the UK there's relatively little economic and social mobility. In some areas in the north of England – as you know better than I – some families are into the third generation of unemployment while staying rooted in their local community . . . Is this another unintentional consequence of the Welfare State? . . .

Silence.

'. . . As I said at the beginning, I see it as my function, as your course lecturer, to challenge you, to unsettle you . . . and to encourage you to think for yourselves.'

oOo

'Hard day at work . . .'

'What?'

'Hard day! – God that music's loud . . . and the strobe's doing my head in . . .'

'Chill out, man . . .'

'Any gear?'

'Blue nitro.'

'Huh?'

'Liquid ecstasy . . . Serenity . . . er . . . GHB whatever y'call it.'

'Yeah . . . I know.'

'Taken it before?'

'Sure . . . body-building shit.'

'Twenty.'

'That's steep.'

'That's the price for good quality . . . Ever had asthma . . . allergies?'

'No.'

'Try it out . . . Not all at once . . . One capful first. – Then wait . . . for the effect . . . No alcohol or other stuff . . .'

'I know, I know . . . Fifteen?'

'Twenty.'

'Ah, who cares about a fucking fiver? . . . Twenty.'

'Here y'are.'

. . . Huh! – What does he know? . . .

* * *

Come on. Come on. Come on, Lizzie! . . . Absolutely not going to let a silly thing like this get me down . . . I'm alive, dammit. – End of story . . . umm . . . I hope. – That stuff on the web about long-term post-traumatic stress disorder affecting 41% of patients with this thing . . . Not me. – I'm in the 59% . . . I don't do 'psychological harm' . . . And I don't do 'panic' – apart from this . . . umm . . . nightmare . . . Understandable that . . . Huh! . . . Haven't got to where I am – professionally – as a female milksop . . . Hmm . . . S'pose I take so much for granted – my mind . . . umm . . . general health, work – even family at times . . . Huh! – I'm not the complaining kind . . . Things go wrong, I sort them. – Do a 'start from scratch' . . . Yep, that's it. – They should do that for the NHS – define what they're not going to do . . . Same for me . . . umm . . . Not going to make a fuss . . . Not give up work . . . Not let people down . . . Not collapse in a heap . . . Huh! . . . Definitely not me . . . That's good . . . Easy really . . . Hmm . . . I thought if anything went wrong it'd be a superbug. – The hospital seems ok – Ha! – so it should be . . . teaching hospital – and 'Now gel your

136

hands' blaring out all the time . . . Got my goat in the NHS . . . Patients getting MRSA – or Clostridium Difficile – 'cos a nurse or porter, student or visitor – even a doctor – didn't do basic hygiene! . . . Yaaargh! . . . Not a matter of budgets . . . common sense . . . umm . . . and consideration for others . . . Hmm . . . Got to make choices – all of us . . . I do . . . all doctors do . . . all the time . . . Administrators aren't the only people who have to think and plan . . . Huh! . . . If they ever do . . . Yep . . . All budgets are limited . . . Staff numbers, equipment, drugs, locums . . . Ha! – There's a thought . . . Locums? – Do they care about anything or anybody? . . . If there's no fat pay packet? . . . Huh! . . . Some earn more than I do – with no responsibility! – Yes, that's it . . . They're just numbers. – The whole NHS is just numbers . . . at times . . . the wrong times . . . Should do comparative studies – state and private outcomes . . . We don't have superbugs . . . Very rare with us . . . Hmm . . . Anaesthetic accidents? . . . Never seen one . . . Must happen, though . . . everywhere . . . Awful . . . Huh! . . . Should cooperate – state and private. – Not the part-private doctors . . . They're not really private at all . . . Not fully committed . . . We've got to get the best ideas, best quality care . . . for everybody . . . staff and patients . . . Yep – We need a real health service . . . Not a ramshackle disease service . . . No. No. No. – Not going to let silly things get me down . . .

* * *

'It's good here in Byron – the smoky hamburger's delicious. I'm glad I suggested it.'

'Try some of my courgette fries. – They're mean.'

'I'll swap you for some of my onion rings.'

'Sounds like a good trade – an ethical trade – to me.'

'Ethics matter to you, don't they, Phoebe?'

'Yes of course.'

'Why "of course"?'

'I want to do what's right, what I believe in. – That's why I like your course . . . It challenges me to think things through.'

'But? . . .'

'But nothing.'

'That's wonderful, very exciting for me. – People usually say, "Mind you, I don't always agree with everything you say . . ." – and then leave me hanging out to dry – without them saying anything specific . . . They leave me with their negative statement – and no chance of discussing anything.'

'Well I've got lots of ideas I want to discuss – if that's ok with you . . .'

'Sure thing. – Remember I said – right at the beginning – healthcare is how I live, why I live and how I hope to be remembered . . .'

'I remember the dancing.'

'So do I – but I guess maybe not here in Byron right now.'

'Why not? – It'd be funky.'

'Ha! You remembered that word as well.'

'Of course . . . Now . . . umm . . . Down to business . . . Why d'you say that doctors who work for the state aren't worth asking the time of day?'

'I didn't say *that*. – I said, "if they allow themselves to become mere units in state provision of healthcare, rather than people who are responsible for their own philosophical and mental integrity".'

'How do you remember it – word for word – like that?'

'Because I thought about it a lot . . . And it's also true for doctors who work in large companies – or in any system where they're not individually responsible for the ideas behind their actions.'

'Yup. I get that. – Then what's the matter with being a super-specialist? My mum's one – in some ways . . .'

'What's she do?'

'Obs and gynae – but she tends to leave ovarian stuff to others.'

'That must be difficult – knowing what's there in advance of the op.'

'S'pose so – but she says you can't be good at absolutely everything.'

'I guess the Greeks admired their polymaths.'

'But science has moved on since Hippocrates. – So have ethics . . .'

'That's for sure . . . And that's my point. – Splitters have to learn to see the big picture and lumpers have to learn to see the details – in clinical medicine and in ethics . . . umm . . . Ideally we should see both.'

'I liked what you said about doctors – or teachers or architects or any professionals – not being the only people who have ideas . . . and insights, I guess . . . into their own subjects.'

'Yup . . . Progress tends to come from the periphery – not the centre.'

'. . . Again?'

'New ideas tend to come from people who see the issue from a bit of a distance, rather than from people who are up to their elbows in it every day.'

'Oh . . . umm . . . And I particularly liked what you said about not letting politicians run our lives without ever being challenged . . . I enjoy the protest marches.'

'They're good theatre – but they're not influential . . . Think-tanks can be . . . and books, of course. – And maybe, on my good days, the occasional lecture.'

'Ha! – You're fishing, Precious. – Fancy that!'

'Fancy what?'

'Now that you ask, a kiss would be nice.'

'With all these onions?'

'We both had them.'

'Umm . . . What other points did you want to make?'

'Hmm . . . They've slipped my mind for a moment . . .'

'You've got a good mind.'

'That's what my mother says – but I'd rather hear it from you.'

'Back to business, Phoebe. – You've got me interested . . .'

'In what?'

Your next point.'

'Oh . . . umm . . . Can the state be relied on to produce responsible clinical care when it's needed?'

'It should be possible – but it doesn't happen often.'

'Why not?

'Because – when people are carried away with the virtue of what they're doing – they don't see their mistakes.'

'Oh . . . And you said that a true sense of commitment comes only from individual minds – not from rules, regulations and committees.'

'That's obviously true – and it's what Mrs Thatcher was on about when she said, "There's no such thing as society".'

'She was a witch.'

'Yes, I'm told she was very bewitching . . . personally.'

'So'm I . . . Mmmm . . . Can I have the oniony kiss now?'

*   *   *

James seems to be getting his head screwed on. – Not before time . . . Hope Phoebe's doing some work for finals – instead of chasing round after a man, as usual. – Can't think what she's up to. – Huh! – No time to worry about that now . . . It's Lizzie I'm worried about, poor love . . . How can it happen?

140

How can it possibly happen? God alive – giving a whiff
of gas can't be all that complicated . . . No whistleblowers?
– 'S'pose not, with the treatment they get nowadays. – Too
frightened to step out of line . . . Thin red line . . . Picket line
. . . Party line . . . All the same. – Pay 'em all the same, that's
what you get. – No pride in their own work. No competition
to be the best – like at the Bar. Ha! – My clerk and secretary
and pupil – all of 'em – out of work if solicitors send cases to
someone else . . . Can't afford to compromise between good
and bad . . . No substitute for talent – or quality. You've got
it or you haven't . . . Huh! How does the state get away with
it? – Costs a fortune in tax. – And then does this to my Lizzie!
. . . S'pose NHS care's a bit like legal aid. – Criminal lawyers
are useless . . . Many of them. – Ha! Not like commercial or
company law and litigation . . . Very competitive . . . Yes,
Dr Anaesthetist, there'll be some of that coming your way
over my Lizzie . . . That'll cost 'em! . . . Huh . . . Cost the
taxpayer, I s'pose . . . And there's so much waste! Spent
all the money on scroungers. – Nothing left to pay good staff
to do good work . . . or get good kit . . . and drugs that work
. . . Dammit, we gotta have limits to demands. – Doctors
and patients . . . And James'll have to find out the basics of life
for himself . . . One day . . . It's a different game when you have
to earn everything and pay everything for yourself . . .

* * *

'Today we're going to examine precisely why supporters of
welfare statism – which is just a sub-category of statism in
general – point to a few people who have been dramatically
helped "at no cost" . . .

    Silence.

    '. . . Perhaps they play on the fear or pity of their

listeners – and in so doing make them into supplicant pap . . .

Shuffles – and again one cry of 'Fascist!'

'. . . Ah, you again . . . Maybe you haven't understood that fascism and communism are two sides of the same statist totalitarian coin . . .

Silence.

'. . . Let me explain how and why statists play on people's fear and pity . . . Newspapers and other media outlets like to personalise their stories. So do politicians. Readers, listeners and viewers identify with a story much more than with an abstract treatise . . . They want to know the basics of who, what, where, when, why and how? Academics and researchers like me tend towards the opposite. We want numbers and reasoned argument . . .

'Poor dears!'

Laughter.

'. . . Yeah. It's a hard life . . .

More laughter.

'. . . But, as you yourselves know only too well, clinical practice is no laughing matter . . . Our trade really is one of life and death . . . Reading the annual reports of the doctors' liability insurance organisations, or details of the hearings of the disciplinary committee of the General Medical Council, is a sobering exercise . . .

Silence – apart from some throat clearing.

'. . . You need to be aware in advance that there are patients who think it's a great idea that the GMC nowadays has a predominance of lay members . . . Since Dr Harold Shipman was convicted of murdering some of his patients – and he may have murdered very many more – it's understandable that there's been a loss of confidence over doctors monitoring the behaviour of their own professional colleagues . . .

Shuffles and more throat clearing.

Part 3

'. . . The GMC today is judge, jury and executioner – and the general public supports that position . . . And politicians, in the promises they give to the electorate, sometimes "name and shame" errant doctors – or those they consider to be errant – in the House of Commons, under parliamentary privilege. This means the MPs can't be sued for slander . . . Errant doctors have nowhere to hide. And it's right that they shouldn't be able to escape proper assessment and sanction . . .

Yet more shuffles.

'. . . But there's a catch . . . Many doctors feel hounded by the GMC even when they've done absolutely nothing wrong . . . And they also feel pestered by the Care Quality Commission, the Health and Safety Executive, the stipulations of the Employment Protection Act and various decrees from the European Union . . . As a result, they'll be more – not less – likely to make mistakes . . . A stressed doctor will commit errors and also transmit stressed feelings to his or her patients. The Law of Unintended Consequences strikes again . . .

Shuffles.

'. . . Yes, it's all very uncomfortable – but that's the way it is nowadays. The end result is that many doctors are considering early retirement . . . There's going to be a significant crisis in manpower . . .

'And woman power!'

'. . . And you, madam, have just made a very important point . . . 60% of the new entrants to medical schools are women. They make excellent doctors. They have a strong work ethic . . .

High-heeled drumming.

'. . . Many of them are Asians who have a cultural commitment to enterprise and excellence . . .

Similar drumming.

'. . . But many of these women make it clear they intend to

work part-time . . . That would be fine in non-clinical work but patients – especially in general practice – tend to like having just one doctor . . . The Law of Unintended Consequences strikes yet again . . .

Shuffles.

'. . . One way or another, patients may be fearful because they have a lot to be fearful about. – So it's very easy for politicians to play into that fear, raising one spectre after another . . .

Silence.

'. . . And patients are frightened – because they perceive no other choice than to stick with the NHS they've got . . .

'Abolish all private practice!'

'. . . as in the Soviet Union, no doubt . . . where patients really did become supplicant pap, pleading to be given their free sustenance – regardless of its quality – and being prepared to do anything to get it . . .

Silence.

'. . . And, of course, in any country where there's – in effect – a monopoly supplier of healthcare and welfare services, they'll be happy to give the credit – and the votes – to the politicians who offer the biggest promises . . . But promises of what quality and at what cost?'

oOo

'Not you again!'

'Wise up! . . . I'm the . . . patient . . . 'n I carn . . . breathe . . . Frighten' . . . gonnadie . . .'

'Sit there.'

'Needa . . . doctor.'

'Sit there!'

'Needa . . . doctor . . . Now!'

Part 3

'What've you taken this time? – apart from the alcohol I can smell?'

'Needa . . . doctor.'

'She'll need to know . . .'

'She? . . . She? . . . I got . . . women . . . doctors . . . everywhere.'

'Well we haven't got enough here . . . And we're busy – this time of night – with people like you.'

'Needa . . . doctor.'

'What – Have – You – Taken?'

'Legals . . . Mary Jane . . . Clockwork orange . . .

'Anything else?'

'Christ . . . I dunno . . . umm . . . GHB . . .'

'How much?'

'One bottle . . .'

'30 mls?'

'Yeah.'

'That's plenty . . . You can damage yourself – hurt your brain – with that stuff.'

'Class C . . .'

'You know too much about it – and too little.'

'You . . . know . . . fuck-all . . . Needa . . . doctor . . .'

'Ah – here she is . . . Yes, doctor – you've met James before . . . One of our regulars . . . GHB – and some legals and alcohol . . . umm . . . I wonder – this time – if he might do best in the . . . umm . . . special unit . . . He's not safe . . .'

* * *

'In one of your lectures you said that the NHS is totalitarian. – That's ridiculous.'

'It's ridiculous because I didn't say it. – You're making the same mistake that lots of people make when they let their feelings cloud their rational judgement.'

'The NHS is important! – Vital to lots of people! – Of course they have feelings about it!'

'That's precisely why it's important to think clearly about it. We can't afford simply to take on other people's ideas . . . Remember what I said in one of my earlier talks. – Any thinker who allows himself or herself to be the property of someone else – and be indoctrinated by statist or other corporatist ideas – ceases to think.'

'I'm not going to be indoctrinated by you – if that's what you want.'

'Dingbat! I want the exact opposite.'

'What's a dingbat?'

'Umm . . . usually it's a very derogatory expression but I meant it as a term of affection . . . umm . . . Originally it's a printer's decoration – or a symbol that sometimes gets left in the final copy by mistake.'

'So I'm a decoration or a mistake, am I?'

'Aaargh . . . I'm in trouble here . . .'

'No you're not . . . umm . . . You meant it as a term of affection. – So let's see you prove it . . . mmmmmm . . . Yesss . . . That's better – much better – better even than dancing and just as good without onions . . . But we could do both.'

'Later, later . . .'

'That sounds good.'

'As I was saying . . . It's great that you challenge me. – That way we both learn.'

'Go on . . .'

'As I've mentioned before – and will mention again because it's my most important message – what Ayn Rand said was that the difference between a welfare state and a totalitarian state is merely a matter of time . . . And you can see why this might be true – even with the best of intentions.'

'I very much doubt that I'll see that now or later . . . umm . . . But tell me.'

'Look at the government's concerns over cigarette smoking, alcohol consumption and obesity – and look at what those things cost the NHS.'

'Yes . . . A fortune – enough to build many more hospitals and pay for hundreds of doctors and nurses.'

'That's right. – That's the blackmail.'

'Blackmail?'

'Sure thing . . . The state blames these patients – so does the public generally – despite all they pay in taxes on tobacco and alcohol – and that diverts attention from the government's own failings.'

'But blackmail?'

'Yup. – "Vote for us, trust us and we'll force doctors to do what we say . . . er . . . what you want them to do. – And we'll make sure that self-indulgent people are shown the error of their ways" . . .'

'And?'

'. . . Not 'and' – 'otherwise' . . .'

'Otherwise what?'

'. . . "otherwise we won't be able to provide care for you." . . .'

'Oh.'

'Yes. – By making out that the state is indispensable, they've got the entire population by the . . . umm . . .'

'By the what, Precious? – I'm a big girl now.'

'Umm . . . Yes . . . umm . . . Stick to the point, Precious. Stick to the point. Don't let yourself get carried away . . . umm . . . They make out that if there were no NHS, people – those who could provide for themselves – would do so . . . And the rest would have nothing.'

'But the NHS means that nobody has to pay . . . Or do without.'

'Does it really?'

'You know perfectly well it does.'

'I know perfectly well that it *doesn't* . . . Healthcare and welfare services are very unevenly distributed in the UK – and the people in greatest need of help are least likely to get it . . . The Salvation Army – The Sally Anns – and various other charities are the people who care for the truly destitute.'

'Well, umm . . .'

'What we're looking at is not a compassionate state but health fascism . . .'

'That's way too much for me . . . What on earth are you going on about?'

'At the origin of the Welfare State, people gave up their real birthright – the right to care for themselves and their families and help each other – in exchange for being ruled by a paternalistic and patronising state . . . And they sold themselves for so little! – A promise of free prescriptions, free teeth and free spectacles – and even they're not free nowadays for most people . . .'

'But really important things are.'

'No they're not. – They're rationed by queue – and by postcode . . . And look at how the state tries to implement its ideas. – You'll see immediately that the concept of a state implementing ideas can't possibly be true. – It's a contradiction in terms. – The state's inanimate . . . like the money you took from me . . .'

'You threw it away.'

'. . Yes ok . . . But the state can't *do* anything . . . Only people can do things – for themselves and each other. – Or not, if they're not motivated.'

'So?'

Part 3

'That's the blackmailing catch of health fascism . . . If there were no NHS, pretending to pick up the pieces, there'd be no blackmail.'

'But there've been dramatic improvements in healthcare and welfare since the birth of the Welfare State.'

'It came into being after the utter destruction of two world wars . . . and the experience of the whole population working together to fight – and defeat – a common enemy . . . Twice . . . But that shared motive didn't survive for very long in peacetime.'

'It should've done.'

'Ah well, maybe – but it didn't – the pre-existing fissures in society reasserted themselves . . . from both sides . . . I'll be referring to that in one of my lectures later on . . . And anyway, how many improvements d'you think came about specifically as a result of a welfare state? – That's what we have to look at.'

'Where? – In the UK yes . . . But absolutely not in the USA. – It hasn't got one. – Don't make me laugh!'

'I'm deadly serious – just as you were when we last came to Byron's . . . A great many advances in healthcare – surgical procedures, scanners, drugs, all sorts of things have come from the USA. Nothing new came from the USSR, China, Cuba and other socialist countries . . . And, as I showed in one of my lectures, the UK – with its Welfare State – lags behind many European countries in the outcome of many important clinical conditions... The NHS isn't as indispensable as the health fascists would like us all to believe.'

'I do wish you'd stop referring to "health fascists". – You'll undermine people's faith in their doctors and in sensible advice.'

'So I should . . . Well . . . in the system, I should say. – There's nothing wrong with British doctors . . . or there used not to be

149

until the last brain drain when so many emigrated to Canada, Australia and New Zealand . . . and some to the USA.'

'Before my time, Precious, before my time – you dingbat.'

'And mine . . . But that's a major legacy of the Welfare State.'

* * *

'Oh Roddy, Roddy, Roddy, I couldn't do it . . .'

'Couldn't do what?'

'Operate . . . I had to leave the theatre . . . I was all scrubbed up and everything . . . Then I saw the machine.'

'What machine?'

'The anaesthetic machine – and the tubes . . . and the mask – and I couldn't go on.'

'Why not? – You've been fine . . .'

'I . . . I . . . I suddenly thought the patient might be awake . . .'

'Oh Lizzie, my poor Lizzie. – That's dreadful . . . That bloody locum! – And the bloody Health Service . . . We pay enough for it . . . Good quality care should be available for everybody – rich and poor, black and white, you and me . . .'

'Don't go on about it . . . It was an accident . . . Accidents happen. – In the private sector as well – He didn't do it deliberately and I expect he feels a bit grim about it.'

'A bit . . . A bit? – He should be struck off.'

'No . . . It's just the way it goes.'

'So what'll happen to him?'

'They'll hold an enquiry – as if the cause wasn't obvious . . . what happened – and then they'll say that lessons have to be learned – which they won't be . . . because they never are. – It's just human error. That's all.'

'Why don't they just say that and be done with it?'

'Ha! Roddy – You of all people, asking that! . . . Lawyers . . . sweetheart . . . Lawyers. – There's nothing in life that lawyers can't make more complicated . . .'

'Well thanks – and here I am being nice to you.'

'You are . . . very nice . . . but I'm allowed to tease you. – I've got to keep my spirits up . . . somehow . . . But I wish it hadn't happened to me . . . And what's going to happen to me now? – if I can't work?'

'I'll look after you, sweetheart – as much as I can . . . with all my own work . . . I'm not so tied up I can't spare some time for my own wife and family . . . a bit . . . God knows what would happen if we were both knocked off . . .. umm . . . ill . . . We can't rely on the state – or anyone else – to do our thinking and planning for us . . . We've got to survive on our own . . . Somehow.'

*   *   *

Typical! – Sent from one person to another like a kid's game. – Ha! 'Pass the parcel! Pass the patient!' . . . First a psychiatric nurse in A and E . . . Now a 'health worker' – whoever – and told I've got to be here till Monday to see the shrink . . . Huh! . . . Very basic medical check. – Could've died and they wouldn't notice . . . Very basic washing things as well . . . and pyjamas . . . Wha'do I need them for? . . . Wonder who had them last . . . No introductions to anyone – staff, patients – nobody . . . Ha! No surprise to me Africa has no nurses. – They're all here . . . Talk about communication! – No sympathy, no compassion. Huh! . . . Probably little or no training . . . And me not searched at all – but had to hand in the fags! . . . fire risk, cancer risk, whatever. Bloody ridiculous . . . And nothing decent to eat on the ward . . . if you get peckish . . . one loaf of bread – no butter – for 20 patients! . . . Told by one of them the night staff pocket the food money . . . Then the doctor turns up and offers me drugs – to help me with a drug problem! . . . It must get to him – all the shouting and screaming – and no intervention at all from staff – except when they threaten to sedate someone . . . Then at last they take me to the canteen . . . 'basic' isn't the word for that! . . . 'Primitive' more like . . . And then the outside smoking area – the only comforting place in the whole fandango for some of the patients, poor buggers . . . Staff present – but with no interest in what's going on . . . They know – they must know – the dealers drop drugs through the fence in the smoking area . . . and they must know the long-stay patients prey on the new ones – vulnerable ones like me – to 'borrow' some dosh – or a mobile to call a dealer. – But the staff are just not bloody interested . . . They don't give a fuck . . . Ha! If I wrote a book about this, they'd say it was all exaggerated . . . But what would Phoebe say about it? – She must've seen all this in her training . . . And Mum as well in hers . . . Ha! But now she's cherry-picking the easy private patients . . . It's all right for some . . .

* * *

'We must'nt worry Phoebe . . . with her finals.'

   'Agreed.'

'It may be a mother's instinct – to protect . . . like the pious pelican . . .'

   'The what?'

'. . . plucking her breast to feed her young on her blood.'

'That's a bit gruesome – a bit medical – Lizzie.'

'It's a symbol of Christ's sacrifice . . . for the church . . . umm . . . for us – His children.'

'You know I don't do religion . . . but I s'pose . . .'

'. . . a bit of prayer wouldn't come amiss?'

Part 3

'Wouldn't know how.'

'No matter . . . Could do with a bit right now . . . for myself – with this thing . . .'

'. . . God bless my Lizzie . . . – That ok?'

'That's lovely. – Because you meant it.'

'Yeah, well . . . umm . . .'

'Dear Roddy . . . You're such a paradox – so precise in your work and so mushy with me . . . sometimes.'

'Time and a place . . . umm . . . Y'know, I was thinking about these medical insurance people – all of them the same, I expect . . . wriggling to get out of paying up . . .'

'They'll have good lawyers.'

'Ha! – You're teasing me again.'

'Yes . . . as I said. Keeps my spirits up.'

'I s'pose they'd go out of business – the insurance companies – if they covered everything for everybody.'

'That's what the State's for really.'

'I don't see that . . . And the State'll go bust on the same principle – though I s'pose it can't really . . . The state hasn't got any money of its own. – It's yours and mine.'

'That's good.'

'Legalised theft's good?'

'No – that the State can't go bust.'

'Well it can – theoretically – and, come to think of it, in reality . . . sometimes . . . Iceland defaulted . . . Did very well out of it . . . but a lot of private individuals and companies . . . and local authorities and our government itself – gamblers, the lot of them – lost their shirts.'

'Serves them right . . . But not the taxpayers like us . . . It's our money they're gambling with.'

'And Greece is a basket case even now after all the bailouts – most of southern Europe is . . . Spain next. – Then France . . . Only kept afloat by Germany's thing with the EU

153

. . . They'll get tired of that one day . . . the people, not the politicians.'

'You always think so commercially, Roddy.'

''Smy job.'

'Yes – and thank God for that . . .'

'And a bit of hard work.'

'Oh sweetheart. – Just because I mention God – it doesn't mean I don't appreciate what you do . . . After all, you kept us afloat when I was having the children . . . And we're going to need you again if I can't . . . umm . . . function.'

'You'll be fine . . . You'll be fine. – My Lizzie's made of stern stuff – nothing southern European about you . . . Ha! We pay a fortune keeping those people in their Welfare States . . . and us in ours.'

'What's the alternative? – Riots on the streets when nobody can get a job – particularly in Phoebe's and James's age group . . .'

'Governments pay for it by what they call "quantitative easing" . . . printing more money – devaluing it. Steals the value of our savings and pensions.'

'We can afford it – and I feel so sorry for the youngsters . . . not getting a proper start.'

'Nobody'll get a proper start – or finish – if they kill the goose . . . take even more money from the private sector . . . And if the insurance companies go down and if the State has to pay out any more claims for malpractice . . . like they should for you.'

'I'll be fine, Roddy love, just fine . . . You'll see . . .'

'I hope so . . . I just hope we never become dependent on the State . . . Too much power over other people's money – and then they throw it away . . .'

'Phoebe says they haven't got enough power . . . to protect people . . . when they can't look after themselves.'

154

Part 3

'Phoebe's young – idealistic. – Got to grow up sometime . . . and James.'

* * *

'And there's another reason why welfare statists aim to focus people's attention on a few fortunate – or unfortunate – patients in particular . . . It diverts attention from what's happening in general to the Welfare State . . .

Mutterings.

'. . . You'll remember Al Gore, the former Vice President of the United States, talking about "an inconvenient truth" when he tried to make the public more aware of the effects of global warming . . .

Applause.

'. . . He ran the emotional stakes very high and was very persuasive – to a willing audience – when presenting data and images in support of his case . . . He still believes significant environmental problems are man-made and therefore the solution must also be man-made . . .

Applause.

'. . . I reckon he believes the solution should be primarily at the expense of the industrialised world . . . especially America – his own homeland . . . and therefore America would have to foot an enormous bill . . .

'Uncle Sam kills people. He deserves to die!'

'. . . Ahem . . . I'm making a different point . . . Does the emperor have new clothes? or is he, as Danny Kaye sang, "as naked as the day that he was born"? Was Al Gore right? The current evidence seems to be against him . . .'

'No. No. No.'

'. . . Yet still he clings to his own truths . . . He says they're "inconvenient" for the climate change deniers . . .

'True! True!'

'. . . Who – or what – is true?' . . .

'Too-wit. Too-woo. Hoo-hoo.'

Laughter.

'. . . Good one! . . . umm . . . Good-ish... Where was I? – Oh yes . . . How do we know what's true? . . .

'Evidence!'

'That's absolutely right. – You got it. – But here's a dilemma . . . the evidence is conflicting . . . So the debate is often decided by the heart rather than by the head . . .

'Yeehaw!'

Laughter.

'. . . Thank you. – You're doing great today! . . . Many debates are decided by the heart rather than the head. – Getting married, for one . . . Independence for Scotland, for another . . .

'Och aye the noo!'

'Huh?'

'Yessss!'

'No!'

'. . . Hey! This is getting out of hand . . . Settle down . . . Settle down . . . Thank you. – Now, maybe you can see where this is going . . . We've had some fun here even though the issues are serious . . . And don't forget about healthcare systems . . .

Silence.

'. . . Medical students are famous for their sense of humour – but can any of you afford to ignore what's happening in general to the NHS when the focus is on a few fortunate – or unfortunate – patients in particular? . . . I don't think so – but we're looking at your future career and the healthcare and welfare of your patients . . .

Silence.

'. . . That's right. You yourselves – It's probably too late for Al Gore – might like to consider the "inconvenient truth" I've been putting forward in these sessions.'

oOo

'Father? . . . James . . . umm . . . Father, I need your help . . . I . . . umm . . . took something at a party – maybe my drink was spiked. I dunno – but it didn't do me any good . . . Yes, I agree – very stupid, very immature . . . Yes. – Sorry, father. – Lost the plot . . . Yes I am . . . umm . . . I'm in the Mental Health Unit . . . Yes, that's the one . . . I needed a hospital – I couldn't breathe . . . No. – I don't know what it was . . . You know me – alcohol's my thing . . . like in your club . . . Sorry, father, didn't mean to cause you any offence . . . after your kindness . . . umm . . . I gotta get out of here, father. – I was crazy when I came in but I'm ok now. – The other guys in here are as mad as yer actual box of frogs . . . Yeah. – barking, croaking, whatever . . . Talking to themselves – and shouting or screaming . . . at themselves or the others . . . Aggressive? . . . Yes, they get locked up if they're too much trouble . . . Some of them'll never get out of here, I reckon . . . More like a prison than a hospital . . . No . . . No – I've been here a week and I've never seen staff sitting down to talk to a patient – or even call a doctor . . . That's it – the patients are a nuisance to them . . . We get in the way of whatever it is the staff are doing on their computers all day . . . Yes . . . The one time I saw a psychiatrist, there were two nurses taking notes – risk assessments, something like that. – Ass-covering I reckon . . . or ass-licking, one of the two . . . umm . . . Nobody asks me how I'm doing – or if I need anything . . . No – no activities at all – except a bit of basketball on Monday . . . but only a few turned up . . . And the group therapy's a joke. – How can some poor bloke on a load of different psychiatric drugs make any

157

sense? . . . No, there's a waiting list for individual therapy . . .
Months, they said . . . I need to get out of here, father . . . Help
me . . . Please . . .

* * *

'I'm sorry I called you a dingbat last week, Precious . . . umm
. . . I was afraid you wouldn't turn up today.'

'I keep my word. We agreed to meet here every week at
this time – so here I am . . . Anyway, you meant it as a term of
affection. – As I did earlier.'

'No I didn't.'

'Ha! – Then I'm very glad you turned up today.'

'I wouldn't miss it for lots of reasons. – Here's one . . .
mmmmm . . .'

'Good. – That's settled then.'

'No it isn't . . . I want another one – with onions on the side
. . . mmmmm . . . That's better.'

'What happened to the courgette fries?'

'Later.'

'All this delayed gratification stuff is a false promise.'

'Is that what happened to the last one?'

'Last what?'

'Last woman in your life.'

'. . . Umm . . . Later.'

'Now who's delaying the gratification?'

'I am . . . It's a sad story – but I'll tell you some day.'

'Not now?'

'No . . . I want to be happy with you right now . . . Today . . .
I don't look back.'

'Right then. – Down to business . . . Why were you
emphasising there's a difference between men and machines?
– That's obvious.'

'Not in a regimented system, it isn't.'

'Huh?'

'The NHS is a numbers business . . . I told you.'

'Yes – but that was about patients . . . umm . . . Treating large numbers.'

'It also applies to employees. The NHS is the fifth largest employer in the world – after the American and Chinese armed forces, Walmart and McDonald's. – The Indian railways come eighth.'

'Indian railways?'

'Yeah. – It may not be a popular idea nowadays but colonialisation wasn't all bad . . . And representative democracy was a great gift to the world.'

'Not in Iraq, it wasn't.'

'It's what Dubya Bush intended – but they didn't follow it through . . .'

'Now who's talking about unintended consequences?'

'Yes . . . umm . . . Well . . .'

'Yeah – Got you there!'

'Sure did . . . umm . . . What I was saying – intending to say – was that people themselves shouldn't be treated as numbers. – Patients or staff.'

'They're not.'

'Yes they are. – Particularly by the trade unions, such as Unison and Unite and the British Medical Association.'

'The BMA isn't a trade union. – It's not affiliated to the TUC – The Trades Union Congress.'

'I know what the TUC is. – I've lived here long enough.'

'But the BMA certainly isn't a trade union.'

'It certainly is already – and it certainly will be even more so one day. – It already holds joint rallies with the TUC . . . Its primary concern is for its members – not for its customers.'

'They're not customers. The NHS isn't a business.'

''Fraid not – but it should be.'

'Privatised? – What would poor people do then?'

'Be looked after very well . . . As I said in one of the talks, the state can fund the NHS – but the private sector should run it . . . That's their skill. – Look at Walmart and McDonald's.'

'I'd rather not.'

'They're very fine employers – with great training schemes.'

'McJobs.'

'Better than the dole . . . More dignity. And great service to customers.'

'So all we have to say is, "Would you like a bag with it?" and "Have a nice day"? – It makes me sick.'

'Sounds good to me.'

'Me being sick?'

'No, dingbat . . . Whoops! . . .'

'No that's fine – provided you pay the customary penance . . . mmmmm . . . Better and better.'

'That's what the NHS could be if they ran it properly. – Better and better. – Treat people with respect and dignity and they'll behave with respect and dignity.'

'Well maybe . . .'

'And Ayn Rand . . .'

'Her again? Don't you read anyone else?'

'Tolstoy, Dostoyevsky, Victor Hugo, Goethe, the Brontes, Mark Twain, Aristotle . . .'

'Enough, enough . . .'

'Never enough . . . Anyway, Ayn Rand – in *Atlas Shrugged* – showed what happens when capitalists, who she said drive the motor of the world, go on strike.'

'I wish they would.'

'No you wouldn't. Being a rebel is easy – when you agree with your band of brothers and sisters – but it's difficult when

160

your whole business depends on finding new ideas and new ways of doing things.'

'Such as?'

'Dyson, the vacuum cleaning and hand-drying man. He spent £45m on research and development in 2010 and filed the second-highest number of patents in the UK – and made great profits . . .'

'Yuck.'

'You'd rather he made losses?'

'. . . Hmm . . .'

'Remember that the state – in itself – has no power to create or destroy. Only people can do that – with their actions based on their ideas . . . As I pointed out in a lecture, the question is whether individuals – by nature – are altruistic or mean-spirited and demanding . . .'

'Nature or nurture?'

'Either way. – As I asked, do we have a generous society or an entitlement culture? Does the Welfare State make the situation in general better or worse? – and individuals more compassionate or less?'

'Hmmm . . . I'll have to think about that some more. – Later . . . Onion time!'

*   *   *

That's a worry . . . Getting me down a bit . . . What'm I going to do with myself? – Got to get back to work somehow . . . Admin's a bore. – Paperwork! – Research? . . . I'm a surgeon dammit . . . practical . . . I like cutting . . . and sewing. – Bit of a tailor really . . . Problem is my whole life's turned around . . . Different priorities . . . Got to get this sorted, Lizzie . . . Somehow . . . Huh! . . . NHS doctors can be off work on full pay for ever! . . . Too bad. – My choice. Private. – That's ok . . .

Hmm . . . Time-limited private insurance . . . Not like the state system... But I'm not dead yet . . . Not by a mile! . . . Hmm – That's a thought. – I'm fit. – Not going to die of anything . . . Not a care in the world until now . . . Ought to be able to sort this out, Lizzie . . . Huh . . . The web data's really grim. – Yes, I remember – 41% long-term psychological harm . . . Not good, Lizzie, not good . . . Nope. – And the state money's all going on welfare . . . Could do with some welfare myself . . . Ha! . . . And the clinical outcome's behind half of Europe – old Europe . . . And some new. – No help for me when we can't even treat cancer and heart disease properly . . . Come on, come on Lizzie. Snap out of it! . . . P'raps treatment for people like me – no fault of ours – would last for ever . . . And cost a fortune . . . state or private . . .

* * *

'Right then, young James . . . We got you out of there – and I could see precisely why it was inappropriate for you – whatever you'd done.'

'Thank you, father.'

'Well I hope it taught you a bloody good lesson.'

'Yes, father.'

'So . . . What's it all about?'

'I made a mistake . . . and I've learned a lesson . . . umm . . . Not the one I expected to learn.'

'I hope it's the one I want you to learn.'

'Umm . . . More than that . . . umm . . . I think.'

'That's interesting . . . Tell me.'

'Well . . . I was shocked and appalled . . . At the way the most vulnerable people in our society are treated when they're most in need . . . They had nothing when they went in – and they got nothing in there . . . just drugs.'

'I expect they're very busy . . . The staff . . . The need is huge – if what I read in the press is reliable.'

'The press wouldn't believe what I've seen – and experienced. – They'd be frightened of undermining people's faith in the only system that's available to most people.'

'Go on . . .'

'The treatment – Ha! – such as it was – is mediaeval . . . The staff don't appear to be properly trained for the job they should be doing . . . They treat patients as a nuisance – and they take advantage of them.'

'In what way?'

'They're dishonest. – I told you. – It's reckoned they take the food money on the ward.'

'You'll need proof, James. – I'm a lawyer.'

'Yes, father . . . umm . . . I know. – But I'm not making it up when I tell you that one of the staff asked me for money.'

'He what? . . . She what? . . . umm . . . What for?'

'He didn't say . . . Just said he's a bit short – until the end of the month.'

'That's dreadful.'

'The whole place is dreadful . . . Well the building's all right – but it's not looked after properly.'

'Forgive me . . . This is you speaking, is it James?'

'Yes, father . . . I saw things I'll never forget – or want to forget.'

'Go on . . .'

'I felt a great deal of sympathy for the inmates . . . umm . . . patients. – Surely, in the 21st century in a so-called civilised and caring society – we should be able to treat these poor souls, with their mental afflictions, in a more humane and compassionate and caring way.'

'James, is this really you? . . . You're not on something are you?'

'No father. – This is the real me . . . umm . . . Now . . . I think.'

'Well if you are on something, I . . . er . . . I suspect your mother would like you to give some to me – all this talk about "souls". Ha! – Maybe I should buy some from you.'

'Hear me through, father. It's not a joke. – Nobody should be treated like that . . . I just hope I never end up in a place like that again – unless it's as someone who can help to make these people's lives better in some way. – That's what I'd like to do with my life . . . From now on.'

'This really doesn't sound like the James I know.'

'I'm not.'

'Oh . . . umm . . . What d'you think should be done? – With these people?'

'Well – for a start – they need to find staff who want to make a difference. – Then train them . . .'

'And? . . .'

'. . . Right now the staff – not just the patients – don't have even a glimmer of hope . . . You can see that in their eyes. – They look right through you. They don't really notice you at all.'

'This is remarkable . . . I never thought – after all your mother and I spent on your education – that you'd learn such important lessons in a . . . umm . . . in a . . .'

'Nut house?'

'Not the best description, James – Not one I'd use in court . . . And your sister would throw a wobbly for a start. – But she does that anyway. – Or did . . . What on earth's got into the pair of you?'

'I saw something I've never seen before.'

'Well I have to say . . . I'd have paid good money – on top of being a top rate taxpayer – to have you learn that . . . Not in this particular way, of course . . .'

'Thank you, father . . . umm . . . The people I've been with have probably never paid any tax in their whole lives.'

'Nor they should – if they're that desperate – and I'd be glad to pay tax to help those people if I felt it was money well spent.'

'It didn't seem that way to me, father.'

'Oh . . . I . . . er . . . Why not?'

'The patients wouldn't benefit. – Not from that treatment . . .'

'Or lack of it, by the sound of things.'

'I can speak only from my own experience . . . I saw no compassion, no thought . . . And nothing that works.'

'But you told me that some of those people might be there for the rest of their lives . . .'

'Short lives would be my guess.'

'That's tragic . . . But surely the doctors want to do something about it – clearing out the stables . . . Like your mother says.'

'Like you sorting out the legal aid system?'

'Careful, James . . . Careful.'

'I'm full of care – now, father.'

*   *   *

'Now that we're almost half way through the spring term, we've come to the final talk about specific ideas that underpin the Welfare State. We've looked at three questions . . .

'What happens if the state takes over ultimate health-care responsibility from the individual? . . . 'What happens if resources are distributed according to need? . . . and 'What happens if services are free at the time of need? . . .

Coughs.

'. . . A number of you have expressed concern –

understandably – over people who cannot afford to pay . . .

'Yes! Yes! Yes!'

' . . . We need to ask a very simple question . . . "Cannot afford to pay for what?" . . .

Silence

'. . . Have a look at this chart based on the official figures of the UK Office for National Statistics in 2013 showing average weekly living costs and food expenditure. This answers the question, "What do we spend our money on?" . . .

Table 5.3
Weekly household expenditure in Great Britain. 2009-11
Commodity or Household service weekly expenditure (£) and percentage of total

1. Transport	77.40	17.76%
2. Recreation and culture	68.80	15.79%
3. Housing (net) fuel and power	58.30	13.38%
4. Food and non-alcoholic drink	57.60	13.22%
5. Miscellaneous goods and services	39.60	9.09%
6. Restaurants and hotels	39.00	8.95%
7. Household goods and services	32.90	7.55%
8. Clothing and footwear	21.30	4.89%
9. Alcoholic drink, tobacco and narcotics	13.00	2.98%
10. Communication	12.80	2.59%
11. Education	8.30	1.90%
12. Health	6.80	1.55%
Total	435.80	100.00%

Silence

'. . . Note – at the bottom of the chart – how little is spent on education and health . . . This, of course, is a result of the Welfare State . . .

Loud drummings.

'. . . Not so fast . . . Not so fast . . . Have a look further up the chart and you'll see where people spend the money they save on education and health . . .

Silence.

'. . . Yes, that's right . . . After housing, fuel, power and transport, they spent it on having a good time . . .

'Why not?'

'. . . Yes why not? . . . This chart shows just how much money is spent on recreation and culture – such as pop concerts, football matches and gambling . . . My point is not that they shouldn't spend their money in any way they wish – although other charts show that compulsive gambling is a major problem in some families, with 10% of gamblers spending nearly 60% of the total – but rather to show where they *do* spend it . . . They've *got* money . . . Many of them . . . And they spend it . . . Not on additional healthcare and education – some do – but not all . . .

'Shame.'

'. . . but on recreation and culture, holidays – mostly to foreign countries – and all sorts of things that have a higher priority in their minds . . . The Welfare State has changed their priorities . . .

'So it should!'

'. . . Yes . . . Some of you – many of you – will consider this a good thing . . .

'Yes. Yes. Yes.'

'. . . Others may not . . .

Silence.

'. . . You may wish to note that more money is spent on alcohol, tobacco and narcotics than personally on education and health . . .

Silence.

'. . . Now. – For the remainder of this term and for the six sessions of next term, before you take your finals – I'll look at one more question . . . "What happens if theory doesn't convert into practice?" . . .'

'It never does!'

'. . . You may be right . . . We'll find out . . . But – for now – let's see what happens when a welfare state takes root in a country. – It becomes a norm, a basic, an expectation . . . And alternatives may be inconceivable . . . So – in time – the state comes to be thought indispensable . . .

'It *is* for the poor!'

'. . . We covered that ground earlier when we were looking at social and economic mobility . . . Remember? . . . You see, it's so easy to get stuck in one particular mindset. – We put ourselves into a trance. – We see what we expect to see and what we want to see . . .

'Ho ho!'

'. . . I should have known I'd be in trouble making that statement to a group of medics . . . Anyway, there's a fundamental inertia in ideas in any community . . . Professor Richard Dawkins calls them "memes" – like genes. They're handed on from one generation to another. Slight modifications occur all the time but occasionally there's a quantum shift – the whole caboosh changes . . .

'Ouch!'

'. . . "Ouch!" indeed. – It can be very unsettling when the "status quo" is no longer the "status quo" but the "status something else" . . . That's what happened in the UK after World War II, when the Welfare State was brought in on a wave of hope . . .

Applause.

'. . . Soldiers, sailors and airmen of all social backgrounds – and both sexes – had fought and died together. – Now the survivors saw their chance to build a new – more equal – society . . .

Applause.

'. . . A quantum shift occurred. A new norm, a new basic, a new expectation became established . . .

Applause.

'. . . Who's to say it couldn't happen again? . . . In a different direction? . . .

'Never!'

'. . . Never evolve? Never progress toward something better? . . .

'Never!'

'. . . That was the attitude they had in the USSR. – Why should they change the structure of their society when they already had what the people in power believed was the perfect set-up – the dictatorship of the proletariat? . . .

Scattered applause.

'. . . That's interesting. I'd have expected more applause than that. – But I keep forgetting . . . you're Generation Z, not Generation Y . . . You're less belligerent and more cooperative than your predecessors . . .

'Don't you believe it!'

'. . . I do believe it – and there's plenty of sociological evidence to support that belief . . .

'Al Qaida!'

'Islamic State!'

'. . . Well yes. I take your point – but it could be argued that those memes have been brought into the UK, rather than being a wholly indigenous development . . .

'Sieg heil!'

'. . . That one as well . . .

'No! It's here now! It must be stopped! We must fight!'

'. . . I agree. – I set you up for that one . . . There are

destructive memes as well as creative ones . . . We have to be constantly vigilant and constantly aware that there are forces – within each one of us as well as in our community – that could destroy us from the inside . . .

Silence.

'. . . And sometimes, as you know from childhood stories, wolves can come dressed in sheep's clothing . . .

'Baa!'

A few nervous laughs.

'. . . Hang on. – This is a serious point. – We have to look at all our ideas, not just the messy ones but the shiny ones as well . . .

Silence.

'. . . Because – otherwise – we'll never know what hits us . . . I suggest to you that the state may in time – perhaps already – be thought to be indispensable . . .

'Yes!'

'. . . and with that goes every last individual freedom.'

oOo

Part 4

If theory does not convert

into practice . . .

'I've been thinking more about wanting to do something with my life . . . umm . . . helpful – making a difference.'

'Yes, James. – So have I... on your behalf – and your mother has as well – umm . . . We've both been thinking about you.'

'D'you still think I'm on something?'

'No . . . I certainly hope you're not . . . umm . . . Precisely what's got into you?'

'Nothing . . . well – inspiration maybe.'

'Oh dear . . . Have you got God or something?'

'No chance.'

'Then what's it all about? – And what are you going to do now?'

'I thought I should learn about rehabs . . . I phoned one and . . .'

'Slow down . . . slow down . . . What about your job? . . . er . . . Commodities?'

'That's over . . .'

'God help us, James. – You're so impetuous! – One moment you're locked up . . .'

'Voluntarily . . .'

'. . . and then you want to save the world!'

'Yes.'

'Yes?'

'Yes.'

'Oh . . . umm . . . How?'

'Most of the people in that place, the Mental Health Unit –
Ha! What a totally inappropriate name! – had drug problems
. . . or alcohol . . . but they're not getting any help . . . They
get told they're depressed . . . or bipolar – God knows what
that is . . . They certainly don't – and then they're given drugs!
Anyone can see – even they themselves see it – their problem
is and always has been drugs . . . and booze. – Same thing
really . . . I found.'

'Slow down . . . Slow down . . . You're all over the place . . .
Now then. – Precisely what is it you want to discuss? . . . Or ask?'

'I want to go to rehab.'

'You what? . . . I've just rescued you from one . . . er . . .
institution – and you want another?'

'Yes.'

'Why?'

'I want to learn to do it the right way.'

'To do what? – drink sensibly? . . . umm . . . use drugs safely
and not catch . . . er . . . things – or overdose?'

'No. – They told all the patients that stuff in the Mental
Health Unit . . . umm . . . It doesn't work.'

'So here you are . . . after ten days . . . and you're the
expert!'

'I learned from the other patients. – There's nothing else to
do in there.'

'The blind leading the blind!'

'Yes.'

'Yes?'

'Yes. – It's obviously sensible . . . Listen to the patients – if
you really want to learn . . . But they don't . . . the staff . . .
They talk to each other – just like some of the patients talking
to themselves . . .'

'Well you're not going to be able to help those patients . . .
Are you?'

174

'I dunno . . . They're not getting well where they are . . . Some of them are drugged out of their skulls – shuffling about. – Call that treatment?'

'I really don't know, James . . . umm . . . Ask your mother.'

'She's a gynae, not a shrink.'

'All right, ask your sister.'

'Phoebe?'

'Why not?'

'I can tell you all sorts of reasons . . . but I won't.'

'That's very loyal of you . . . You've got some principles, I'm glad to see.'

'I've got lots . . . but I keep them hidden.'

'Ha! This really is a remarkable conversation . . . umm – Now then . . . taking you seriously on your wish . . . umm . . . You have to be aware that there are some people who can't be helped . . . They go round and round the loop – criminal, medical, social services, housing . . . and never get off. – But we've got to give help – expensive help as it is – to people who can make the best use of it . . . benefit from it. Otherwise it's a bottomless pit. – The whole country goes bust.'

'But how can you know what will help – or who can be helped – if you don't try things out?'

'Hmm . . . True. – But not indefinitely . . . There has to be a time when enough's enough . . . And then try something else . . . Maybe. – So what's this idea of yours about rehab?'

'I want to learn about myself first.'

'You think you can learn that in a rehab? – rather than in real life? . . . umm . . . in a proper job?'

'Brokering's a proper job – of a sort – and I learned a lot of things I don't value any more.'

'Slow down . . . Slow down . . . for my sake. – I can't keep up with you.'

'I phoned a drug and alcohol unit the . . .'

'Drugs? – You've not been taking drugs, have you?'

'Alcohol's a drug.'

'Well . . . umm . . . it's legal.'

'Ha! – So are lots of other drugs nowadays . . . But, anyway, I spoke to them and they said I'd have to go on their waiting list . . . even if I was desperate.'

'Ah! . . . Here we go at last . . . You've found some private place you want to go to . . . And you want me to pay for it . . . for the good of your soul.'

'Yes, father.'

* * *

'Precious? . . . That book you mentioned – about doctors undermining any healthcare system anywhere in the world . . . Why do they do that?'

'They don't like being controlled. – Nobody does.'

'But people can't be allowed to do things all on their own, any old way.'

'Why not?'

'Because the people at the bottom of the heap have no voice. – There's no one to shout for them, fight for them.'

'Do they have a voice now in the NHS? – even a proxy voice on their behalf?'

'Yes – all sorts of voices. – The Patients Association, charities that cater for particular clinical conditions, stake-holder representation on Trusts, the GMC, the government itself . . . Lots of voices.'

'Are they heard?'

'They should be.'

'That's not the point. – Do any of these voices make a discernible difference up at the sharp end of clinical practice – where you'll be very soon?'

'They should do.'

'You said that . . . But *do* they?'

'Umm . . . I don't know. – You're the researcher.'

'Yes, I am . . . And I've shown you in the lectures that – for all the multi-disciplinary team discussions, focus groups, judicial enquiries, royal commissions and endless structural and administrative reorganisations – the clear evidence is that the NHS doesn't do particularly well in comparison with other developed countries.'

'But people believe in the NHS – and repeated surveys, according to the newspapers, say how satisfied they are with their GPs. It's difficult to get appointments – but government underfunding gets the blame for that . . . And there aren't enough doctors.'

'You've bought into the BMA line . . . I've said before that a national health service can be run on any budget whatever – and with however many doctors are available – provided that governments define what *can't* be done . . . They get themselves into trouble by promising everything to everybody.'

'That's what people deserve.'

'Yes – in an ideal world where there's no limit to resources . . . But see it from a realistic point of view as a patient. If resources are limited, would you compete to establish how well you can do? Or how badly? – I asked that question in a lecture . . . and I got no answer from any of the students . . . Ha! . . . Because you all know perfectly well what your answer will be.'

'That's very cynical.'

'Realistic.'

'You're exasperating sometimes, Precious. You don't seem to feel things . . . umm . . . naturally – the way other people do.'

'With or without onions?'

'That's different – that's passion.'

'Healthcare is how I live, why I live and how I hope to be remembered . . . That's my passion.'

'Oh.'

'Oh what?'

'Umm . . . I was beginning to hope it might be me.'

'Of course it's you, dingbat. I've got no one else – and I wasn't looking for anyone until you came along and nicked my money clip.'

'I told you before . . . You threw it away.'

'Well I'm . . . umm . . . not going to throw you away.'

'Ha! You dug yourself out of that one neatly. – Plenty of practice, I guess.'

'You guess wrong – on that and on the NHS.'

'Huh?'

'I'm passionately committed to working towards getting the best healthcare and welfare system possible – anywhere.'

'It doesn't sound like it. – You're a right-wing nut.'

'In America a right-wing nut is an outspoken, irrational person.'

'That fits.'

'If you insist . . . umm . . . Would it help if you see me as a devil's advocate? – Setting up a position so that you have to argue against it . . .'

'Now you're telling me something I know perfectly well . . . Why d'you defend yourself so fiercely when I tell you you're a right-wing nut? – Ha! You know it's true, don't you?'

'It's a sore point . . . It's what my girlfriend called me – a wingnut, a crazy person.'

'She was right . . . umm . . . Is that why you broke up?'

'She died – of undiagnosed carcinoma of the ovary.'

'Oh! . . . I'm sorry.'

'You didn't know.'

'Umm . . . You know – as my mum knows – it's a very difficult diagnosis to make. It's all over by the time the symptoms become obvious.'

'An MRI scan would have found it.'

'But . . . umm . . . umm . . . Aaaargh! – No buts . . . umm . . . Sorry, Precious.'

'Yes. – I guess you were about to say that we can't do scans on everybody with a stomach ache.'

'Yes, something like that . . .'

'Well that's the difficulty, isn't it? – When real life collides with theoretical principles.'

* * *

'It's very kind of you to see me. – You – as a private GP – have referred so many patients to me over the years, I thought I'd return the complement.'

'It's always a privilege to see a professional colleague . . .'

'Yes . . . But I'd like to clarify . . .umm . . . I do want you to charge your proper fee.'

'Wouldn't dream of it. – You didn't charge my wife.'

'It's kind of you to remember . . . but that was a straight-forward medical thing – fibroids, I recall.'

'You've got a remarkable memory – with all the people you see . . .'

'I cheated . . . I looked up my notes on private GPs I'd met in the Independent Doctors thingy. – I always respect the ones with higher qualifications . . . You'd know how to deal sensibly with a silly problem like mine.'

'I doubt I'd find it silly . . . You wouldn't be here for something trivial . . . and I think I might know why you're here . . . umm . . . It's a small world in the IDF.'

'Hmm . . . S'pose it is . . . I remember the time everyone

got salmonella at a pathologist's Christmas party. – Nearly closed down the whole private sector. One chap – a surgeon – was very ill . . . Hospitalised for ages . . . Story's gone into the folklore.'

'Your chap was a locum, wasn't he?'

'Could've happened to anybody.'

'Doubt it . . . We look after our own . . . I feel – if I may say so – very concerned for you . . . dreadful thing to happen.'

'Seems so silly I just can't get over it.'

'No – it's not like that . . . These . . . umm . . . emotional things take a third of my time.'

'Really? – Even in the private sector? . . . I'd always reckoned that the mark of a good GP is knowing which specialist to refer to.'

'Well there is that – but, y'know, I refer only one or two patients a day . . . Couldn't make a living on that . . . Mostly I sort things out myself.'

'S'pose you would – with your higher qualifications . . . Forgive me asking . . . umm . . . Why didn't you specialise?'

'Ha! I'm often asked that – by all sorts of people – I . . . er . . . I see general practice as a specialty in its own right . . . early diagnosis, that sort of thing.'

'Oh yes . . . of course . . . Rude of me.'

'Not a bit, not a bit . . . You intended a compliment. That's how I take it . . . umm . . . I was wondering what to do for you . . . umm . . . Tricky.'

'Yes.'

'The gold standard's CBT and antidepressants . . . umm . . . even for a colleague.'

'I think I just need to be seen as a patient – like any other – but what I really want is to get back to work . . .'

'Not so easy.'

'No – as I found.'

'Well then . . . Shall we try that approach? . . . A CBT chap comes here twice a week – and we could book you in on Thursday . . . if you want.'

'I wouldn't want to jump a queue.'

'That's very thoughtful of you – but there's no queue . . . If there's more work, I ask him to come on more days. – That's the privilege of private practice, isn't it? . . . Being able to treat patients as individuals instead of numbers . . .'

'Yes – There's so much less stress . . . Some of my NHS contemporaries tell me they can't wait to retire early . . . Lost all the go, the . . . umm . . . love of the work itself – and the love of people.'

'Yes . . . We're very fortunate men – and women – in the private sector . . . Might have been like that before the NHS . . . But, of course, anyone can run a health service if you have to see only a few patients each day . . . Same's true in general practice . . . Even in the private sector. – Can't make a living off one or two rich Arabs.'

* * *

What an awful thing for Precious to go through, poor man – poor love . . . Don't know if I could pick myself up like he did . . . After her death . . . He's some other kind of guy . . .

* * *

'Roddy, I need to talk to you more about my anaesthetic aware-ness . . . Huh! – I'd have thought "terror" was a better word than "awareness" . . . but maybe they can't say that because everybody would sue.'

'Quite right! – So they should.'

'But there's no proof of what the patients are going through

... It's like people complaining of whiplash injuries – when they're faking it.'

'But you remembered the conversation about football.'

'I did. – Yes . . . But how could you prove someone did or didn't wake up? . . . umm . . . or if there was or wasn't a memory? – And what about False Memory Syndrome?'

'What on earth's that?'

'When people have clear memories of things that didn't actually happen.'

'Ah . . . That's what you call it . . . In law – well, to ourselves and sometimes in court – we call it lying.'

'No . . . "Denial" isn't lying . . . It's firmly believing something that isn't actually true.'

'In law it all comes down to a burden of proof . . . on who has to prove what – in order for a clear judgement to be made one way or the other.'

'Well I don't want to make a fuss . . . It's just – for the first time in my life – I can't pull myself together . . . umm . . . sort myself out.'

'Ha! You'll never make a lawyer! – or a claimant . . . not wanting to make a fuss . . .'

'But if I can't get back to work – really can't – I'll be in a dreadful mess . . . umm . . . work, money, what to do all day . . .'

'You need to establish the claim straight away . . . with the malpractice people – yours and his and the hospital's . . . Modify it later – when you see how things go . . .'

'Well, I've been given SSRIs – antidepressants . . .'

'I'm not a doctor . . . But wouldn't a tranquilliser – or sleeping tablet – be better?'

'I don't want to get into all that . . . I'll do whatever's suggested. Ha! – There's a saying . . . "A doctor who self-diagnoses and self-treats has a fool for a physician".

'Yes . . . Like lawyers who act for themselves – costs more in the end, particularly when things go against them and they get heavily stuck into appeals . . . umm . . . Is that all he's given you?'

'I'm booked in for some Cognitive Behavioural Therapy . . . CBT . . . They give it for everything nowadays . . . It's very logical . . . Doctors love it.'

'Does it work?'

'I'll find out.'

'That's not good enough . . . really.'

'I have another choice?'

'Dunno.'

'Nor do I.'

'But you're the doctor.'

'Not now, I'm not . . . I just don't know . . . umm . . .'

'Umm what?'

'. . . umm . . . anything. – Dammit . . . This is so unlike me . . . I've been brought to my knees – praying even – by a silly little neurosis . . .'

'Lizzie, sweet Lizzie . . . Nobody else would see it that way. – A judge wouldn't. – You're a totally credible witness.'

'I do wish you wouldn't talk legal stuff . . . It's so un-nerving.'

'You won't say that in a year's time . . . if you're still like this.'

'A year! . . . God in heaven! – Something's got to work before then . . .'

'Let's think about this . . . umm . . . Would you do better flying over to the States?'

'That's a possibility, I suppose . . . I advise patients – sometimes – to go to Mayo Clinic in Minnesota . . . or the Sloan Kettering in Manhattan.'

'Why?'

'If money's no object . . . and if I think they'd do a better job.'

'Than you? . . . in private work?'

'Yes – than me or anybody in the UK. – They've got fantastic services in the States – in the right areas – all the kit you could dream of, excellent staff – the lot . . .'

'Why not here?'

'Well . . . It's cultural really . . . Over there they look for new ideas, new ways of doing things . . . better and better.'

'Not here?'

'Not to the same extent . . . There's an arrogance – a belief that we're the envy of the world. That leads to inertia . . . a mind set . . . stuck in superglue . . . And then we have to get un-stuck – and that's difficult.'

'But the big private hospitals in London are American-owned.'

'Yes – but English-staffed – with English training and English low level of expectation. It all comes from the NHS . . . except the nurses of course.'

'Huh?'

'They don't come so much from the NHS. We steal them from countries who can't afford to lose them. – Even the NHS does that . . . advertises for them.'

'Ha! – So much for its morality!'

'Yes. S'pose so . . . But I'm more concerned with competence.'

'But the GMC – like the Bar Council – can surely cope with that problem.'

'Not nowadays . . . It's become judge, jury and executioner all rolled into one . . . Bad doctors need to be got rid of – but bullied doctors become dangerous doctors . . . Their minds aren't on the job . . . umm . . . Some control-freaky patients – and politicians – approve of that approach . . . bullying by the state . . .'

Part 4

'Why?'

'They dislike American free enterprise so strongly –
blaming it for all the wrongs in the world – they don't see
how creative and productive it is – especially in helping the
poor and needy . . . They just don't want to know – don't even
want to look. – And they don't want to give credit to American
industry – for creating the wealth – or the philanthropists and
the tax system that makes their universities and hospitals so
rich . . . They want the Cuban situation where the government
has total control over the doctors – and there's lots of them
. . . on very poor salaries. – That tends to happen every time in
totalitarian regimes . . . Politicians say what the doctors have
to do. – It's getting progressively closer to that here.'

'Wow, Lizzie – What a speech! . . . But, with all those doctors,
do the patients get well looked after? . . . umm . . . in Cuba?'

'I don't doubt the doctors care for them but after the
collapse of the Soviet Union that supported Cuba financially,
many Cuban doctors went to Venezuela to get better salaries
and working conditions.'

'Understandable.'

'But with Venezuela now in trouble because of falling oil
prices heaven knows what will happen . . . The Cubans lack
the facilities . . . and the medicines . . . and decent buildings . . .
for proper clinical care . . . and I doubt the new accord with
President Obama will have much effect.'

'Why not?'

'He's looking to his legacy . . . Wants to bury the Bay of
Pigs disaster from 50 years ago . . . But the Cuban government
says it's still communist. – He's given something for nothing. –
He's compromised American values . . . and one compromise
always leads to another.'

'It's not really going to go that way over here. – Is it? . . .
D'you reckon?'

'Well Phoebe made an interesting comment to me – ages ago when she was still with that . . . umm . . . what's his name? . . . umm . . . Nate, that's it.'

'What did she say?'

'She said, "If you listen carefully you can hear the ice cracking underneath everything you stand for." . . . She meant our society – yours and mine. – But I think it's happening to hers as well . . . And America's. – All those high-minded socialist ideas are coming unstuck.'

'They always do – Socialists come unstuck when they run out of other people's money . . .'

'True.'

'. . . Same thing here. Our hospitals – and schools – are worse now after 60 years of the Welfare State.'

'That's a bit unfair . . .There've been great advances. – You – as a doctor – know that.'

'Not as a result of the system itself . . . Those advances would've happened anyway – importing ideas and new specialist equipment from Germany, Israel . . . the States, of course . . .'

'And exporting some.'

'Yup . . . We still rank very high in the international league tables for universities – but we're not so good at putting new ideas into practice.'

'Why not?'

'I told you . . . Why should we change if we believe our system is already the best?'

'It's lovely hearing you on your high horse, Lizzie . . . Nothing wrong with your mind . . . Or body . . . Fancy a turn at being Lady Godiva? . . .'

* * *

Part 4

'In the remaining sessions of this term, leading up to the Easter break and then the intensive four-week revision course up to your final examinations . . .

Groans.

'. . . we're going to look at one vital principle. – If the ideas and principles of the NHS are wrong then the practice will inevitably fail . . .

'*Hissss. Hissss. Hissss.*'

'Underfunded!'

'. . . I hear the reactions from some of you. – But these are not answers to the point I made . . . Let me say it more simply: If the theory is rotten, the practice will rot . . .

'*Hissss. Hissss. Hissss.*'

'. . . No. That's an opinion – a forceful one, even if not verbalised. – But it isn't an answer to the philosophical principle that, in some situations, A inevitably leads to B . . .

Silence.

'. . . In our particular concern for healthcare systems, we have to acknowledge – regardless of issues of funding or manpower or other practical considerations – that a poor outcome is inevitable if the theory is shaky . . .

Silence.

'. . . Our first responsibility therefore has to be that we put our ideas into the crucible . . .

'Un-der-*fun*-ded!'

'. . . That's not an idea. It's a practical consideration – an important one . . . Some of you may be familiar with the business principle that any successful entrepreneur will tell you . . . if a business is making a loss, expanding it will lead to a bigger loss . . .

'The NHS isn't a business!'

' . . . Oh yes it *is* . . .

'Oh no it *isn't!*'

187

'Ha! This session isn't what you English would call a pantomime game . . . Perhaps the greatest danger in any enterprise is when we fail to examine it dispassionately . . . Anything that requires money to run it is a business. – If we choose to make a profit, it's a business. If we run it on a not-for-profit basis or as a charity, it's a business . . .

'No! No! No!'

'. . . On this, Sir, we'll have to disagree. Let's leave it at that . . . I accept your right to disagree with me. – My experience is that I learn most from people who challenge me.'

'I'm off. I've got better things to do than listen to any more of this crap.'

'And me.'

'And me.'

'. . . I respect you for acting on your beliefs. – And I do not assume that those of you who are still here necessarily agree with the ideas I'm putting forward . . . Each of us learns from our own experience . . .

Silence.

'. . . In childhood we observe our environments – at home, at school and in our community. – Initially we may trust what we're told but in adolescence we begin to think for ourselves . . . Then in adulthood we create our own system of values. These determine our behaviour and on that we form our relationships – tending to be friends with people who agree with us and who largely behave as we do . . .

'Homer Simpson!'

'D'oh.'

Laughter.

'. . . Yes, if you wish. – It's your life . . . The important point is that you'll get the consequences of your beliefs, your behaviour and your relationships . . . You can change these at any time – or you can choose to stay as you are . . .

Silence.

'. . . The same principle applies to political philosophy – like the ideas that underpin healthcare systems. – Ideally, a clear set of principles is established, plans are made on how to implement them, and the people involved then cooperate to convert theory into practice . . .

Laughter.

' . . . Yes . . . It's sad when ideal worlds clash with real worlds . . . Only in a totalitarian state does everything work according to the Grand Plan – but look at the end result, for example in North Korea . . . And observe what happens in a theocracy like Iran, where religious beliefs and political ideas are tied in together . . .

Silence.

'. . . In a representative democracy there will be constant conflict . . . Of course there will – because differing political philosophies co-exist and each is periodically voted upon . . .

'Get rid of the toffs!'

'. . . Yes, that's one view . . .

'Home rule for England!'

'. . . That's another . . . Political parties form when people come together in a common cause . . .

'Legalise cannabis!'

'. . . Yes, that's an excellent example . . . In the USA the states of Colorado and Washington have done exactly that . . .

A few drummings.

'. . . Ah. – Not as much approval as there might be generally in your age group. – As medical students, you'll be familiar with the consequence of that policy in clogging up the psych wards. – But how about free beer? . . .

Heavy drummings.

Laughter.

'. . . Well that's even more interesting. Every day on the general wards – not just in the psychiatric unit – you'll see the damaging consequences of high alcohol consumption . . . But you would support free beer . . .

Silence.

'. . . Now consider the broader picture in healthcare systems. . . . We see different ideas put into practice in various parts of the world – private insurance-based systems in the USA, now being superceded in part by ObamaCare . . .

Drummings.

'. . . And variations on the state and private sector inter-relationship in many parts of the world – as illustrated in the book I mentioned – *The Public-Private Mix for Health* . . .

Yawns.

'. . . Yes, maybe I do go on about it a bit . . .

Laughter.

'. . . The important principle – we learn this from personal experience as we grow older . . . as you will have done over some of your childhood beliefs and experiences . . . is that we need to observe what happens when ideas are put into practice. It's on this basis that I ask you to consider a clear scientific postulate . . . If the ideas and principles of the NHS are wrong then the practice will inevitably fail.'

'Un-der-*fun*-ded!'

oOo

'This really is dreadful. We pay shedloads of tax – and a hefty whack on private medical insurance . . . and it all counts for nothing.'

'Really, Roddy?'

'. . . Umm . . . I phoned the insurance company to see if we

190

could get James into a private rehab – if he needs it – but they said no . . . because addiction and alcoholism and long-term mental health problems are excluded in our policy . . . As I feared they might be . . . I seem to remember something like that.'

'Well at least he's not really an addict or anything like that . . . Though I did tell him he ought to cut down on the alcohol a bit.'

'Yes . . . umm . . . good. – But my point, members of the jury . . .'

'Roddy?'

'Sorry, dear – quite forgot . . .'

'No you didn't, you cheeky monkey.'

'Ahem . . . My point is that when we need serious help we can't get it. – state or private.'

'What's happened now?'

'I told you I spoke to James about that so-called "Mental Health Unit" he was in. – Nothing healthy in it . . . staff or patients . . . Food . . . or even furniture . . .'

'Oh.'

'. . . James said if the patients haven't got problems when they go in, they'll certainly have plenty by the time they come out.'

'It can't be that bad, Roddy. – Not like when I was a medical student . . . The long-stay institutions in those days were left-overs from the Victorian days.'

'They still are . . . More like Georgian – mad King George – or like the Industrial Revolution sweat shops and satanic mills . . . except that they're hanging around doing nothing.'

'That doesn't add up, Roddy.'

'I mean . . . the doctors didn't do much for James – or for King George.'

'They couldn't. – He had Porphyria . . . King George, I

191

mean – not James . . . They didn't know about it then . . . And how can the patients be hanging around doing nothing in a sweat shop? – That's like politicians going around whipping up apathy.'

'The patients and the staff do nothing all day. – That's the impression I had from James . . . Talk to him yourself.'

'I certainly shall – if he's made the turnaround you say he has.'

'Only on the Hilaire Belloc principle . . . umm . . . patients and staff.'

'Huh?'

'. . . "And always keep a-hold of nurse
For fear of finding something worse".'

'I don't understand.'

'What choice did James have – or any of the other patients? . . . Or the staff?'

'You're still talking in riddles . . . Imagine you're in court – addressing a jury.'

'Ha! That's exactly what you tell me not to do when I'm talking to you.'

'This is an exception . . . Woman's prerogative . . .'

'I should have known . . . Well, as I see it, ladies and . . .'

'Stop it, Roddy. – This is serious.'

'Right then . . . People have to trust the doctors and nurses they've got . . . because – for the vast majority – they have no other choice . . . That's what James wants to influence.'

'Poacher turned gamekeeper?'

'Umm . . . Yes. – Why not? – Ideal training if you ask me.'

'What? – Barristers have to have criminal backgrounds?'

'Not allowed. – Bar Standards Board Handbook for Rules and Guidance . . . Section 301 a i . . . "Conduct which is dishonest or otherwise discreditable to a barrister." . . . Ha! Fine line sometimes . . . "Spent convictions have to be disclosed when applying for a Practising Certificate.". . . umm . . . A panel decides fitness to practise in the light of the conviction.'

'Yes... There's a very similar procedure for doctors – for the GMC putting a name onto the Medical Register. – But you do like having a dig at your professional colleagues, don't you?'

'We all do . . . umm . . . in the snug. – Chatham House rules of confidentiality, of course.'

'No whistleblowing in the snug?'

'Certainly not . . . umm . . . Aah . . . I see what you're getting at. – One rule for the NHS and one rule for the rest of us . . . umm . . . James was saying the staff probably moonlight here and there – earning loadsamoney as locums in other hospitals when they should be resting between shifts in the unit they're employed to work in full time.'

'Maybe they're not paid enough.'

'That too.'

'What else?'

'James says they just don't give a damn.'

'Well he would, wouldn't he?'

'The old James yes.'

'Is the new James all that different?'

'I think so. – He convinced me.'

'Ha! Dear Roddy . . . You get caught every time.'

'Well I . . . er . . .'

'Yes you do. – Admit it . . .'

'Hmm.'

'All right . . . What's the big deal?'

'What he saw in that place – I can't imagine it would be worse than any other. It's part of the teaching hospital set-up – was enough to make him want to spend his life trying to make a difference.'

'He's had no training.'

'He says it doesn't look as if the staff have either – except for the doctors . . . He says he could do a better job even with no training.'

'Of course he'd say that. – He was in a very vulnerable position.'

'So were the other patients . . . That's what he saw – and he wants to try to help people who are like them . . . Anything would be better than what they have now . . . But they're all frightened of letting go of nurse . . .'

'But you said they were dreadful – the nurses . . . health assistants – whatever . . .'

'Belloc again . . . They may be dreadful – but they're all that the patients have got.'

'. . . Until James comes riding in with the cavalry?'

'Got any better ideas?'

'Well it's true we can't give all the people everything they want all the time . . . And I expect it's the paperwork and the committees and the training courses . . . and the constant inspections and revalidations . . .'

'That's the same for you.'

'. . . No it isn't – not all of it – I breathed again when I went fully private.'

'Yes – and I'm glad you did . . . even though we don't need the money.'

'Don't speak too soon, love . . . I really don't know when I'll be able to get back to work . . . S'pose I'll have to ask someone for help . . . But who?'

'Yes . . . That's what James was saying. – Who is there to ask? . . . On anything . . . when what's to do isn't obvious?'

* * *

'Why did you come to work in the UK, Precious?'

'I didn't. – My mother had died and I came over to be

with my English girlfriend. I met her when she won a place at Columbia. – Oxford and Cambridge were turning up their noses at students like her . . . from private schools.'

'Why didn't she stay with you in the USA?'

'She never really settled in. – She didn't get the American dream.'

'I don't get it either.'

'The land of the free?'

'And the home of the belligerent.'

'Ha! – We bailed out Europe twice – in two world wars.'

'And you bankrupted us by making us pay for a Lend-Lease loan afterwards – when the Labour government wanted to spend more money on welfare reforms.'

'And then we sold you the Lend-Lease equipment at ten cents in the dollar... We give a great deal to the world . . . We're expected to contribute to everything – war repairs, disaster relief, floods, famine . . .'

'You cause them through your war-mongering... and through the global warming you cause.'

'Ah . . . You've bought into Al Gore's crap.'

'It's not crap . . . There's lots of evidence . . . You – of all people – should appreciate evidence.'

'I would if I believed it.'

'So the great researcher, the impartial scientist, picks and chooses the evidence he wants to hear and believe . . .'

'Maybe we all do. – My girlfriend and I disagreed about the UK Welfare State. She didn't like the evidence I showed her.'

'Well I don't either. – And you may be letting your damaged heart rule your determined head.'

'Yeah, maybe . . . maybe.'

'Sorry . . . umm . . . I didn't want to be insensitive to you.'

'I don't hear it that way . . . You've every right to challenge me . . . After all, I challenge you – and the other students – in every lecture.'

'You certainly do . . . umm. – In return, try this for size . . . You said that NHS patients may be fearful because they've got a lot to be fearful about . . . and they're fearful because they've got no other choice than to stick with the NHS . . . Well great! You frighten them by saying it's useless . . . and then you say they've got no practical choice but to stick with it . . . You forgot. – You were addressing a couple of hundred students. – What choice do they have? Many of them are building up huge debts because they – and their families – can't afford the tuition fees . . . They don't all come from privileged back-grounds like mine . . . Some of their families slaved night and day – in corner shops or God-awful jobs – to get the basics for a decent life. You've forgotten your own background. – What would your mother say about you now – with all your smart ideas?'

'She was very proud of me for improving myself, rising above my background. – That's the American dream . . . The British dream seems to be to win the lottery or shack up with a celebrity – Ha! – or, more likely nowadays, get compensation for a non-existent whiplash injury.'

'And where's the research that supports those statements? – In the *Daily Mail*, I suspect . . . You don't seem to realise – dreams are broken on the wheel of despair . . . There's great swathes of the north that have no hope. – You yourself said that there are third generation dole-seekers up there. How would that feel to you? – if you were a third generation dole-seeker? . . . with no hope and no prospect of hope?'

'We're looking at the same evidence and coming to different conclusions. – You see communities downtrodden by Mrs Thatcher and forced into penury . . . I see people trapped in their own mind-sets – "Ain't it awful? Who's going to do something for me?".'

'Well who *is* going to do something for people who can't help themselves? . . . If the government doesn't help them, nobody will.'

'There you are . . . That's the blackmail – the indispensable state.'

'But it's true.'

'Only if people *believe* it's true. – It's not like that in the States. The "Can do . . ." society is still alive and well – an enterprise culture, rather than an entitlement and benefits culture.'

'Yeah – And in the States you've got gated communities – too frightened to come out from behind their barricades . . . And, most recently, gradually, you're getting politicised communities – Democrats in some neighbourhoods and Republicans in others – all in the same city . . . Your country is breaking apart into little bits. – You can hear the ice cracking underneath your society . . .'

'Over here, on this side of the pond, it's already broken. It's just that you haven't seen it yet – because you're so busy blaming everyone else.'

'Huh!'

'Huh! – Now you know why I came over here – to see things for myself, to see what's likely to happen in the USA if President Obama gets his way.'

'As he damn well should . . . Yeah . . . You look at things, Precious, and you talk about them – but you do sweet FA.'

* * *

'That son of yours . . .'

'Ours.'

'I was going to say something nice about him . . .'

'Ah! – I'm all ears . . .'

'He's made an extraordinary turnaround.'

'Oh Roddy, dear Roddy . . . You're such a sucker. – He sees you coming . . .'

'Well try this out . . . He wants to go to rehab.'

'What on earth for? – His drinking?'

'Yes. S'pose so – but really in order to learn how to help others . . . umm . . . like the ones he met in that . . . umm . . . place.'

'Then why doesn't he become a doctor – like Phoebe?'

'He seems to have some idea that the doctors in the place he was in didn't do much . . . other than write out prescriptions – probably too many.'

'What gave him that idea?'

'Well they didn't do anything else – not really . . . as far as James could see . . . So they give out scrips . . . James said some of the patients were just shuffling about.'

'Yes . . . "the Chlorpromazine shuffle". – It's a side effect of anti-psychotic drugs.'

'That's a side effect? My God! – The treatment's worse than the disease.'

'An acute psychosis is very frightening – for everybody . . . The treatment keeps them on the planet . . . and the nurses can get on with their work.'

'Hang on . . . They make one patient into a zombie so they can help another? . . . and have a quiet life?'

'Well yes. – That's probably the way it works.'

'But that's barbaric.'

'Would you want to work in that unit? . . . every day?'

'I'm not a doctor.'

'All right then . . . Would you do legal aid work – in criminal law – every day?'

'Umm . . . No . . . er . . . James was challenging me on that . . . umm . . . It's not my skill.'

'Or commitment . . . Geriatrics and Psychiatry tend to be like that . . . They're the dumping ground after all the good jobs – hearts, lungs, obs and gynae, neurology, orthopaedics – have gone.'

'Why are they "good"?'

'They attract private patients . . . middle-aged middle-class people spending their money on themselves – and finding excellent doctors very willing to take it.'

'Gosh! – You sound just like Phoebe.'

'I was once . . . Surely you remember . . . The idealism of my youth. – Just like hers.'

'What happened?'

'I love surgery – like you love the commercial bar.'

'But surely doctors have a vocation . . . Hippocrates and all that . . . Wanting to help those most in need.'

'Dream on . . . That's the BMA line – the emotional black-mail so they can screw the government for more money . . . and the patients buy into it because they're frightened of having no medical care at all.'

'Well that's fair enough.'

'Ha! . . . You buy into it as well . . . umm . . . When the whole medical profession went on strike in Canada some years ago, the death rate went down.'

'Good God! . . . I bet they hushed that up.'

'Too late . . . And iatrogenic disasters – things caused by doctors . . . like my problem – are in the papers every day . . . in very large numbers. But people cling to the NHS – as God's gift – because they believe they have no alternative.'

'They don't have an alternative . . . They don't all have our income.'

'They don't need to . . . Common things occur commonly – and they don't cost much to treat.'

'They would in the private sector.'

'Only when the doctors run a closed shop . . . instead of competing with each other.'

'Ha! That's what Mrs Thatcher was going on about.'

'Yes – and a fat lot of good it did her . . . or the Health Service – Doctors know how to protect their own interests . . . The BMA is the most unscrupulous trade union of all.'

'If Phoebe could hear you now! . . . Or James.'

'What about James?'

'He's on a crusade . . .'

'Good for him! – He should be at his age.'

'But he'll have to come face-to-face with reality sometime – inequality in needs and provisions, postcode lotteries, one set of rules for the Scots, the Irish and the Welsh and another for the English, the worst clinical services in the poorest areas. – All this in the Welfare State! . . . and, to give him credit, that's what James wants to change.'

'He'll need a thick skin – on his back – and a lot of luck . . . But his heart's in the right place – apparently – and so's Phoebe's.'

'So were the hearts of the people who created the Welfare State.'

'Yes they were – but their minds went walkabout . . . It doesn't work in practice and it costs progressively more and more. People think they're getting something for nothing – but they're not . . . They say healthcare's a birthright – but that belief will bring us all down . . . And the Americans – with their ObamaCare . . . With or without all the current opposition from the medics and the insurers and the pharmaceutical companies – they'll find the same . . . Give people a sense of entitlement – rather than responsibility – and it'll run and run.'

Part 4

* * *

'Why d'ya come to Hazelden, Jimmy . . . er . . . James?'

'I needed a breath of fresh air.'

'Ya come to Minnesota at dis time o' year for fresh air? – Go outside and ya'll freeze ta death. Dis is Scandinavia, USA.'

'What are those things on the lake?'

'Dem's ice-fishin' huts. Dey bores a hole through da ice, puts in a baited hook and waits for da fish.'

'Just sitting there? . . . in those little shelters? . . . reading or something?'

'What sort o' alcoholic are you, man?'

'Oh! . . . I see.'

'Come in the summer and ya'll be bitten to death . . . Mosquito's da state bird.'

'This your home area?'

'Nah . . . I'm Noo Yawk, Noo Yawk, born and raised.'

'Why d'you come here?'

'Too much cocaine . . . Company sent me here . . . on employment assistance programme.'

'What's that? . . . umm . . . What does it do?'

'Employment assistance? . . . Don' you Brits have that? . . . The company pays in – an' we pay some – and then we're covered, see? . . . Couldn't afford this place – even not-for-profit – without EAP.'

'And what d'you do . . . umm . . . for a living?'

'Me? – Security guard . . . ex-cop.'

'You . . . an ex-cop . . . on the white stuff?'

'Sure . . . NYPD's full of it . . . specially in the Bronx – my neighbourhood.'

'And the company . . . the EAP . . . pay for you to come here – one of the top rehabs in the world? . . . for addiction problems?'

'Sure thing . . . Why not?'

'It's not quite . . . umm . . . what we do . . . umm . . . back home.'

'But you got ObamaCare already.'

'Yes . . . That's the theory.'

*   *   *

'I want to notify you of a claim I shall be making on a policy . . . Roderick Finch . . . Yes, that's right . . . It's about me leg . . . right leg . . . It's gone wrong . . . Not working properly. – Dragging me foot a bit, tripping over things occasionally . . . When I'm not careful over where I'm going . . . Yes – a couple of times . . . When did it begin? . . . er . . . Three or four months ago, I s'pose. Maybe more . . . not sure . . . It gets better – or not so troublesome – without me doing anything . . . Then it comes back again . . . umm . . . worse than before sometimes . . . I thought me GP would send me to an orthopaedic surgeon – but he's sent me to a consultant neurologist for some reason . . . Yes – he's on your list of approved specialists. – I checked . . . Oh . . . Why not? . . . Neurological problems are excluded? . . . But that silly little thing with me leg last time is nothing to do with what's happening now . . . I see . . . I see . . . Seems to me that almost every time me family has a medical issue – and we pay our premiums regularly so we're good customers of yours – you do your best to get out of paying . . . Yes . . . Yes . . . I understand. – Yes . . . If that's in the policy, that's the way it is . . .'

*   *   *

'Today I'm going to begin with a statement that should be obvious . . . True compassion can only be individual. Whether

I help you or not is up to me – but I'll reap the consequences. I have to earn my place in a compassionate society through my actions for others . . .

Silence.

'. . . By contrast, the state can never be compassionate . . .

'Rubbish!'

'. . . Hear me through, please . . . I did not say that individuals working for the state cannot be compassionate. – Of course they can . . . and a great many are. – But the state is a disembodied entity. It has no feelings. Irrespective of the motives of its founders and the determined commitment of many people in its workforce, the state – like money – as Miss Finch helped me to demonstrate . . .

'Pfwooar!'

'. . . Ahem . . . is inanimate. It needs people to bring it to life . . . But now hear this . . . When A gives the life of B for the benefit of C, but A expects the credit for himself or herself, this is the essential prerequisite for totalitarianism . . .

'That's not people – it's algebra!'

'You're right. – This simple algebraic statement shows how people behave in a top/down directed healthcare system . . . The politician A gives away the life of the healthcare worker B for the benefit of the patient C. But then – guess what? – the politician wants all the credit . . .

Shuffles.

'. . . All politicians want to be seen as the guardians of healthcare – protecting quality and reducing costs . . . They know only too well that protecting the NHS – or the social welfare system in other countries – is a top priority in the minds of the electorate. No politician in the UK would be elected on a promise to reduce services . . .

'Tory cuts!'

'. . . Even Margaret Thatcher didn't mess with the NHS

... And Prime Minister David Cameron ring-fenced its income ...

'Tory cuts!'

Drummings.

'... The only cuts made were in the previous Labour government's projected expenditure – because, as the brutally honest Labour Party Chief Secretary to the Treasury wrote to his successor, "I'm afraid there is no money" ...

'Healthcare's a birthright!'

'... At whose expense? ...

'Rich people!'

'... We've covered that ground before. – But let's spell out some clear facts ... Modern medical practice is expensive. NICE protects costs. That's its remit, no matter what government is in power ...

'*Hissss. Hissss. Hissss.*'

'... I understand your displeasure but that doesn't covert into cash ...

'*Hissss. Hissss. Hissss.*'

'... New methods of clinical investigation – scans and so on – are expensive. New pharmaceutical drugs are expensive. New advances in surgical procedures are expensive ...

'Psychiatry's a rip-off!'

'... Well you may have a valid point there. – Big Pharma makes vast profits from antidepressants that have little evidence of efficacy ... And although Big Pharma supports research and post-graduate education, there are good reasons – and maybe some bad reasons – for that ... They get a hefty return on their investment, particularly from drugs prescribed in the NHS ... Have a look at the Fortune 500 companies in the USA ... Big Pharma's right in there. Several times ...

'*Hissss. Hissss. Hissss.*'

'. . . even though drug channel companies – the distributors – easily outrank them . . .

Silence.

'. . . But there's another serious concern . . . Big Pharma and the American Psychiatric Association – the APA – and the private medical insurance companies between them stitch up the DSM and ICD . . .

Silence.

'. . . No hisses? . . . Ah, maybe you don't know that the psychiatric diagnoses listed in the Diagnostic and Statistical Manual and the International Classification of Diseases are there just as the result of a show of hands – or some equally casual vote – in the APA . . . But, based on this, the private medical insurance companies agree to pay for the treatments – including the fees of the consultant psychiatrists . . .

'Hissss. Hissss. Hissss.'

'. . . Yes, it's a nice little earner – and what in any other profession would be called "insider trading" . . .

'Hissss. Hissss. Hissss.'

'. . . As I said at the start . . . True compassion can only be individual . . .

Silence.

'. . . This again shows why – even in America, where the private healthcare system is dominated by the big corporations – no system anywhere in the world is perfect . . . Far from it – although the Chinese "barefoot doctor" system has a lot to recommend it . . .

Laughter.

'. . . Don't laugh . . . Look it up . . .

Shuffles.

'. . . Even in the rudimentary universal welfare system in the USA, powerful interests in the medical profession, Big Pharma and the medical insurance companies try to run things for their own benefit rather than primarily for the care of patients . . .

'Boo. Boo. Boo.'

'. . . But any universal welfare system anywhere in the world can get out of control . . . Ayn Rand is right when she says that the difference between a welfare state and a totalitarian state is merely a matter of time.'

'Boo. Boo. Boo.'

oOo

'That session today, learning the story of Hazelden, was fascinating. – Starting from nothing in Hazel's den at the bottom of her garden . . . and then joining with St Paul's hospital . . . in what you people call the twin cities – Minneapolis St Paul – where I flew in . . . to make the "Minnesota Method". The AA counsellors say, "Hand it over" . . . umm . . . I don't do God, by the way . . . and the psychologists say "Work it out" . . .'

'He really say dat? . . . You weird, man . . . We see da chicks – from da other unit – an' you listen to da lecture!'

'It's my money I'm spending here . . . well my dad's . . . and there's totty back home.'

'Totty? . . . Wassat?'

'Hotty totty . . . a hot woman . . . London Cockney rhyming slang . . .'

'Huh?'

'. . . er . . . Forget it.'

'Fergedaboudit? . . . How can I fergedaboudit? – Locked in here wid you for 28 days.'

'No . . . Forget about the rhyming slang . . . umm . . . too difficult to explain. – But don't forget about the crumpet.'

'Huh?'

Part 4

'. . . er . . . hot chicks.'
'Why dint you say dat, man? – Don' ya spik English?'

* * *

'I'll tell you something, Phoebe . . . It's a credit to our relation-ship that either of us is here in Byron's this week.'

'Yes, I was thinking that as well . . . Umm . . . Onions?'

'You betcha . . . Mmmmm.'

'Wow, Precious, it gets better and better.'

'Of course. It's more real . . . Otherwise it's Sonny and Cher all over.'

'What's that?'

'They were singers – a married couple – in the 60s and 70s. They had a hit called *I got you babe*.'

'You heard them? You were there?'

'Ha! Cheeky! . . . It's still played sometimes – I heard it last week. It's all about young love surviving being misunderstood – I don't remember any of the other words . . . umm . . . They divorced.'

'Oh yeah . . . I know Cher . . . She's still around as an actor – and what some people call a "media personality" . . . umm . . . What happened to Sonny?'

'He became a Republican congressman.'

'What! A right-wing pop star?'

'There's plenty – and actors . . . Ronald Reagan became president.'

'Don't we know it – Mrs Thatcher's boyfriend . . . They should've sung *I got you babe*.

'Left-wing Luvvies aren't the only people with feelings.'

'Right-wingers can't possibly have real feelings – or sound minds.'

'Well thanks for that.'

'You don't count . . . You're just a researcher and lecturer. It's your job to look at all ideas.'

'Thanks for the "just".'

'Oh . . . umm . . . Sorry about that . . . You've got lots of feelings – with or without onions.'

'Everybody has – but some people wear them on their sleeves. Ha! I remember a guy in San Francisco, just by the Golden Gate Bridge, selling T-shirts saying, "Thank you for NOT sharing your feelings".

'Ha! Fair enough.'

'And – while we're on the subject of politics and the arts – There's a saying that the problem with left-wing people is that they read only left-wing literature . . .'

'Yeah – and the problem with right-wing people is they read nothing at all. – Heard it.'

'And it's largely true . . .'

'. . . but it needs more research . . . umm, Precious . . . Do you ever forget your day job? . . . umm . . . when you're with me?'

'Ronnie Scott's.'

'I can imagine you – even there – whispering into my ear, "Let's look at the evidence . . .".'

'Well ok . . . Let's do exactly that . . . Very soon you'll be on the wards – not as a student but as a qualified doctor making clinical decisions. – Each decision will have cost implications for the NHS . . . And anything you do for one of your patients will mean there's less to spend on others.'

'Umm . . . I've never thought of it that way – so personally.'

'But that's the truth – even though the senior consultants who trained you won't see it that way.'

'Why not?'

'Because their greatest fear is missing something – and being found out by their colleagues . . . and by students . . . I remember reading an insensitive obituary about a consultant who committed suicide. His research student proved that the chief's big idea – over the previous 20 years – was based on a false premise.'

'Poor man.'

'Yes – but maybe a silly man as well . . . If you come up with better ideas than mine, I'll be delighted. I'll hug and kiss you.'

'You can do that now – and more . . .'

'But you haven't had a better idea yet.'

'Don't tempt me . . . mmm . . . It might be rather fun here in Byron's. The sofas are comfortable. – I bet the staff have given them a try after work.'

'I'm a spoilsport.'

'But you said in a lecture that you want us to be individuals – rather than mere units in someone else's grand design . . . Why should we obey other people's customs and boring norms?'

'You've remembered the principle very well – but applied it out of context.'

'But you told me that new ideas come from the periphery – from the oddballs . . . Ah! That's my destiny – to be an oddball.'

'Dingbat's good enough.'

'I'll settle for that . . . Right then . . . New ideas . . . umm . . . okay, try this . . . You said that patients see themselves as individuals, rather than as mere numbers . . . Let's brighten them up in the wards by getting them some silly hats.'

'That's been done already – well, the other way round really . . . Dr Patch Adams – Robin Williams made a film about him – used to dress up as a clown . . . His humour had a positive effect on physical outcomes.'

'His own or the patients?'

'Both, I expect.'

'Don't you know?'

'No – I don't know everything.'

'Then look it up before you quote it . . .'

'Ouch!'

'. . . That's what we're taught nowadays. – There's no shame in not knowing . . . and it's so easy to access stuff on the web.'

'Yes. – That's Larry Weed's big idea, from Vermont . . . He said students are forever being asked, "Whaddyaknow? Whaddyaknow? Whaddyaknow?" – when they should get used to looking things up . . . They make mistakes – we all do – if they guess . . . and then they try to justify them . . . umm . . . He also said that patients are the most important members of his staff. – They're motivated, there's one for every patient and they pay him while they're doing their work.'

'Ha! That's great! – but I'm not sure about the last bit.'

'Well it shows that American doctors aren't stuffy – not all of them – and Patch isn't the only one to use humour . . . It heals – and it's memorable.'

'Right. Here's another idea . . . Easy answers to easy questions might be the ones that work.'

'Yeah, could be . . .'

'But you said in a talk that facile solutions will be no comfort to those of us at the sharp end of medical practice.'

'Hey! You're a sharp one yourself – turning things around on me like that.'

'It's good for you . . . Otherwise an MD becomes an MDeity.'

'That's an American joke – an old one – Where did you get it from?'

'I looked it up – on the web. – It suits you very well, pontificating away every week.'

'Wow! You certainly know how to cut me down to size.'

Part 4

'I told you – it's good for you.'
'You're going to tell me I'll get used to it.'
'Yes.'
'Is that all? – Just "Yes"?'
'Yes.'

* * *

Mustn't bother Phoebe . . . Important time – finals – coming up soon . . . Hope she's working – not with some man or other. – So different from my time . . . Hmm . . . Would've been nice to keep an eye on Roddy . . . hmm . . . He'll be ok in the Garrick. – No difference there . . . really . . . Hope James isn't off – again . . . Oh dear. – on a mad-cap scheme . . . Still . . . he's young . . . plenty of time . . . Ha! . . . for more mistakes . . . Hmm . . . before settling down . . . Got to get married . . . sometime . . . grandchildren . . . Hmm . . . Nasty time for him in that Mental Health Unit. – Might learn from it . . . I s'pose . . . Hey-ho . . . We'll see . . . What's this family week thing like? . . . in America? . . . Hope I'll be ok . . . and on the plane . . . Oh Lizzie, oh Lizzie, oh dear, oh dearie me . . . What's happening to me? – and the family? . . .

* * *

'Thank you for seeing me at such short notice, within a couple of weeks, and for arranging the tests. – It's amazing you were able to get all the results back within a few days and see me again within the week.'

   'Yes . . . It's the advantage of the private sector – to get things dealt with straight away . . . In your case, as I mentioned when we first met, there were clinical signs of damage to the nerve pathways to your right leg . . . There's some spasticity – tightness – in

211

the muscles and you had very brisk reflexes when I tapped your right knee and ankle . . . And your big toe went up – instead of down – when I scraped the underside of your foot.'

'I was trying to get away.'

'No . . . It's a reflex action – the Babinski reflex. – You can't control it.'

'I certainly couldn't . . . umm . . . Why's it got that funny name? – Babinski – Is it something done on babies?'

'Ha! Yes it is actually – to test their nerves . . . right from birth. – But it's named after Dr Joseph Babinski who first described it . . . Great man, fine doctor . . . French . . . Late 19th century . . . umm... A positive result – like yours – means the nerve impulses . . . all the way from your brain and through your spinal cord and down the whole length of your leg . . . were impaired for some reason.'

'Why?'

'That's what we don't yet know . . . The rest of the examination showed that your balance was impaired – inevitably from your right leg not functioning as well as the left – but maybe for other reasons.'

'Oh. I thought that might have happened when I've had just a bit too much of a good thing – at the club.'

'There's some sign of that on the blood tests . . . but nothing dramatic . . .'

'That's good . . . Ha! – I'm sure my wife'll be pleased . . . umm . . . reassured. – She worries about me sometimes.'

'Well I'd suggest that you cut right back on alcohol. – It's a neurotoxin . . . specifically damaging brain and nerve tissue – and we don't want any more of that in your case . . .'

'Indeed not. I . . .'

'Forgive me . . . I'll just take you through the full set of results . . .

Part 4

'Yes . . . umm . . . Sorry about that. – Bit nervous, y'know. – Seeing a neurologist.'

'Yes. I understand . . . All my patients have similar concerns – when they see a neurologist like me . . . The other blood tests were fine. No sign of anything wrong in your general blood tests – no anaemia, no kidney problems, no vitamin deficiencies, no problems with your thyroid. – And the results of all the other blood tests we've done so far were negative . . .'

'So far?'

''Fraid so . . . We gradually narrow down the possibilities.'

'Why don't you test for everything straight away?'

'Not good clinical practice . . . We have to think and plan – rationally – and it'd be hugely expensive.'

'Oh. Thank you for that . . . umm . . . My insurance won't pay . . . They said I'd made a previous claim for a neurological problem – when I slipped a disc.'

'Strictly that's orthopaedic – or neurosurgical – rather than neurological . . . although it has neurological consequences.'

'Huh! . . . No use being strict with them . . . Law into themselves when it comes to paying out.'

'We'll see what the other tests show . . . but . . . umm . . . it might be best for you if your GP refers you to my NHS clinic . . . if this drags on. – Could be very pricey.'

'Oh . . . umm . . . Thank you . . . I'll ask him . . . umm . . . if this does go on and on – and builds up.'

'I think it might . . . But at least the MRI scans of your brain and spinal cord were completely normal . . .'

'That's a relief . . . I thought – just having that test – I might have a brain tumour.'

'No sign of one.'

'Brain or tumour?'

'Ha! . . . I must say, you certainly know how to keep your spirits up.'

'Got to . . . Me wife's not too great at present . . . Some idiot anaesthetist didn't see she was awake during the operation . . . On her gallbladder.'

'That's bad.'

'Yes . . . Gotta make sure I'm in fine fettle.'

'Yes . . . umm . . . The nerve conduction studies showed some fibrillation... a sort of fluttering. – The impulses down the nerves aren't working quite as they should.'

'Can you wake 'em up? Gee 'em along a bit?'

'I wish we could . . . Not as easy as that . . . First we've got to check for all sorts of infections . . . Some fairly common, some rare . . . D'you travel much? – Exotic places?'

'I wish . . . Me work takes me to Europe all the time – and America sometimes – but nothing "exotic", if I've understood you correctly.'

'Well, the point of my question is this . . . Some neurological conditions – like those caused by infections – are treatable and others are not . . . More or less . . . We've got to look at the possibility of the treatable ones first of all. – To give the patient the best chance.'

'Oh . . . umm . . . Yes . . . Very much so . . . umm . . . What d'you think I've got?'

'Can't say at this stage . . . All sorts of possibilities . . . Let's just do the further tests . . . umm . . . with your permission.'

'What will they show?'

'Most likely they'll show what you haven't got . . . or less likely to have . . . Few tests ever are totally "yes" or "no".'

'But, putting everything together so far, what do you think?'

'I think you have the early symptoms and signs of a neurological illness – but I can't say which at this stage . . . Let's do the tests.'

'Oh.'

'And I'll need to keep a close eye on you – as time goes on – regularly . . . so we can see what develops.'

'Or not.'

'Yes, of course. – "Or not".'

'Umm . . . Will I be able to work?'

'Yes . . . I believe so . . . For now at any rate.'

'But you're not sure?'

'It's so unpredictable . . . Patients differ – no two are the same . . . And the same illness can behave very differently in different patients.'

'Oh God . . . Hmm . . . Time for prayer, I s'pose. – My wife's good at that . . .'

* * *

'The gateway to any healthcare system is its family doctor system. In sparsely populated rural areas there may be no doctors for miles around . . . This situation is common in some parts of the USA. Local communities may club together to put up the money to pay for a doctor to work there. Sometimes nurse practitioners are the best they can get . . .

'Lucky them!'

Laughter.

'Sexist!'

'. . . Thank you, thank you. Settle down now . . . In Russia, "Feldshers" – paramedics – serve a similar function. In the People's Republic of China, as I mentioned previously, "bare-foot doctors" – often farmers who work barefoot – are given minimal medical training so they can diagnose and treat a few common clinical conditions . . . They're also responsible for educating the local population in basic hygiene, prevent-ative health care and family planning. All other conditions come under the categories "Something else" or "Don't know".

Patients with those diagnoses are referred on up the line to people who've had more training . . . The system works insofar as it's a lot better than nothing. You might like to go see it one day . . .

Silence.

' . . . The barefoot doctor system operates on the principle that they're paid by the people who are well . . . Those who are sick don't contribute – because their doctors are deemed to have failed them . . .

Some uncomfortable shuffles.

' . . . No volunteers to work in that system? . . . No, maybe not . . . I make this point in order to counter the belief that there is "poverty" in the UK or the USA. There certainly are areas of *relative* poverty but only in contrast to areas where there is a very high standard of living . . .

Shuffles.

' . . . Have a look at this chart from the United Nations in 2007:

Highest number of physicians per 100,000		Lowest number of physicians per 100,000	
Cuba	591	Tanzania	2
Saint Lucia	517	Malawi	2
Belarus	455	Niger	2
Belgium	449	Burundi	3
Estonia	448	Ethiopia	3
Greece	438	Sierra Leone	3
Russian Federation	425	Mozambique	3
Italy	420	Togo	4
Turkmenistan	418	Benin	4
Georgia	409	Chad	4
Lithuania	397	Bhutan	5

Israel	382	Papua New Guinea	5
Uruguay	365	Lesotho	5
Iceland	362	Eritrea	5
Switzerland	361	Rwanda	5
Armenia	359	Burkina Faso	5
Bulgaria	356	Senegal	6
Azerbaijan	355	Uganda	8
Kazakhstan	354	Angola	8
Czech Republic	351	Central African Republic	8
Portugal	342	Mali	8
Austria	338	East Timor	10
France	337	Congo, Dem. Rep. of the	11
Germany	337	Gambia	11
Hungary	333	Guinea	11
Spain	330	Mauritania	11
Sweden	328	Vanuatu	11
Lebanon	325	Côte d'Ivoire	12
Malta	318	Guinea-Bissau	12
Slovakia	318	Zambia	12

Whistles.

'. . . In the UK there are 236 doctors per 100,000 people. In the USA the number ranges from 169 in Idaho and 172 in Oklahoma to 415 in Maryland and 462 in Massachusetts . . . But in Tanzania, Malawi and Niger there's only 2 . . .

Silence.

'. . . Yes, the contrasts between the richest and the poorest countries are astounding. There are no two ways about it . . . doctors – and the populations they serve – in the UK and the USA are very privileged . . .

Silence except for a few throat clearings.

'. . . We can see clearly that the expectations of doctors and patients in the UK or the USA will be vastly different from those in Tanzania, Malawi or Niger – and many other . . . er . . . developing countries. – We've got it made . . . over here and Stateside . . . in terms of healthcare services. But still – both as doctors and as patients – we complain . . . Ha! – So much for "Tory cuts" . . .

'Boo. Boo. Boo.'

. . . or for the Republican defence – or denial – of healthcare inequalities in the USA . . .

'Boo. Boo. Boo.'

' . . Are you booing one or the other or both? . . .

'You!'

'. . . I'm merely the messenger . . . But let me draw your attention now to some features of general medical practice in the UK, bearing in mind that – whatever your hopes and intentions now – the same proportion of you will become GPs as will become hospital specialists . . .

'Aaaaargh!'

Laughter.

'. . . Career GPs would consider themselves specialists in their own right, seeing as they deal with the vital early diagnosis of significant disease as well as the management of today's emotional and social *dis*-ease so that it doesn't become the physical disease of tomorrow . . .

'They failed!'

'. . . That's what Lord Moran, Winston Churchill's doctor, said – "GPs are the failures of the medical profession . . . They fell off the ladder" . . .

'Poor dears!'

Laughter.

'. . . Times have moved on – but they could easily regress if GPs are not given ready access – preferably on their own premises – to diagnostic facilities, like simple X-Ray units and pathology labs . . . This "one-stop-shop" would be clinically exciting for the doctors and save the patients a huge amount of time and travel and general hassle. After all, their time's as valuable as the doctor's time . . . Treat GPs and their patients as idiots and they will surely become idiots . . .

'D'oh.'

Slightly less laughter.

'. . . The economic implications of failure to use highly trained staff to the best of their ability is huge . . . At present nurses are often doing the work of assistants, GPs are doing work that could often be done by nurse practitioners – and consultant specialists spend a significant part of their time in outpatient clinics doing work that could have been done beforehand by GPs . . . Work out the cost implications of that! . . .

Silence.

. . . In America there's not such a clear physical divide between hospital doctors and GPs as there is here in the UK – give or take GP clinical assistantships in some hospital departments . . . American doctors work hard for higher qualifications so they can get their patients admitted to the best hospitals . . .

'And more money for themselves!'

'. . . Yes – and more money – and why not? . . . But, in the UK, GPs are now often paid more than hospital specialists . . .

'*Grrrrrr.*'

'. . . and their patients may still have to wait a week or more for an office appointment . . . And if they're ever too ill to get into the doctor's office they'd commonly be seen at home by a deputising service . . .

'*Grrrrrr.*'

'. . . Yes. – There are fundamental flaws in the structure and function of medical services in the UK . . . For a start, GPs are given little training in medical schools – like this one – for the work they'll actually do in practice . . . They learn, alongside future hospital doctors, about rarities. These can lead to the highest attainment of all – an eponym – a disease or a test named after the doctor who first described it. Nowadays – with distinguished exceptions – that may mean that he or she did the least good to the smallest number of people . . .

'Hissss. Hissss. Hissss.'

'. . . And to treat GPs merely as sorting offices so that important consultants are not troubled with "trivia" – whatever that may be – is a phenomenal waste of GPs' training and skill . . .

Silence.

'. . . Might it not be a good idea for future hospital doctors to be required to do six months in general practice, just as future GPs have to do several six-month training stints as junior hospital doctors? . . .

Shuffles.

'. . . Maybe in this way the ghost – a very patronising and expensive ghost – of Lord Moran can be laid to rest.'

oOo

'I like the idea of "barefoot doctors". I love walking barefoot – wriggling my toes in the sand.'

'One day I'll do a timeline exercise with you – just for fun – looking forward into the distant future of your life . . . Eventually you get to the time of your death. You sit down on the end of your timeline and twiddle your toes in the infinite . . . the ultimate expression of innocence when all the hard times in life are over . . .'

'You gaze at the stars . . . and you see something written in the sky . . . the number 42 . . .'

'You what?'

Part 4

'Dear Precious . . . Where have you been all my life? . . . 42 – the ultimate answer to the ultimate question . . .'

'Huh?'

'Douglas Adams – *The hitch-hiker's guide to the galaxy.*'

'Really?'

'Precious Ellington, you really are what you Americans would call "something else" . . . Douglas Adams was poking fun at convergent thinkers. They search for the ultimate answer – the holy grail . . . He was a divergent thinker – always looking for the next question. I am too – and I guess you are . . .'

'So, if 42 is the answer, what's the question?'

'He never said. – It's irrelevant.'

'But if . . .'

'English humour, precious Precious . . . English humour.'

'You'll have to teach me.'

'Can't be done.'

'No?'

'No. – But I'll teach you something else . . . if you let me . . .'

'Umm . . . umm . . .'

'Umm what? – I may be a dingbat but I'm not that much of an old bat, am I? . . . Not yet.'

'You're fantastic . . . but I'm . . . umm . . . I'm shy.'

'Ye Gods and little fishes! – You're what? – You, the lecturer who can hold an audience of 200 stroppy students. You . . . shy?'

'Umm . . . yes.'

'Oh . . . umm . . . All right then. – Shall we save it for a special time? . . . when the course is over and I'm no longer your student? . . . I can be your teacher then . . .'

'Umm . . .'

'I give up.'

'Don't do that. Don't do that . . .'

'Oh well, if you really mean that . . . umm . . . delayed gratification will be rather fun . . . Right then. – Down to business.'

'Phew!'

'Sweet love, you really are shy – aren't you?'

'Yes.'

'That's sweet.'

'I think it's stupid – but it's the way I've always been over things like this.'

'If anything, I've been the opposite.'

'I . . . umm . . . mm.'

'You noticed?'

'Just a bit . . . I . . . er . . . I like it . . . umm . . . Down to business now?'

'Penance first.'

'Why? – What've I done?'

'Nothing yet – but you might.'

'So I pay a penance in advance?'

'Get on with it you . . . you . . . umm . . . dingbat. – Now you've got me at it! – Me! Shy! Come here, you lovely lovely man . . . Mmmmm . . . That's better . . . Now then. – Where was I? . . . Oh yes . . . You mentioned "barefoot doctors" because you said that no system in the world is perfect . . . umm . . . Something along the lines of us needing to learn from anyone.'

'Yes.'

'Is that it? – Just "Yes"?'

'Yes.'

'Mmm . . . Try this . . . If free market capitalism's so wonderful, why do senior doctors – not just Big Pharma and the medical insurance companies – run things for their own benefit rather than for patients?'

'They don't – not all of them . . . There's kindness and compassion all over the world – as well as hatred and cruelty . . .

Part 4

No group of people – doctors, lawyers, accountants, builders, housewives, politicians – has a monopoly on all human virtues or vices.'

'That's obvious.'

'You wouldn't think so from the verbal – and physical – attacks people make on each other . . . umm . . . personally and politically . . . People are always dividing themselves into opposing camps – left or right, right or wrong.'

'But the middle ground's so boring, so pathetic . . .'

'Not to me as a researcher, it isn't. I want to find out what works and what doesn't – what's useful or crazy.'

'Can't we be all of those things?'

'We are – but my job is to be a splitter and lumper with the data until a clear pattern emerges.'

'You wish . . .'

'Yes, I do . . . Then I can present my points in a clear way – which is what I've been trying to do on the course.'

'You succeed – but it doesn't mean that we have to agree with you.'

'No. But it does mean – if you're honest . . . if you value the integrity of your own mind . . . that you'll try to work out exactly where I'm right or wrong – and why – and then come up with some ideas of your own.'

' . . . But I've noticed even some students – some of my mob – don't want to think for themselves. – They want to be force-fed . . . You'll make a lot of enemies.'

'That's fine. – You know a man by his enemies.'

'Huh? . . . How?'

'If he's got anything worth saying, he's bound to rattle some cages and make enemies. – And that shows the quality of his mind.'

'Or hers.'

'Yes, of course.'

'Not "of course" at all.'

'Umm . . . Sorry . . . umm . . . It was a woman – Eleanor Roosevelt – who said, "Great minds discuss ideas; average minds discuss events; small minds discuss people".'

'She got that right! Good for her!'

'What I said on the course was that we get the consequences of our beliefs . . . They lead to our behaviour and that determines our relationships . . .'

'Yes, I can see that.'

'. . . And this principle applies to governments as well as individuals . . . None of us gets very far just shouting at each other . . .'

'I love you, Precious.'

'Oh . . . umm . . . er . . . Thank you . . . Umm . . . We've got to get our ideas right first of all – on healthcare and welfare systems or anything else.'

'I love you, Precious Ellington . . . I want your babies.'

* * *

'Isafunnyting . . . dis "disease" business. – I ain't got no disease . . . not since the last time I . . . er . . .'

'I think what he meant was it's a "*dis*-ease" . . . something that throws us off balance – and makes us do stupid things.'

'Like a line-backer charging down?'

'Line-backer . . . What's that?'

'Football . . . forward trying to sack the quarterback before he throws the pass.'

'Hey! – That's good! – Charging down on me! – Feels just like that when I try to avoid the next drink or line or pill . . . If I start, I can't stop.'

'Yeah . . . me neither, man.'

'I think what he meant was that it's not our fault, see?

– being addicts . . . but we're still accountable – responsible – for what we do.'

'Yeah . . . Makes sense when you says it . . . umm . . . I hears it from you. – Umm . . . Ah'm not fixed on dis AA shit.'

'Well . . . as I see it . . . maybe . . . it's a sort of preventive medicine . . . umm . . . stops the craving for the next drink.'

'Oh dat's it!'

'Just my opinion . . . I'm no expert.'

'You'se nuff expert fer me.'

'Ha! – I've come over here to learn from you guys . . . There's nothing . . . umm . . . sensible – back home. – A few in the private sector but no real rehabs – like this one – in the National Health Service.'

'We gottem all over . . . Betty Ford, Arizona places, Ashley – Father Martin done dat . . . in Baltimore, Maryland.'

'Who's he?'

'Catholic priest . . . Saw his "Chalk talk" on film – 'fore you come in . . . Great stuff . . . He's one of us. – Dead now.'

'A Catholic priest . . . drunk?'

'You betcha.'

'And he built a rehab?'

'Sure . . . Why not?'

'Because priests don't have any money . . . The church does – loadsamoney, megabucks – but not the men in frocks . . . umm . . . How did he get it?'

'People give it. He's good man – an' he earn it . . . from "Chalk talk".'

'I wish I'd seen it.'

'Still on YouTube.'

'Oh . . . Good . . . umm . . . How did he get the money?'

'I tells ya – He good man . . . Help lotsa people.'

'But why didn't the United States government give him the money?'

'Nancy Reagan say, "Just say no" – Dat's da way to stop.'

'But it doesn't work.'

'You knows dat . . . I knows dat . . . But dey don't ask *us*.'

'Then why didn't they ask Betty Ford?'

'Good question . . . umm . . . Maybe dey pitied her – and da President . . . fallin' on da stairs.'

'But he wasn't drunk.'

'No – but she was – and dat's not pop'lar . . . not what First Lady's meant to do . . . She gotta look serious . . . an' pretty – or smart – an' do charity an' stuff.'

'Yes – but why doesn't your government – or ours – build rehabs?'

'Dey don' givashit.'

'But my dad told me America spends twice as much on healthcare as we do . . . There must be some money to look after people properly . . . like in here.'

'We don' count, man . . . We's da pits . . . But the EAP helps. – If it lasts . . .'

'How d'you mean?'

'De toll-free number's 1800-NO . . . Whatever you asks them, the answer's "No" . . . Dat means I don' get anudder chance if I screws dis up.'

'I didn't get a single one – not a civilised one.'

'Ya crazy, man . . . We's been envying you all dese years – wid your Health Service annat – likes we seed on da 'lympics . . .'

'Well dream on . . . umm . . . Where does Hazelden get its money?'

'Crock Foundation or summat . . . McDonalds.'

'McDonalds what?'

'Hamburgers . . . Don' you have 'em? – Dey's everywhere.'

'Are you telling me that McDonalds hamburgers pay for Hazelden?'

'Sure . . . partly . . . Don't know da details . . . And de IRA . . . used to.'

'Jesus! You'd better not let my dad find that out . . . He'd go white.'

'He black?'

*   *   *

'That Zoffany is magnificent . . . I always sit on the window side of the long table – if there's room – so I can look at it . . . umm . . . if the conversation goes off a bit. – It's the one disadvantage of filling up the table from the end . . . Never know if you might get lumbered with the club bore – or a gushing guest hoping you'll sign his page . . .'

'Should be safe on Club day – and the food's great – with the new chef . . . umm . . . Fancy yourself wearing pink trousers, Roddy?'

'I beg your pardon?'

'The portrait upstairs . . . Another Zoffany.'

'Oh . . . umm . . . No thank you . . . Wig's enough dressing up for me.'

'Going on the bench one day? – Judge's robes might suit you.'

'Umm . . . No . . . umm . . . Not really on the cards now.'

'Glory be, Roddy! – Not you as well?'

'Ha! No. – Very happy with Lizzie . . . Red-top journos won't catch me in a sting.'

'Then why not? . . . You've got a fine record.'

'Umm . . . Chatham House?'

'Yes of course. Won't tell a soul.'

'Saw a neurologist today . . . Nice chap . . . Wonder which club he's in. – Must see if he'd like to be put up here . . . Not on the members list . . . Yep . . . umm . . . Told me I might have a neurological disease.'

'Not good, Roddy. – You poor man.'

'Not dead yet . . . Diagnosis not confirmed anyway . . . See how I go . . .'

'But your wife . . . umm . . .'

'Haven't told her yet . . . She's on her way to America right now . . . I needed a bit of Dutch courage first. – Before telling her on the phone . . . She'll want to know what he said. – Oh! – Dammit! . . . He told me I had to cut down . . . umm . . . Damages nerves. – Alcohol.'

'Oh . . . Not good, Roddy, really not good at all . . . umm . . . You won't resign . . . From the club . . . umm . . . Will you?'

'Lord no. – I'll need the support.'

'Wheelchair?'

'God! – Hadn't thought of that . . . Only saw him today . . . umm . . . No. – the understanding . . . no faffing about, just time with congenial people.'

'But I was going to ask you about your wife . . . Is she over her . . . umm . . . difficulty now? – Back to work?'

''Fraid not.'

Oh . . . umm . . .'

''S'right . . . Bit of a rough time. – Not sure how I'm going to tell her about my business.'

'Tell you what, Roddy . . . There's a chap I know . . . member of another club actually . . . umm – one of us . . . does counselling work . . . stress, that sort of thing. – Runs a good shop, good team . . . Like his number?'

* * *

'In today's session we'll look at a belief that underlies – and undermines – state health and welfare systems . . . the belief that the government ought to do something. This belief is at the heart of the dependency culture . . .

'It should be!'

'It must!'

'Yes!'

'. . . These comments precisely illustrate my point . . . When people say, "The government ought to do something", they assume a particular type of political culture – one that is top/down directed . . . They want the government to determine how people should live their lives and how to solve all their problems . . .

'That's democracy!'

'. . . No it isn't. It's dictatorship. – In a democracy people retain free choice of action – which means the right to make mistakes, pay the price for them and learn from them . . .

'They vote!'

'. . . Ah, so that's it . . . By putting a cross on a ballot paper, they hand over all responsibility for their own lives . . .

'And other people's!'

'. . . I take it you mean that the government will act with the interests of the entire community in mind . . .

'And at heart!'

'. . . So your concept of a representative democracy is that a government – the correct government, when the people have chosen wisely – will know instinctively, not just on evidence, what to do for everyone's benefit? . . .

'Yes!'

'. . . Thank you for being so clear – and so honest . . . But it would appear, in some people's view – perhaps in yours – that people who disagree with the approach of a particular government are confused, deluded – even wicked . . .

'Thatcher!'

'. . . and have to be re-educated . . .

'Yes!'

'. . . About what? – And what should happen to them if they stick to their own viewpoints? . . .

'They can vote!'

'. . . I recall that Pol Pot didn't give people that choice. Stalin didn't. Hitler didn't. The Mullahs don't. Al Quaida doesn't. Islamic State doesn't. No dictators throughout history have done . . .

'But we can vote!'

'. . . Provided we vote the right way – as several European countries have discovered – or else have a government imposed upon them by unelected commissioners or commissars . . .

Silence.

'. . . Let's go right back to considering why representative governments were first invented . . . The ancient Greeks formulated a particular concept of democracy . . . but let's go back even before that – to primitive man . . .

'D'oh.'

Laughter.

'. . . Some leaders of the tribe will have taken their positions by force – but others may have been chosen for their wisdom or magnanimity . . .

'Their what?'

'. . . Being high-minded, noble, forgiving . . . These people had a value to society . . .

'There's no such thing as society!'

Laughter.

'. . . You've anticipated me . . . I knew this would be useful some time . . . Have a look at this record of what Mrs Thatcher actually said in an article in *Woman's Own* in 1987 . . .

"I think we've been through a period where too many people have been given to understand that if they have a problem, it's the government's job to cope with it. 'I have a problem, I'll get a grant.' 'I'm homeless, the government must house me.' They're casting their problem on society. And, you know, there is no such thing as society. There are individual men and women, and there are families. And no government can do anything except through people, and people must look to themselves first. It's our duty to look after ourselves and then – also – to look after our neighbour. People nowadays may have got the entitlements too much in mind, without the obligations. There's no such thing as entitlement, unless someone has first met an obligation."

Silence.

'. . . As I understand it, Mrs Thatcher was saying that the belief "the government ought to do something" leads to a de-skilled, dependent population – and increasing central government expense – with no benefits . . .

'Tory cuts!'

'. . . No . . . We're not referring here to social security benefit payments but to the advantages – or disadvantages – of devolving personal responsibility to government . . . Maybe at times we get the politicians we deserve or need . . .

Hoots of derision.

'. . . Well let's look at something that Mrs Thatcher did *not* spell out with her customary clarity . . . The NHS is a bottomless financial pit. The belief that "the government ought to do something" in healthcare and welfare services has no limit . . .

Silence.

'. . . As I see it, the challenge – for all of us here as well as everyone in the wider community – is that doctors and politicians must agree on what will *not* be provided . . . Otherwise a dependency, entitlements and benefits culture is here to stay for good . . .

'Good!'

'. . . As we saw in a previous session, the major government expense is health, welfare, education and pensions . . . Now we're observing that it will continue to grow indefinitely while the belief, "The government ought to do something" is in the front of people's minds . . .

'Yes!'

' .. Yes it should be? Or yes it will continue to grow indefinitely? . . .

Silence.

'. . . Ultimately we – all of us – have to look at the conflict between wants and needs . . . Where does one reasonably equate with the other? And where – in a representative democracy – can a government put limits to people's expectations?'

oOo

'So kind of you to come all the way over for family week, mother.'

'How's it been?'

'Umm . . . I was worried about it at first . . . Y'know – American emotionalism . . .'

'Yes.'

'Umm . . . There's a lot of hugging. – All the time in the unit. – You get very fond of each other . . . umm . . . bonded . . . 'S'pose that's why they separate the sexes . . . umm . . . I'll miss these guys a lot after the leaving ceremony tomorrow.'

'You sure it's wise to bond with a group of addicts? . . . I thought we sent you over here to get new ideas . . . new relationships.'

'It's the way it works here. – We hardly see the counselling staff . . . except for process group in the morning and an occasional one-to-one.'

232

'We pay all that money to . . .'

'Worth every dollar.'

'Thousands of dollars.'

'Still worth it . . . I love these people . . . umm . . . They're my people.'

'Mmm?'

'We understand each other – learn from each other – instinctively . . . Odd that . . . Just like when we were using . . .'

'And precisely what were you using, James?'

'Not good for you to know . . .'

'But it's what I want to know . . . I'm your mother . . . Oh! . . . This is what they've been saying in our family group all week. – We need to learn from each other . . . umm . . . about our "family disease" – doing too much for others and not enough for ourselves – how to get well.'

'Same for us . . . But they sent me to join you today . . . umm . . . They don't do that for all of us . . . spending a day in family group . . . to learn about the other side . . . umm . . . what it's like for families to live with us.'

'Very good for you . . . umm . . . Several of us – in this family group – said we wanted to learn about addicts . . . umm . . . about why you do these things . . . But they – the specialist family counsellors – said all we needed to know was we didn't cause your addiction, can't control it and can't cure it.'

'Seems right to me . . . And in the unit we've been told to sort ourselves out . . . umm . . . alongside each other . . . in AA . . . and not live off you – or bother you. – It's what they call a "selfish" programme.'

'I thought you'd all been self-centred enough . . . certainly felt like it.'

'Yes . . . True . . . umm . . . Sorry, mother.'

'That's all right.'

'Well it isn't really . . . We're told we have to learn the true meaning of "selfish" . . . It's in our self-interest to be kind and considerate . . . because then you'll be the same to us.'

'Oh. – Well I always intended to be . . .'

'You are . . . You have been . . . umm . . . Too much for my own good – specially father – sometimes . . .'

'Yes . . . Well . . . Maybe he could come over for this family week sometime – even though you won't be here . . . Come to think of it, there's some like that in the family group now . . . I'd wondered why . . . umm . . . James? . . .'

'Yes, mother?'

'Umm . . . You haven't been using injectables, have you?'

'Ha! – Ask your group if you should be asking that question.'

'. . . But have you?'

'Not yet.'

'James! Really! – Now you're just winding me up . . .'

'Yes, mother . . . umm . . . Time to go back into group.'

*   *   *

'I was thinking about our babies . . .'

'Hey there! Whoa! That's a bit fast – even for you.'

'That's not very gallant of you, Precious.'

'Oh . . . umm . . . Sorry. – I was tied up in my own head . . . on my issues with commitment.'

'Aah . . . Now it's my turn to be sorry. I was preoccupied with family stuff. – My brother's just coming out of rehab . . . My mother's been over there – in Center City, Minnesota – on the family programme.'

'What's that got to do with you and me having babies?'

'Is addiction genetically inherited? – There's stuff on the web but it doesn't add up to very much.'

'Oh, I see . . . umm . . . It runs in families – in one way or another – but association doesn't imply causation.'

'Again?'

'Just because A and B go together, it doesn't mean that A causes B.'

'Wow, Precious! – I love it when you talk dirty like that.'

'Huh?'

'Hah! – Don't worry . . . Just my English sense of humour again . . . Well is there? – Is there any addiction in your family?'

'My mother was overweight, God bless her – but that sort of thing's hardly noticed in the USA nowadays . . . Except by researchers like me. – It's become the norm. – Almost everybody's overweight.'

'It's getting that way here . . . And your dad?'

'Well, as you know, he was killed in Vietnam . . . I didn't know him . . . umm . . . The Vietnam War Veterans Study showed that a lot of GIs used drugs . . . Why not if you're going to die at 19?'

'19?'

'That was the average age of combat troops killed . . . My mother used to play a song about it – made to sound like machine gun fire – *N-N-N-N-N-N-N-N-N-Nineteen* . . .'

'That's terrible.'

'Yes it was – for them and for families like mine.'

'But did A lead to B?'

'Huh?'

'Did the combat stress – Jesus! *Apocalypse Now* was dreadfully frightening . . .'

'And *Full Metal Jacket* and – saddest of all, with that incredible theme on the guitar – *The Deer Hunter*.

'. . . Did the combat stress – and the drug use – lead on to addiction?'

'That's what the study tried to find out ... The results showed that something like 90% of the GIs got off but 10% stayed on drugs ... The 10% seemed to be made that way – or maybe they were just stupid, or maybe some form of chemical switch was thrown in the brain ...'

'Couldn't they sort that out ... umm ... in the research?'

'Ah well ... That's where observer prejudice came in ... Some shrinks said the 10% were stupid or deranged – because the 90%, in the same situations, got off ... And some psychologists said it was more likely genetic – the 10%. – That's what rehab people tend to believe nowadays.'

'Oh.'

'Oh, I see ... You're wondering whether your brother and my father – two first degree relatives of ours – were both addicts ... and therefore if you and I have addictive genes ... That's way too much conjecture. – And anyway the Twelve Step programme from AA can deal with it – nature or nurture ... That's what your brother will've learned in rehab.'

'He's actually in Hazelden – in Minnesota ... The London rehab he went to first of all wasn't a rehab at all – just a dumping ground.'

'... But, of course. – We're 30 years ahead of you.'

'Why?'

'We started the rehab idea.'

'Well I've never been taught about any of that – in five years of medical school.'

'That's dreadful ... We teach the Twelve Steps – as a preventative – in some high schools ... We do what works – and we don't do what doesn't work ... It's what I said about free market capitalism – the power of the buck even in health-care, welfare and education – helping people who are most in need ... and making sure that resources are focussed on those with the greatest capacity to benefit.'

* * *

'That view last night – in Manhattan . . . looking downtown across Central Park – is the most wonderful thing I've seen in all my life! . . . I thought the idyllic view of rural England from the stand at Goodwood or the wildness of the west coast of Scotland was as good as it gets . . . but this place is amazing! . . . Particularly yesterday at the Frick Museum – and now here at the 9/11 memorial.'

'That's why I thought it worthwhile to stop over for you to see it . . . not fly back direct to London . . . New York City is the most wonderful creation of the mind of man . . . It's alive!'

'I can see that – and feel it.'

'Remember . . . New York has its own special way of doing things.'

'It looks so different in real life . . . I thought I knew it from films.'

'There's never any substitute for personal experience.'

'Ha! . . . I never thought I'd enjoy going to a museum. – Funny that.'

'The Frick's very special . . . The Guggenheim's gone a bit fancy – putting up a plain sheet of silk and calling it "art" . . . And the Museum of Modern Art – MoMA – has some very well known works . . . Picasso, Chagall, Jackson Pollock . . . but the sum's less than the parts.'

'Huh?'

'There's so much . . . They detract from each other.'

'But that's America, isn't it? – Always going for the biggest.'

'Texas maybe – but that doesn't make it the best . . . though the public sculptures in Houston are very striking . . . But the Hermitage in Leningrad . . . ah, silly me . . . St Petersburg – We'll go there one day – it's fabulous . . . Needless to say,

237

the Russians don't know how to look after it . . . umm . . .
incidentally . . . You could do worse than walk round to the
Saatchi at home. – That's very exciting. – So's the way Isabella
Stewart Gardner did her place in Boston . . . Someone stole
the Rembrandts and they never got them back . . . Frick had
the same idea.'

'Stealing Rembrandts?'

'Ha! – Sorry – No . . . putting works of art in context – like
in a private home . . . furniture, carpets, sculptures, china . . .
anything beautiful . . . if it all fits together.'

'It certainly did.'

'Well the reason was that Frick actually lived there.'

'He lived in a museum?'

'He created it – a whole block – as his home, but with the
intention of leaving it behind as a museum . . . That's typical
American philanthropy – look at Bill Gates and Warren Buffet
. . . They're not exceptional . . . other than in the sheer quan-
tity of their donations . . . Universities, hospitals, museums like
the Guggenheim – and all sorts of places – have huge endowments from lots of people . . . Bill Gates does a lot for Africa
– malaria – on his own. He's not a country . . . And our Charles
Saatchi gives free entry to his museum in London – more than
the government does to the state ones – and there's lots of
people in the UK doing charitable things.'

'And we've got the NHS – not always brilliant – and state
welfare and all that.'

'But, y'know, our state involvement is probably why people
don't give more – nothing like the Americans . . . Our people
assume the state will provide . . . And they don't see what you
told us about the Mental Health Unit . . .'

'Ugh! . . . Don't remind me . . . It's light years away from
Hazelden . . .'

'. . . but when we prove to people that the state doesn't

provide, they say it should do – and they don't actually do things themselves . . . other than give money to Oxfam and run marathons, make cakes and hire bouncy castles to raise cash for a scanner in a local hospital – making up for deficiencies in the state services . . . And then the Great Ormond Street "Wishing Well" appeal for sick children cleaned out so much charitable money – in the eighties – there was little left for any other charity.'

'Oh.'

'And look at what we're seeing now at the 9/11 memorial . . . Prime real estate left empty out of respect – two enormous holes in the ground, with sheets of water disappearing into the depths of the earth – just like all those poor souls.'

'The poppies around the Tower of London were pretty impressive.'

'They certainly were . . . umm . . . not on quite the same scale as this memorial – even though the numbers of casualties were much bigger . . .'

'Oh! . . . Oh my God! . . . Look at that! . . . Jesus – that's awesome . . . All those inscribed names . . . all those people killed – all at once like Hiroshima and Nagasaki . . . on a vastly smaller scale but just as terrible – and for less reason . . . the firemen, the brokers, everybody . . .'

'Yes, James – people like you – in conflicts that were nothing to do with them . . . to begin with . . . and all because America volunteers to be the world's policeman – and benefactor – and then people come to expect it . . . No good deed goes unpunished . . . And they say, "The Americans are rich. They can afford it" . . . Ha! Americans are expected to sort out the Middle East – somehow – and the Ebola mess . . . But the Chinese buy up Africa – on condition that the countries see Taiwan as Chinese – like Tibet . . . And then India and Pakistan – nuclear powers – take Western aid, fight each other and foster sectarian divisions that affect all of us . . . And we stand back – the whole of Europe stands back – doing very little – but expecting America to do our dirty work . . . I brought you here, James, to show you how hard – efficiently and effectively – Americans work for what they've got . . . and give away . . .'

'Bravo, mother! . . . That's quite a speech! – worthy of the old man – and yes . . . I've seen the Yanks in the City – and now in Wall Street . . . and they were probably – certainly – working their asses off in the twin towers before all this. – And these . . . these massive holes in the ground . . . are what they get for it . . .'

* * *

'It's very kind of you to see me.'

'Do sit down . . . either of the armchairs.'

'This place is beautiful – like a private home . . . and your staff are so welcoming . . . I feel at ease already . . .'

'That's the idea – in my work . . . What would you like to tell me?'

'Nothing really – but I've got no choice . . . I'm in the schtuk.'

'That's precisely why most people come to see me . . . What's been happening? – What's the story?'

'Well – hopefully it'll all blow over – but maybe best to talk about it . . . I s'pose . . . Ha! I'm the one usually asking the questions . . . Feels odd – being in the witness box.'

'Bit pointless being in a witness box in here . . . There's no judge.'

'S'pose not . . . Right then . . . My wife's got what they call, "anaesthetic awareness" – woke up in the operating theatre.'

'That's dreadful . . . Very frightening . . . Upsetting for both of you.'

'And my son's just come out of rehab . . . In America . . . Hazelden . . .'

'Yes, I know the place . . . We all do – in my trade . . . Should do . . . It's the first ever rehab.'

'Seems to have done the trick . . .'

'Takes time . . . time after rehab.'

'Yes . . . That's what my wife was told – on the family programme . . . She's just left there now . . . She told me.'

'Any other children?'

'Daughter's just about to take finals . . . Bit of a wild one . . . Medical student. – Following her mother's example.'

'Wild?'

'Ha! – No . . . Medical practice.'

'What does she do?'

'My wife? . . . She's a consultant gynaecologist – fully private . . . umm . . . Not working at present . . . Scared off by seeing the anaesthetic machine when she tried to get back to work . . . Frightened the patient might be awake . . . Can't get it out of her mind . . . Can't focus on the surgery she's meant to be doing.'

'No . . . I can understand that . . . It sounds like the way it would be . . . umm . . . with PTSD – post traumatic stress disorder . . . What are they doing for her?'

'Usual treatment, I gather – Cognitive whatsit . . . Not really got going yet . . . and antidepressants of course . . . Not been on them long enough to see any effect . . . She's itching to get back to work . . . Bit in limbo at present

'What's the fourth thing?'

'Huh?'

'You rattled off those three things quickly enough . . . Anything else . . . umm . . . In you personally?'

'Oh . . . umm . . . I may have a neurological illness . . . The specialist said.'

'It's interesting you mentioned yourself last ... It isn't every day you get told you might have something like that.'

'Haven't really told anyone else yet – Not Lizzie. – She knew I was going to see him ... Not spoken to her yet on the phone.'

'Because?'

'She's got enough on board ... without worrying about me ...'

'Are you able to do your work?'

'Yes ... at present. I go to chambers every day – but me foot's ... umm ... not working well and I can't carry me briefs ... Too wobbly on me pins.'

'Ha! ... I misunderstood you for a moment ... umm ... You mean legal briefs – your files ... umm ... How long d'you propose to keep yourself ... umm ... last in the queue? – before you allow people – even your wife – to care for you? ... and even care for yourself?'

'It's not the way I do things ...'

'You push the feelings down?'

'Yes ... s'pose so ... Seems to work.'

'Yes – for a time ... But then what?'

'Nothing so far ... I always get by somehow.'

'Not necessarily the best plan ... with everything you've got on your plate right now.'

'What's my other choice? ... Got to keep things together.'

'Until they pop?'

'Hopefully not.'

'The thing is ... The body's not a machine and the brain – the mind – isn't a computer ... We're flesh and blood ... We can't discipline the feeling brain – in the way we do the thinking brain ... It rebels.'

'What happens then?'

'It doesn't function . . . Best to help it first . . . before it goes wrong – just like a car . . . or a child . . . really.'

'Oh . . . umm . . . How?'

'We've got a range of approaches here – with specialists who come in . . . according to the needs of the individual clients . . . I'll probably keep you myself . . . if you feel that would work for you.'

'Yes . . . umm . . . Yes – no choice really . . . As I said . . . umm . . . as I inferred.'

'Well I need to get to know you better – just listening to you – before we discuss which approach might work best for you . . .'

'Sounds good . . . and for my wife?'

'Oh . . . I hadn't realised she wanted to see me as well.'

'I'll suggest it to her.'

'It might give you the opportunity to tell her about your own . . . er . . . difficulties at the same time . . . You can do that here – together – if you wish.'

'That's very kind of you . . . umm . . . I've never been a patient . . . er . . . client . . . before – in this sense.'

'You don't want to get too used to it . . . It's not good for clients to become dependent on therapists. – Too close, too dictatorial . . . too much like school – or hospital.'

* * *

What is it about Phoebe? . . . She makes it obvious she likes me . . . umm . . . more than that – a lot more . . . but I've got nothing – really – to give her . . . I'm no catch . . . not financially . . . Ha! – I got plenty o' nuttin' . . . People imagine – and sing – *Money can't buy me love* . . . Ha! Try loving – or basic living – without it! . . . Hmm . . . Mustn't hurt her – take advantage of her – or

. . . umm . . . hurt myself, I s'pose . . . Done that before . . .

* * *

'Your husband mentioned you might come to see me . . . I gather you've just been in America . . . Welcome back.'

'Thank you . . . He said how kind you are.'

'That's nice of him.'

'He's a good judge . . . as a result of being a good QC.'

'Aha!'

'He finds it very difficult . . . allowing himself to be put at ease . . . Cross-examining people day after day in court . . . you know – makes him very wary.'

'Yes . . . I imagine.'

'Ha! – except in his club, of course.'

'And at home?'

'Most of the time.'

'Why not all?'

'When he's got something on his mind . . . Like now.'

'Yes. – He told me about your difficulties. – Dreadful.'

'Yes . . . and he's told me about his own . . . with the neurological problem . . .'

'Ah.'

'It was very kind of you to offer to see us both.'

'Another time – if you'd find it helpful.'

'I'm sure we would . . . umm . . . later . . .'

'Hmm.'

'Not now . . . umm . . . I didn't want that.'

'Because?'

'Because we're both capable of looking after ourselves . . . in our own way – and each other . . . when we want to.'

'Not always?'

244

'Ha! – I didn't mean it that way . . . I meant we've given each other lots of support over the years . . . establishing careers . . . having young children . . . Ha! – and grown up ones.'

'I understand.'

'We've grown together . . . umm . . . We don't need to live out of each other's pockets . . . all the time.'

'Meaning?'

'Umm . . . meaning we don't have to spell things out – all the time . . . to each other . . . Instincts, mostly.'

'Yes.'

'Why "Yes"?'

'Must be true in any close relationship . . . and in your professions – the two of you – and mine . . . But not at this particular time . . . for you?'

'Roddy's got a very real problem . . . Mine's in my head.'

'Heads aren't real?'

'Umm . . . not in the same way . . . umm . . . As a surgeon I'm used to separating the two . . . thoughts and feelings.'

'Which two thoughts?'

'Ha!' – separating thoughts from feelings.'

'Yes . . . umm . . . Maybe you're doing that now. – You've laughed several times . . . but the reason you're here is very serious . . . very distressing.'

'Yes . . . Habit.'

'Yes.'

'Don't want to break it now . . . I need to survive . . . Get over this silly thing . . . Get back to work.'

'If it were silly, you'd have got over it by now . . .'

'S'pose so . . . umm . . . What's to be done? . . . Practically – not just tablets . . . Don't like taking anything . . . Ha! – I'm the doctor . . . umm . . . Will the CBT work? . . . Seems like I'm back at school – so far.'

'I don't know . . . There's no magic fix – in this type of

challenge . . . umm . . . Nothing surgical . . . so to speak . . . except possibly hypnotherapy . . . and EMDR.'

'I don't like the sound of the first . . . umm . . . too spooky . . . too theatrical . . . umm . . . What's the second?'

'Hypnotherapy can be very helpful – in really skilled hands . . . EMDR helps the thinking brain to talk to the feeling brain . . . again only in skilled hands. – Not a party trick . . . neither of them.'

'Neither of what? . . . The sides of my brain?'

'Ha! Now you've got me laughing . . . 'S'pose it's part of your stock in trade – putting people at ease – as a surgeon.'

'Yes . . . Try to.'

'I meant neither hypnotherapy nor EMDR are party tricks . . . Shall I explain more about them?'

'I'd rather look them up on the web . . . umm . . . My natural way of doing things.'

'Yes . . . I understand that . . . Me too . . . I like finding out about things – and people – before jumping in with recommendations.'

'D'you reckon this could get sorted out . . . this anaesthesia thing?'

'I really don't know . . . You're the first person I've ever seen with this – but I know someone who might help . . . I'd trust him myself . . . That's why I refer people to him.'

'Yes, that's the way it works . . . Isn't it? . . . umm . . . in the private sector.'

'I can refer you if you wish . . . We could give him a ring now . . . see if he's available . . . He can usually fit people in . . . Works all hours.'

'Thank you . . . umm . . . I think I'll look these things up first – hypnotherapy and EM . . .'

'EMDR.'

What's it stand for?'

Part 4

'Eye movement desensitisation and reprocessing.'

'Eye movement . . . Eye movement? . . . Sounds a bit odd . . . umm . . . more than a bit.'

'Yes – but it works . . . I've seen it done – very effective – and lasting . . . First tried in rape victims – and Vietnam War veterans.'

'American? – The process I mean?'

'Yes . . . originally . . . Done all over the world now . . . not much here.'

'Why not?'

'Ha! We're always suspicious of American things . . . here.'

'Why so?'

'Stiff upper lip I s'pose . . . And government tardiness. – Takes a generation to get round to a new idea . . . Force of habit . . . Intellectual and clinical inertia . . .'

'Yes . . . That's why I left the NHS . . . umm . . . I'll look these things up – and get back to you . . . Thank you for seeing me . . . There's hope, d'you think?'

'Always.'

* * *

'In this session we'll look at who's in greatest need. In previous sessions we've looked at the difficulty of getting doctors to work in areas of sparse population. We've also looked at countries where it's difficult to get any medical services at all . . . Today we'll look at the UK – and the USA and other economically developed countries – to observe the people who fall through the government safety nets . . .

'There's no safety net in the USA!'

'. . . Interestingly, in my five years over here, I've noticed that's a common assumption. – But let me tell you about the land of my birth and the government programmes that benefited my own mother . . .

Silence.

'. . . Medicare looks after the elderly. My mother had excellent care for ten years, when she was in increasingly poor health. She died five years ago and I came over here. Medicaid looks after the poor, which we certainly were . . . Many people were poor in our neighbourhood when I was young. Medicare and Medicaid particularly helped families like mine . . .

'Not fully – like the NHS!'

'. . . Let me give you the figures for the USA . . . Today, Medicare provides health insurance cover for more than 45 million Americans – about 38 million elderly people and an additional 7 million younger people who have certain types of disabilities, like end-stage renal disease . . . Medicare covers hospital insurance – inpatient care at a hospital, skilled nursing facility and hospice care. It also covers services like lab tests, surgery, doctor visits, and home healthcare . . .

Silence.

'. . . Medicare medical insurance covers doctor and other healthcare providers' services, outpatient care, durable medical equipment, home healthcare and some preventative services . . . Additionally Medicare provides medical care and prescription drugs in disaster or emergency areas . . . As you can tell, the cover is extensive . . .

Silence.

'. . . Yes, I thought that might surprise you – just as it surprised students in previous years. The USA and the UK have many misconceptions about each other's healthcare and welfare services . . .

Shuffles.

'. . . Medicaid is a USA government insurance programme for people of all ages whose income and resources are insufficient to pay for healthcare. It's the largest source of funding for medical and health-related services for people with low income in America . . . It's jointly funded by the states and the federal government – but it's managed by the individual states . . . It's a means-tested programme . . .

'*Hissss. Hissss. Hissss.*'

'. . . That's interesting . . . You don't like means tests? . . .

'*Hissss. Hissss. Hissss.*'

'No! No! No!'

'. . . But, when budgets are finite and there are no means tests, rich people – who have other choices – compete for services with poor people – who have no choice . . . The idea that rich people will then clamour for improvements in state services is completely wrong. – They go to other countries for their healthcare if they're really sick . . .

Shuffles and throat clearings.

'. . . Medicaid recipients must be US citizens or legal permanent residents. They may be low-income adults – or their children or people with certain disabilities – but poverty alone does not necessarily qualify someone for Medicaid . . .

'Shame!'

'. . . Medicaid and CHIP – Child Health Insurance Programmes – provide health coverage for nearly 60 million Americans, including children, pregnant women, parents, the elderly and individuals with disabilities . . .

Silence.

'. . . The Affordable Care Act of 2010 – "ObamaCare" – created a national Medicaid minimum eligibility level of 133% of the federal poverty level – $29,700 for a family of four in 2011 – for nearly all Americans under the age of 65 . . .

Drummings.

'. . . Responsible medical practice – in any country – is essentially a numbers business. It's easy to design and run a healthcare system that would work effectively for well-off patients in a settled community. – The greatest challenge is in areas of sparse or dense populations and areas of high turn-over of population – like inner cities . . .

Silence.

'. . . The most challenged patients – those who have mental problems or addictive behaviour – drop down through the social and economic strata and move to the poorest areas. This is the same problem in the UK and the USA and other countries . . .

Silence.

'Let's look at the numbers . . . Schizophrenia causes people to have hallucinations – hearing or seeing things that don't exist – and delusions – unusual beliefs and muddled thoughts, leading to strange behaviour . . .

'Psychiatrists!'

Loud laughter.

'. . . Calm down, calm down . . . Schizophrenia affects 1% of the population in developed countries . . .

'Why there?'

'. . . That's an interesting question. – The diagnosis is rarely made in countries where they have an extended family system. Relatives care for those members of the family who are disturbed in this way . . .

'They haven't got any doctors!'

'. . . Yes, that too. – And in the developed countries there's a debate on whether psychoses – thought disorders – as opposed to neuroses – emotional disturbances – are genetically linked or due to "unexpressed emotion" in childhood environments . . .

'What's that?'

'. . . Sigmund Freud said, "Unexpressed emotions will never die. They are buried alive and will come forth later in uglier ways."

'Ugh!'

'. . . John Nash, an American mathematician, showed signs of paranoid schizophrenia during his college years. Despite stopping his prescribed medication, he won the Nobel Prize in 1994. His life was depicted in the 2001 film *A Beautiful Mind* . . .

Applause.

'. . . Some evidence suggests that antipsychotic medications may have adverse effects on brain anatomy and function . . .

'*Hissss. Hissss. Hissss.*'

'. . . Schizophrenia is a major cause of disability. Active psychosis is ranked as the third most disabling condition after quadriplegia and dementia – and ahead of paraplegia and blindness. Three quarters of people with schizophrenia have ongoing disability with relapses – but some people recover completely . . . and many others function well in society. Most live independently with community support . . .

Silence.

'. . . In people with a first episode of psychosis a good long-term outcome occurs in 42%, an intermediate outcome in 35% and a poor outcome in 23%. The suicide rate is 49 per thousand people with schizophrenia . . . In 2011 in the UK, there were 6045 suicides in a population of 63.26 million . . . That's less than 1 per thousand . . . And, incidentally, the gender ratio in suicide is three and a half men to one woman.'

Silence.

'. . . Yes. Schizophrenia is a very frightening illness . . .

'Are neuroses real?'

'Another good question . . . Anxiety, depression, obsessional thoughts and compulsive behaviours are very real. Physical symptoms – when there's no evidence of disease – and personality disorders with indecision and interpersonal maladjustment are also very real . . .

'That's normal before finals!'

Silence.

'. . . Yes. – You're right. Doctors may diagnose illness when there's none at all – just normal reactions to stressful situations . . . And they commonly diagnose a Valium deficiency . . .

Strained laughter.

'. . . To be fair, doctors have at last recognised that benzo-diazepines – like Valium, Diazepam – are addictive but they prescribe antidepressants instead – or some other "magic bullet" – to suppress symptoms rather than provide personal care . . . And bear in mind that any of these drugs – including antidepressants – may be addictive in people who have addictive natures . . .

Silence.

'. . . Either way, the doctors say there's little time to do anything else but prescribe for these patients . . . Currently, just providing continuing supervision and antipsychotic medication takes a huge amount of the very costly time of consultant psychiatrists . . .

'Send the patients to hairdressers!

Laughter.

'. . . Yes. That's been my suggestion. – They're good listeners, they can't prescribe and you get a short back and sides . . .

'Give the psychotic patients a job and a home!'

'. . . Hey, you've studied this – haven't you? – There certainly is evidence from New York that these social treatments can be significantly effective . . .

Drummings.

'. . . Depression, which has to be distinguished from sadness – a natural response to distressing circumstances – may be due to genetic disorders in the dopamine, serotonin or other neurotransmitter pathways . . . It may be a precursor of addiction – the discovery by the patient of chemicals that have a mood-altering effect . . .

Silence.

'. . . No cries of "Gimme gimme"?

Silence.

'ADHD – which may not exist at all . . . except in the concerned minds of ambitious mothers . . . may also be a precursor of addiction and therefore an early indicator of an addictive nature. The standard treatment is Ritalin which is amphetamine based. Of course that drug would help ADHD. – So would cocaine . . .

Shuffling.

'. . . Yes. – It's a worrying thought that children are being given speed as a medicine . . . Anyway, instead of trying even more drugs, why not give them a computer game? – Then see if they really have any attention deficit – or whether they were just bored . . .

More shuffling.

'. . . Bipolar disorder is said to affect 1% of people. As you know, the treatment is mood-stabilising drugs and lifestyle changes – but it may be significantly over-diagnosed because mood swings are common in alcoholism and other addictive behaviour . . . which affects 15 to 20% of the population . . .

'You bet!'

Muffled laughter.

'. . . "Bipolar disorder" sounds nicer – more acceptable – than "manic depression", its former name, and a lot nicer than "alcoholism" or "addiction" – but we cannot afford to hide behind euphemisms. We have to speak the truth . . . Bipolar disorder may exist – but in nothing like the number of people diagnosed with it . . . By contrast, addiction problems of one kind or another – drug addiction, alcoholism, eating disorders, compulsive gambling, nicotine addiction . . . not just cigarette smoking . . . and so on – affect one in six people . . .

Whistles.

'. . . You yourselves will have seen – in every ward throughout all hospitals – not just in A and E and in the psychiatric units – the devastating effects of alcohol . . .

'Hic!'

Laughter.

'. . . Yes – and in the student bar too. – Remember that addiction is no respecter of persons. One in six of you will develop problems with addiction . . .

Shuffles and throat clearings again.

'. . . And yet, in the UK – unlike the USA – medical students like you will have virtually no training in treating addiction problems. The three approaches that most people – family members, colleagues at work, healthcare and welfare professionals – most commonly try are love, education and punishment . . . They don't work – any more than they would work in appendicitis . . .

Shuffles.

'. . . You're taught about Methadone and Prozac. They simply cause the patient to develop another addiction – a more difficult one because these pharmaceutical drugs are the ultimate "designer drugs" . . .

'Yeeeehah!'

Laughter.

'. . . And you're taught the rudiments of Cognitive Behavioural Therapy. – Doctors like CBT because it shows that we're brighter than our patients . . .

'Do'h.'

'. . . You again? . . . But CBT is an intellectual approach. It aims to change people's behaviour by changing their thinking. – That can't help with emotional problems . . . All behaviour is the external expression of a very complex interaction between cognitive and emotional components . . . Focussing primarily on cognition is patronising. – The vast majority of people can think perfectly well for themselves. – But clear thinking does not necessarily lead to happier lives. Brilliant thinkers may sometimes be profoundly depressed.'

Silence.

'. . . And the root of that sense of inner emptiness may be an addictive nature . . . This may be genetically inherited . . .

'Rubbish!'

'. . . as shown in Scandanavian adoption studies and possibly indicated in the Vietnam War Veterans Study. – Nature may be a more reliable predictor of an addictive tendency than nurture . . .

'Grrrrrr.'

'Boring! . . . Snoring.'

'. . . We can't afford to be bored by a treatable condition that significantly affects one in six people and has serious secondary consequences for their families, their workplaces and their wider communities . . .

Silence.

'. . . The appropriate treatment for the massive number of people who have addiction problems – and the underlying depressive illness – would therefore be a daily programme involving mentors or peer groups or self-help groups – such as those built around the Twelve Step programme of Alcoholics Anonymous . . .

'God help us!'

'. . . Yes. As AA says – any God of your own understanding – but not yourself . . .

'Bacchus!'

Laughter.

'. . . In this clinical area – the understanding of addictive disease and daily recovery from it – the USA is 30 years ahead of the UK and other European countries . . .

'Rubbish! It's not a disease!'

'The Hughes Amendment to the Constitution of the USA – and also a specific declaration by the World Health Organisation – say that it *is* . . .

Silence.

'. . . These mental health issues are huge problems – far more common than anything else you've learned about in medical school, other than cancer, heart disease, diabetes and chronic obstructive pulmonary disease . . .

Silence.

'. . . Maybe, on this occasion, the government – all governments – ought to do something . . . They should – primarily – fund healthcare and welfare services for those who do not have the mental or physical capacity to provide for themselves . . .

Drummings.

'. . . But it might be better, as has been demonstrated in some NHS hospitals already – not always successfully . . . as a result of politically motivated obstruction – if the private sector runs them . . .

'*Hissss. Hissss. Hissss.*'

'. . . Perhaps the NHS is too entrenched in the entitlement culture to be able to be helped from outside . . .

'No privatisation!'

'. . . Well . . . have a look at how other countries manage the relationship between their state and private sectors in healthcare . . . Many allow medical expenses to be tax-deductible . . . Switzerland has a mixture of public, subsidised private and wholly private systems – and a queue of foreigners wanting to pay for treatment. In the UK, there's "health tourism" of a different nature. – There's a queue of foreigners trying to get free treatment in the NHS . . . and often succeeding . . .

Silence.

'. . . That's the evidence . . . The NHS may not be the envy of the world – other than in people who want something for nothing, as they see it – but it may well be the envy of the world's politicians and those who aspire to have political influence . . . because it increasingly controls the medical profession . . .

Shuffles.

'. . . This certainly doesn't mean that the government knows how to run things. – It doesn't. – It's not the field of expertise of politicians and civil servants . . . After retirement they may join company boards – but only to show their new masters how to crack open the state coffers . . .

Shuffles and throat clearings yet again.

'. . . In closing, we need to remember this . . . A healthcare and welfare system – anywhere – that doesn't work in practice is a bad system. Its ideas may superficially appear to be good in theory – but they're no use if they don't work in practice . . .

Shuffles.

'. . . I'm reminded of the story of a communist being shown the perfect capitalist village. He said, "I can see that it works in practice – but will it work in theory?".'

A few uncomfortable laughs.

oOo

Don't need a crystal ball to see my future . . . A neurological illness – of any kind – is no party – probably . . . Ha! . . . All very well reading about spontaneous remission – and variable timescale of decline . . . Let's face it, Roddy. – You're on the way down . . . And out . . . Huh! . . . Never expected much from life . . . Made me own way . . . but, but, but – this is a bit too much. – Unreliable leg, unpredictable nerves, unknown future for work . . . And Lizzie not strong . . . God!

257

You Can Hear the Ice Cracking

– Where's it all going to end? . . . Good job the children are off our hands – seem to be . . . umm . . . What now? . . . That insurance business is worrying . . . If anything else happens . . . Hmm . . . Wonder what the insurance companies stand for – believe in – nowadays. They're not Provident Societies any more. – Ha! More like the accountants Grabit and Runne . . . umm . . . What's to become of us? . . . Lizzie and me? . . . if we're both out of work? . . . and dependent? . . . Hmm . . . Dependent on what? – The state? . . . How do families manage? – I dunno . . . We've got the house . . . no mortgage . . . and our pensions and insurance policies – and a bit in the bank . . . How long's that going to last? . . . with mansion taxes, wealth taxes, inheritance tax payable in advance? . . . or something? . . . What next? . . . What if we've got nothing? . . . Reduced to the bare bones. – That's what. – No . . . Doesn't bear thinking about . . .

* * *

'Phoebe – dear Phoebe . . . I've been thinking about you . . .'
   'Have you really?'
   'Yes . . . It was something you said . . .'
   'Yes?'
   'About a point I made in the last lecture . . . umm . . . living in a democracy like America – and hopefully still in the UK in future – people have free choice of action . . .'
   'Oh.'
   '. . . Are you with me?'
   'Yes . . . Yes, of course.'
   '. . .They have the right to make mistakes, pay the price and learn . . .'
   'I hope that's true for my brother.'
   'Well if all he got in treatment was pharmaceutical drugs,

258

he'll be on his way to a severe dependency – and an entitle-ment and benefits culture . . . I wouldn't want that for him.'

'God, I hope not.'

'That's what I said – in general – about doctors and politicians having to agree on what should or should not be provided.'

'What chance of that?'

'We can live in hope . . . And, in the States . . . and here too . . . the Internal Revenue Services support charitable donations.'

'I don't think we do it to the same extent over here . . . On the web it says American universities and private – even charitable – hospitals are flush with cash from donations . . . Ours are always putting out the begging bowls to government.'

'Yeah – and the prize goes to the politicians who offer the biggest promises . . . But, as I asked the students – including you . . . umm . . . promises of what quality and at what cost?'

'Hmm . . .'

'Got you thinking, Phoebe? – I'll make a free market capi-talist of you yet . . .'

'Ha! – That'll be the day! . . . Let's concentrate on the onions.'

'You think they might run out?'

'No chance . . . Mmmmm . . .'

* * *

'I gather you do a number of different therapeutic interventions in this office . . . umm . . . The counsellor my husband and I are seeing . . . er . . . not for a marital problem, you understand. – That's the one thing that hasn't gone wrong . . . recently . . .'

'Did it before?'

'No . . . not at all. – We've been blessed . . . until just recently.'

'What happened?'

'I woke up under an anaesthetic . . . I can't get it out of my mind . . . umm . . . the terror of being fully aware but paralysed – and not able to communicate in any way . . . And my husband's just been told – by a top consultant neurologist after he did all sorts of complicated tests – that he might have – probably does have – a neurological illness.'

'Gosh! – That's a double whammy if ever there was one . . .'

'D'you think you could help? . . . either me or my husband?'

'I don't think there's too much to be done for him at present . . . umm . . . What's he had so far?'

'He's having some stress counselling – but I don't hold out too much hope for that doing anything dramatic . . . emotionally or physically . . . but anything's better than nothing.'

'Yes indeed . . . but the counsellor who gave you my name runs a very professional establishment . . . If anyone can help your husband – in any way – he will.'

'That's very comforting.'

'You're in good hands with him . . . umm . . . I see you're a consultant gynaecologist . . . Fully private.'

'Yes.'

'Maybe one thing you and I have in common is that those of us in fully private practice have to be very selective in our referrals . . . If anything goes wrong – or even if the patient doesn't take to that person – we get the blame . . . and we ourselves risk losing the patient altogether.'

'Yes, that's certainly true – and it's not at all like that in the NHS nowadays . . . What I keep hearing is that patients get taken for granted – have to go where they're put, wait for ever and may have to tolerate all sorts of rudeness and lack of consideration . . . I dread ever being dependent on it.'

Part 4

'I myself have been treated very well – and with real under-standing and care – on the rare occasions I've asked for help from the NHS . . . Perhaps I've just been fortunate – catching the staff on a good day . . . Hopefully the same will happen to you . . . er . . . if you ever do need it . . . umm . . . What would you like to discuss with me today?'

'EMDR was mentioned by the counsellor who referred me to you . . . umm . . . He obviously trusts you . . . But I googled EMDR . . . umm . . . Some people have had very unfortunate experiences . . .'

'I think it depends who does it – and if they do the proper preparation and follow the correct protocols – Same as in any professional discipline.'

'Well I've been quite put off by the reviews I read. – And I'm in enough trouble already.'

'Yes . . . I can understand that. – I'd hate your dreadful experience to happen to me.'

'I was wondering what other things might help.'

'EMDR is what I recommend for your specific problem . . . mmm . . . Hypnotherapy . . . in the right hands – or voice . . . it's all about voice, not watches and pendulums – could be effective . . . But the man I trust for that has moved to Los Angeles.'

'More money?'

'No . . . More acceptance of the serious side of his work – curing phobias particularly – not the TV stuff. – He comes over here to see a few patients and do training courses a couple of times a year . . . That's how I got part of my training . . . with him.'

'And then?'

'I did more and more training – a bit here but most of my training in psychological techniques has been in the States . . . six weeks each year. – It adds up.'

'Umm . . . I get the impression you're not too keen to help me with that yourself . . . umm . . . Hypnotherapy.'

'That's right.'

'Why not? . . . If you've had the best training?'

'He'd look after you more skilfully than I can. – I'm ok . . . but I'm not in his league. – It might be worth your while flying to the States to get specialist treatment from him . . . It would cost plenty – but it'd be worth it and probably not take longer than a week.'

'That's extraordinary.'

'Well what he says . . . and I find this very persuasive . . . is that the brain learns to be phobic very quickly – almost instantaneously . . . So, if we do the work in the way the brain itself works – not in the way that universities assume – it can *un*-learn very quickly.'

'I've only just come back from America . . . My son was in rehab . . . umm . . . Isn't there anyone else over here?'

'Not in my book – at his level.'

'And you yourself wouldn't take me on?'

'No . . . Essentially I'm an addiction specialist . . . treating all addictive behaviours and – without asking a doctor to prescribe drugs other than for detox – treating the depression, anxiety and poor self-esteem that underlie it . . . And I deal with the traumas that addicts – and their families – experience . . . That's where the EMDR – and the other approaches I use – come in.'

'Oh . . . umm . . . My son – he hasn't specifically told his father yet – says he'd like to be an addictions counsellor . . .'

'And he's only just come out of rehab?'

'Yes . . . He says it takes an addict to help an addict.'

'That's true . . . umm . . . His heart may be in the right place – but his head needs a great deal of training . . . and his timing's wrong . . . It's far too soon.'

Part 4

'Oh, I see . . . umm . . . Would you be willing to see him – I'll pay now for your time – to tell him that?'

'Yes, of course . . . I'll be glad to . . . But don't be surprised if he tells you I'm useless – when I don't tell him what he wants to hear.'

'You're absolutely right! . . . That's my James . . . How did you know?'

'It takes one to know one . . . and help one . . .'

* * *

'Welcome back.'

'Thank you, father . . . and thank you for sending me – and paying for me. – It was great . . . I learned so much.'

'Yes . . . I can believe that . . . umm . . . in the commercial bar – inevitably – I've had to learn a great deal about how the Americans do things . . . umm . . . not always for the best.'

'I learned most from my room mate.'

'A doctor?'

'No . . . a security guard – an ex-cop.'

'Heavens! James . . . We send you all the way over there – and your mother goes too – and you spend your time stuck in your room?'

'Not all the time . . . just in the evenings . . . In the day we had lectures and groups and one-to-ones and things . . . And they've got a gym and a basketball court and an Olympic-size pool. – They treat a lot of athletes . . .'

'Very good for you . . . being with athletes.'

'You wouldn't think so if you knew what the basketball and American football players – some of them – do with all their money . .'

'What do they do?'

'Put it up their noses . . . cocaine . . . Too much money. – Don't know what else to do with it.'

'Well at least you'll have had three square meals a day in there – hamburgers probably . . .'

'The food's good . . . umm . . . They treat eating disorders – a bit.'

'A bit? – With the size of the people I see in airports? . . . They ought to treat them a lot . . .'

'They focus mainly on alcohol and drugs . . . That's what kills people straight away.'

'Well I hope the doctors sorted you out on that – and your resident policeman taught you all the legal risks.'

'Ha! . . . The doctors check you when you first get there – but you don't see them after that . . . The work's done by counsellors – recovering addicts – and by us ourselves . . . with each other . . . And my "resident policeman" was one of us.'

'You're going too fast for me again, James . . . What's a "recovering addict"? . . . And what – or who – is "one of us"?'

'A "recovering addict" is one who's done it all but doesn't do it now.'

'That's good.'

'Yes . . . but it's a relapsing illness . . . some of them go back out.'

'Oh . . . Thanks for telling me that.'

'And Chuck . . . That's his name . . .'

'It would be . . .'

'Huh?'

'These Americans have such strange names.'

'Some of ours are strange to them.'

'There's nothing strange about "James" . . . It's biblical . . . Your mother's choice. – They'd understand that.'

'As feminists?'

'No . . . As God-botherers.'

'Yup . . . We had one chap from Tennessee – a horse thief – who . . .'

'James, this is too much . . .'

' . . . He was preaching the Word all the time . . . He was told – by the staff – to keep it to himself . . . It's our choice what sort of "Higher Power" we have.'

'Well I'm sure your mother will be pleased . . . partly . . . and what about this . . . er . . . Chuck. – I hope he pointed you in a sensible direction.'

'Ha! – He would've done . . . to the nearest dealer . . .'

'James, James, James . . . Tell me the good news – before I die . . .'

'You're not dying are you?'

'Not yet . . . at least I hope not . . . umm . . . I mean before I die of shock – from all you're telling me.'

'The good news is that I know what I want to do with my life . . . I want to train as a counsellor – and set up my own rehab . . .'

'Isn't that rather a lot of carts before very few horses?'

'Well, the man from Tennessee – or someone else – could teach me how . . .'

'Take me seriously, James – for just a bit . . .'

'Yes, father. Sorry, father . . .'

'What's the first step?'

'Admit that I'm powerless over alcohol and that my life has become unmanageable.'

'Huh?'

'Oh – you meant what am I going to do now . . . Ha! – What I've just told you is Step 1 of the AA programme!'

'Well I trust you won't have to do too much of that sort of thing.'

'A chronic illness needs a chronic treatment . . . That's what they taught us.'

'Oh . . . and where does that so-called "illness" come from?'

'Some genetic influence . . . maybe . . .'

'You looking at me, James?'

'Umm . . . No, father.'

'Not too keen on your hesitation, James . . . but my father was always one to find a reason to drink – and your mother's mother . . .'

'You never told us.'

'No need . . . Not the sort of thing you want to talk about . . . As your mother says, "The very best thing about childhood . . . It's over".'

'Mine was very happy – and thank you for that . . .'

'Parental duty.'

'Yes . . . umm . . . But also your choice . . . umm . . . Some of the guys in Hazelden could've benefitted from a bit of your kindness and concern . . . from what I heard . . . Just shows you . . . Environment can contribute – to bad times – but a good one won't buck your genes.'

'Where's this leading, James?'

'Umm . . . There's no point blaming the environment all the time . . . That gets us nowhere . . . It's a bit of both – genes and environment. – And we have to be responsible for our own continuing recovery.'

'That's better . . . Now we're speaking the same language again . . . I was getting a bit worried that you'd gone all "touchy feely" . . . over there . . . umm . . . So what's practical? What are we going to do with you?'

'I thought I might set up a charity.'

'You'll need a good patron – and chairman and board – if you're going to raise any money . . .'

Part 4

'Perhaps we could ask some of your contacts . . . at work or in the club . . .'

'Not keen.'

'Oh . . . umm . . . Why not?'

'Mustn't abuse colleagues – or friendships.'

'But that's the way Freemasons work . . . in the City . . . and livery companies . . .'

'Back-scratching . . . has to be mutual . . . umm . . . What've you got to offer?'

'Not a lot . . . umm . . . A good idea. – Something worth doing.'

'They won't see that . . . "Lock them up . . . Throw away the key" more likely.'

'Oh.'

'Listen . . . James, dear James . . . I don't want to discourage you – I'll be as supportive as I can be – It's just the way of the world . . . umm . . . the commercial world I know.'

'Capitalism.'

'No . . . The socialists are even more mercenary. – Never do anything without demanding that someone else should pay . . . It's not capitalism or socialism . . . It's reality.'

'Oh.'

'Let's look at some basics . . . Never get too emotionally involved – damages your judgement . . . Never expand a loss-making business. – Cut back to profitability . . . Expand on that . . . Remember that cash is king and cash flow is reality. – Balance sheets are vanity . . . Profit and loss accounts are sanity.'

'Is that the way the drug companies work?'

'And the drug cartels, I shouldn't wonder . . . Any business. – You can't buck the market . . . Every chancellor tries – and every chancellor fails.'

'But that's so uncaring . . . so unfair.'

'Life's unfair.'

* * *

'Welcome . . . This is the last of our 24 sessions on healthcare and welfare systems . . .

Applause.

'. . . That's kind of you . . . It's been my privilege to work with such a lively group of students . . . umm . . . Maybe your warm reception just now indicates that you're glad – relieved – to get to the end!'

Laughter.

'. . . This is the big one. – It looks at fundamental principles . . . showing what ideas we might want to challenge and possibly discard . . . And then looks at what ideas we might want to put in their place . . .

Silence.

'. . . Neither America nor the UK has a perfect system. We – I say "we" because by now I feel very much part of you . . .

'Dream on!'

Laughter.

'All right – I'll get on with it . . . Let's now reexamine Dr Julian Tudor-Hart's *"Inverse Care Law"* – to which I referred in a previous lecture . . . It states that, "The availability of good medical care tends to vary inversely with the need for it in the population served." In other words, those most in need of care are least likely to get it . . .

'Hissss. Hissss. Hissss.'

'. . . The corollary would be the "Direct Care Law", which would state, "Those who are least in need of care tend to get it at the expense of those who need it most" . . .

Mutterings.

Part 4

'. . . Yes . . . It's true, isn't it?. – But putting the corollary alongside the *"Inverse Care Law"* shows that the first law is little more than a political Trojan Horse. – It's the method by which principles of genuine concern and compassion for those most in need are subverted to the political ambitions of those who want to have control over absolutely everybody . . .

'*Hissss. Hissss. Hissss.*'

'. . . I suggest that those who invoke the "Inverse Care Law" would not be satisfied merely by action against the "Direct Care Law". It would not satisfy them if care, specifically that provided free by the State, was restricted to those who need it most . . . Their intention is that there shall be no alternative to State care for anybody at any time . . .

'Quite right!'

'. . . For them, the actual level of quality of care given to an individual is not as important in principle as that no other individual shall receive better care – particularly not if it's paid for at the time of need . . .

'Right on!'

'. . . They know very well, however, that the only way to achieve equality of outcome is to damage the more talented, hinder the more industrious and make providers of any service feel guilty rather than proud of their skill. – And then ensure that they have a sense of corporate obligation rather than individual self-esteem . . .

Shuffles.

'. . . Statism – as opposed to individualism – is not an outward-looking philosophy that seeks improvement at each and every opportunity, but a bitter creed that seeks to reduce all to the lowest common denominator . . .

Silence.

'. . . The *"Law of Infinite Resources"* would state that money

269

comes from the money tree . . . But, of course, this isn't true. Money has to be created . . . And it represents units of work . . . Even natural resources have to be harnessed by skill and effort. They don't become a resource in the absence of the application of the mind of man . . .

Silence.

'. . . Inherited or other fortuitous wealth is soon lost by those who don't respect what it takes to earn it . . .

'Good!'

'. . . Money is a philosophical indicator. – The attitude of any man or woman toward money . . . and what it represents – will indicate his or her attitude toward the value of his or her own life and the value of the lives of other people . . .

Silence.

'. . . The provision of health care should be a business, much like any other . . .

'No. No. No.'

'. . . Successful business people take care of their staff, pay them well and appreciate them for the work they do . . . And they take care of their clients, knowing that their own future livelihoods – and the continued employment of those who depend upon the business that they created – only survive on the satisfaction of their clients . . .

Silence.

'. . . If they fail to look after their staff and their clients, they will go out of business and deserve to do so . . .

'Yessss!'

'. . . unless, of course, they have friends in government who agree that their businesses are "essential" and therefore should be subsidised at the expense of others . . .

Silence.

'. . . And this makes it more difficult for other businesses to survive . . . The marketplace may be cruel – but it's much more cruel when the government intervenes . . .

Shuffles.

'. . . It's the same with healthcare. – It should be run as a business, selling a commodity . . .

'No. No. No.'

'. . . Providers should be in direct competition with each other . . . They should know, as business people know, that if their prices rise above, or their standards fall below, those of their competitors they will face dire economic consequences . . .

'*Grrrrrrrrrr.*'

'. . . Again, the intervention of government, however well intentioned, would be catastrophic . . .

Fewer cries of 'No!'

'. . . Despite some concern over falling clinical standards – for which providers usually get the blame – security of income and employment for doctors and other healthcare staff tends to be given a higher priority by their various trade unions than is given to maintaining and improving the quality of care to patients . . .

Even fewer cries of 'No'.

'. . . State healthcare and welfare services become little more than a benevolent – and therefore economically irre-sponsible – employment agency . . .

Silence.

'. . . The providers of medical services should not be immune from the pressures and risks of any marketplace . . . Providers of inefficient, careless, expensive or impersonal services deserve to be put out of business by their competitors . . .

Silence.

'. . . Paying for quality has the corollary that we should not pay for poor quality . . .

Silence.

'. . . Doctors, nurses, technicians, social workers, porters and aids of all kinds, cleaners and all staff associated with healthcare should have minimal security of tenure in their employment . . .

Cries again of 'No!'

'. . . No they should not have security? or no they should?' . . .

Silence.

' . . . The nature of their work is too important for manifest incompetence to be tolerated . . . Peoples' lives are at risk . . .

Silence.

' . . . Doctors and all health care professionals will inevitably make mistakes at times – but we should no more tolerate an inadequate healthcare professional than we should tolerate a manifestly inadequate airline pilot . . .

'Whoops.'

'Yes, I thought that idea might startle you . . . But do those who insist that our state healthcare and welfare services are underfunded really care for those most in need? . . .

'Yes! Yes! Yes!'

'. . . If so, let them define the needy, define the need and define the resources that can be shown specifically to alleviate each need . . .

Silence.

'. . . If they are not prepared to make those definitions, we can reasonably assume that perhaps their true interest is not in helping those most in need, but rather in keeping them needy as a focus of shame and discontent . . . That wins votes – of a certain kind . . .

Shuffles.

'. . . It's surely more practical – and less dreamily idealistic – to believe that talent and human compassion can both thrive when exposed to market forces ... The alternative belief would be that talent and human compassion could survive the lifeless uniformity of state control . . .

'Yes! Yes! Yes!'

'. . . Yes it's a lifeless uniformity? . . .

'No! No! No!'

'. . . Don't get too upset . . . Remember I told you my job is to challenge you and make you think . . . I'm asking you this. – Which is more probable, considering human nature, that people will be prepared to care for others as well as for themselves? instead of themselves? or only for themselves? . . .

Silence.

'. . . Our only defence against the inevitability of a gulag is to be proud of ourselves as individuals and proud of the money that we earn through honest endeavour . . .

Silence.

'. . . We should reject all concepts of a something-for-nothing society. We should pay for quality and expect to get it. We should charge for quality and know that we must give it . . .

Silence.

'. . . We should acknowledge that private healthcare and private education are the first rather than the last things that should be paid for by each individual and family . . .

'No! No! No!'

'What about those who can't afford to pay?'

'. . . Can't afford to pay for what? – For food? For clothing? For shelter? . . . Sure, there are some people who will never have the capacity to pay for any of these things . . .

Silence.

'. . . But please remember the evidence that I showed you about charitable donations from the general public . . . The probability is that millions of people would be more than happy to pay a proportion of their income to help these disadvantaged people – because they're already giving them money voluntarily . . . They want to contribute so that those who are less fortunate can not only survive but live in dignity . . .

Applause.

'. . . But these donors might not be inclined to fight a revolution in support of free paracetamol for all . . . I might add that the NHS spent £7 million on paracetamol in 2013 . . . That's the cost of employing at least 300 more nurses . . .

Silence.

'. . . Yes. It might surprise you that it's as many as that . . . Nurses are not very well paid – in junior ranks – but salaries are by far the biggest cost in the NHS – or, for that matter, in the private healthcare sector . . .

Shuffles.

'. . . But it's the unthinking universality of provision in our state healthcare and welfare systems that causes inequalities . . . It does not concentrate on helping those most in need . . .

Silence.

'. . . Healthcare is not a universal birthright . . .

'Yes it is! Yes it is! Yes it is!'

'. . . I hear you, I hear you . . . But I ask you to consider whether we should have a two-tier system in healthcare . . .

'No! No! No!'

'No means tests!'

'. . . the same as in everything else. – One tier for those who can afford it and one for those who genuinely cannot . . . We already have means tests in our income tax system. Is that wrong? . . .

Silence.

'. . . The idea of a "flat tax" – ensuring that everybody pays the same proportion of his or her income in tax – or the idea of extending the taxation system into negative taxation – in order to distribute financial benefit – are not new ideas . . .

Silence.

'. . . They might work satisfactorily as a replacement for our extremely complicated – and therefore expensive – current taxation and welfare benefit systems . . .

Silence.

'. . . Giving money – hard cash – rather than some goods or services, has been shown to be a better method of achieving improved opportunity and outcome . . .

'Gimme gimme gimme!'

Laughter.

'. . . But now hear this . . . The difficulties of those who genuinely cannot afford private healthcare, private education, and private housing – in addition to private food, private clothing and private entertainment . . . if we are to be allowed to have any of these things privately . . . can readily be seen – and then resolved – by acting on an individual's positive or negative taxation status . . .

Shuffles.

'. . . The poverty trap, like the taxation trap at the other end of the economic scale, could be avoided through sliding scales of positive and negative taxation . . .

Silence.

'. . . And please remember – from a previous session – that most tax revenue is raised from the most numerous social classes – II, III and IV. – Corporation tax is, of course, handed on to the individual consumer in the form of higher prices . . . These same social classes – II, III and IV – also receive the majority of all state benefits simply because they are the most numerous . . .

Silence.

'. . . So what's the purpose of state taxation and welfare

systems that don't rob Peter to pay Paul – which some people would consider commendable – but rob Peter, muck about at great expense, and then give Peter back less than he could have bought for himself in the first place? . . .

'Social insurance!'

'. . . Yes, I understand that – and, as we've seen in the American schemes, this can be funded either by the state or by the private sector or by a combination of both . . .

Silence.

'. . . The point, of course, is political. – Paul is kept in the dark about the true costs of alternatives to State provision . . . He has to be made to believe that without State help he and his family would be diseased and destitute and would almost certainly die . . .

'Poor Paul . . .'

A few nervous laughs.

'. . . Only when state resources – which, even if not infinite, are taken from people who are richer than he is – like Peter – can Paul possibly survive . . .

Silence.

'. . . But this whole charade simply isn't true. – It cannot be true. – The state does not make money or any other resource. It spends it . . .

Drummings.

'. . . And with whatever level of resource the state begins, there must be less after the state has processed it . . .

Silence.

'. . . The only possible theoretical justification for state health and welfare services is the redistribution of resources so that those most in need of help – and most capable of benefiting from those resources – should be those who primarily receive it . . . This the State singularly fails to do . . .

Shuffles and throat clearings.

'. . . The solution should not be more state intervention but less . . .

'Shame!'

'. . . Paul should be left to look after himself . . . unless he's genuinely incapable of doing so . . . Peter should certainly care for himself . . . The arrogance of those who assume that Peter is a complete duffer and would not know how to look after himself is quite astounding . . . They are similarly arrogant in their assumption that nobody would look after Paul and others who have little or no capacity to look after themselves. – The evidence is to the contrary . . .

Silence.

'. . . As I've mentioned previously, even with all our state provision today, it's the Salvation Army and other private charities that truly help those most in need and whom the state pitifully neglects . . .

Silence.

'. . . There is today no shortage of private concern and compassion in our societies – in the UK and in America and in many other countries . . . The non-political aspects of Dr Tudor-Hart's *"Inverse Care Law"* itself illustrate individual concern for the socially and financially disadvantaged members of our societies . . .

Silence.

'. . . There's no reason to believe that this concern is rare. – Quite the opposite. – Certainly there's no reason to believe that resources must be channelled through the State . . . Warren Buffet gave billions to the Bill and Melinda Gates Foundation – because he knew his money would be well looked after and spent wisely . . .

Shuffles.

'. . . By contrast, the indignity of being given state handouts – that represent money that has been unwillingly prised away

277

from others in the form of taxation – is far more degrading than receiving willing gifts from private charities . . .

'No! No! No!'

'. . . Perhaps more importantly, private charity gives credit rather than criticism to the giver or producer, upon whom all future economic activity and welfare payments depend . . .

Silence.

'. . . Nor should we forget the magnificent contribution to clinical medicine and research made by the privately owned multinational pharmaceutical companies . . .

'*Hissss. Hissss. Hissss.*'

'. . . To give just two examples – over and above the beneficial effects of public health services – the invention of anaesthetics and antibiotics has totally transformed surgical and medical practice . . . And, as a result, dramatically improved the quality and expectation of life . . .

Silence.

'. . . And if there is thoughtless overprescription of many drugs, this can only be the fault of the doctors who write the prescriptions, not the fault of the companies who make and market them . . .

Shuffles.

'. . . We should look now to the USA, to the experience of individual free enterprise . . .

'*Hissss. Hissss. Hissss.*'

'. . . and look to the experience of corporate ventures such as the with-profit or not-for-profit Health Maintenance Organisations – HMOs. In these institutions – which combine insurance with service provision – general medical practice and hospitals work closely together . . . The clinical and financial interests of insurer, doctor and patient move in the same direction toward early and accurate diagnosis and treatment . . .

Silence.

'. . . Even so, as with other medical insurance organisations, they sometimes do whatever they can to get out of paying the bill . . .

'Ha!'

'. . . On the other hand, many of these organisations extend their insurance cover to include dependents, be they old or infirm, chronically sick or disabled, schizophrenic, alcoholic, unemployed or whatever. – ObamaCare is only an extension of this principle – that had already been established in the private sector . . .

Drummings.

'. . . It is also seen in the Kaiser Permanente insurance scheme in California. This has been going for over 60 years and currently has 9.3 million health plan members, 167,300 employees, 14,600 physicians, 37 medical centres, and 611 medical offices. For the year 2011, the not-for-profit Kaiser Foundation Health Plan and Kaiser Foundation Hospitals entities reported a combined $1.6 billion in net income on $47.9 billion in operating revenues . . .

Whistles.

'. . . The NHS is not unique. The state is not indispensable. There are alternatives . . .

Silence.

'. . . I suggest that we should re-examine the ideas of the UK healthcare and welfare systems and also continue to reappraise those of the USA . . .

Some drumming.

'. . . And incidentally, we should also have a good look at the the private medical system in the UK. – It's currently largely parasitic on the state system . . . Apart from doing major surgery, it most commonly treats only the least problematic clinical conditions . . .

Loud drummings.

'. . . We should start again with clear ideas about what we're trying to achieve and how it can be done . . . We should begin by adopting the prime principle of true capitalism – not the corrupt version seen in the behaviour of some bankers and brokers. We should pay for quality . . .

Drummings.

'. . . Ladies and gentlemen, as I said at the beginning, it's been my privilege to share these two semesters . . . Aaaargh! . . .

Laughter.

'. . . terms with you. I wish you well in your finals . . . I know that you will not be examined on anything that you may have learned here – whether you agree with my challenges to your thinking or not – but I hope you will understand me when I say that I believe these questions – and your own answers to them – will be fundamental to your future lives as working doctors.'

oOo

'You won't leave me . . . umm . . . will you, Lizzie? – as I progressively fall to bits? . . . My consultant told me good news and bad news . . . The good news is that the results of all the tests for weird and wonderful infections were negative.'

'Go on . . . What's the bad news?'

'The same as the good news . . . I haven't got an infectious cause.'

'So it's likely to be a neurological illness . . . umm . . . Untreatable – more or less.'

'Yes.'

'Oh . . . Oh my dear sweet Roddy, my lovely husband, my

hero . . . What a couple of crocks we are . . . What's to become of us?'

'That's what worries me . . . umm . . . You won't leave me? . . . Will you?'

'Umm . . . Let me think about this . . . er . . . Yes. – I'll leave you to the Garrick . . . in a brown paper parcel . . . done up with string and sealing wax.'

'No . . . really . . . Will you?'

'Let me read something to you . . . Yep . . . here it is . . . I keep a copy of it in my bag . . . always . . .

"And Ruth said, Intreate mee not to leave thee, or to returne from following after thee: for whither thou goest, I will goe; and where thou lodgest, I will lodge: thy people shall be my people, and thy God my God".'

'Yes . . . The 1611 King James Bible . . . The Book of Ruth.'

'You really are remarkable . . . dear Roddy . . . I do love you.'

'Even now?'

'Especially now. – You profess . . . in your precise way . . . to have no religious belief . . . and you know exactly where that quotation comes from – and even the date.'

'Of course I do . . . It's one of the finest pieces of literature in the English language – up there with Milton and Shakespeare . . . and Keats.'

'But it has no deeper significance for you? . . . umm . . . spiritually?'

'You've asked me that before . . . about the Bible . . . and religious belief on occasions . . . but we never really talk about it . . . Keep ourselves to ourselves – in some things – I s'pose.'

'And your answer's still the same? . . . even now? . . . with all this – for both of us?'

'Yes . . . and I doubt I'll change my beliefs – even now – when the chips are really down . . . umm . . . for both of us.'

'Yes . . . That's you – sticking to what you believe in . . . through thick and thin.'

'So do you.'

'I find the Bible such a comfort.'

'Even with your scientific training?'

'You forget . . . I deliver babies . . . I see real-life miracles every week – or I did.'

'D'you miss it?'

'Yes . . . a lot . . . Will you? . . . if it comes to that?'

'Yes . . . umm . . . Does the power of prayer . . . umm . . . help you – at a time like this? . . . practically?'

'Well I don't believe it's a magic fix . . . as some people do. – That's the scientist in me, I s'pose . . . healthily skeptical.'

'What is it then? . . . prayer?'

'For me? . . . umm . . . A psychological reminder . . . I pray for things like acceptance . . . and gratitude – not a shopping list.'

'Even at a time like this?'

'Yes – particularly at a time like this.'

'And you don't expect miracles?'

'Of course I expect miracles . . . They happen all the time . . . if we look for them.'

'But not for you and me? . . . umm . . . personally? . . . in the messes we're in now?'

'Not really . . . Maybe I don't pray hard enough . . . umm . . . I don't know.'

'You're a remarkable woman, Lizzie . . . I do love you.'

'Umm . . . Why did you mention Keats – almost as an afterthought?'

'Endymion . . . with Cynthia – right at the end of Book Four . . . "There is not one, No, no, not one, But thee.".'

* * *

'Oh Precious, you've really got me thinking now . . .'

'About me?'

'You as well.'

'Oh.'

'Umm . . . No, it was what you said about a healthcare and welfare system – anywhere – that doesn't work in practice is a bad system . . .'

'As you've said to me before now – and John Cleese says in *Fawlty Towers* – It's "bleedin' obvious". – Ha! – I loved those programmes when I watched them in the States . . . and now there's *Downton Abbey* . . . so British . . .'

'Yes – A joke and a caricature . . .'

'Well at least you know how to laugh at yourselves. One of the best comedians we had was Bob Hope – and, of course, he was English. – I remember seeing a replay of the crack he made when the Ruskies beat us in the space race, putting a bleeping Sputnik up there – and then a dog . . .'

'What did he say?'

'In that laid back way of his – when we needed our national pride bolstering a bit – he said something like, "What does it prove? – It only means their Germans are better than our Germans".'

'Ha! Yes . . . That's good . . . They still are. – They're running the whole of Europe now – and putting in puppet governments and dogmatic bureaucrats to run countries that borrow too much or don't vote the right way.'

'Hey, Phoebe . . . What's got into you? . . . I could've said that.'

'You probably did . . . hypnotising me.'

'I wouldn't do that . . . It's a serious clinical tool – in properly trained hands.'

'I'll have to take your word for it . . . They don't teach us anything like that here . . .'

'What do they teach you?'

'Drugs and CBT – just as you said.'

'Well I do know something about the system over here . . . As you know, the UK has been my home for five years now . . . except for trips back to Columbia.'

'Don't push your luck.'

'Huh?'

'You may know *about* the UK – but that doesn't mean you know it.'

'Yeah . . . That's what they used to say about some of the whiteys in Harlem. – They may know a lot about music but it doesn't make them into musicians . . .'

'You racist pig! – But I guess that knowing a lot about medicine and surgery, and the rest, doesn't make us into doctors . . .'

'You got that right! – And the same's true in the big picture too . . . Ideas in healthcare and welfare systems may superficially look good in theory – but they're no use if they don't work in practice.'

'Well the NHS – that you're always going on about – works very well in practice for people who have no financial choice.'

'Umm . . . You really believe that, don't you? . . .'

*   *   *

'My mother saw you recently. She recommended me to come to see you. Evidently you told her that you built and ran a rehab.'

'Yes, I did . . . It was a wonderful time in my life. – I loved every minute of it . . . even the difficult times . . . In some ways the bigger the challenge the more determined I was to defeat it.'

'I understand that very well . . . umm . . . Why don't you do it now – work for someone else . . . or set up another rehab?'

'I doubt anyone would employ me – certainly not the state . . . I'm too old for them – past it.'

'But, with your experience, you could teach them all sorts of valuable things.'

'Thank you – but all any teacher can do is to help people to learn . . . I gather your sister's a medical student. She'll understand that principle . . . umm . . . It depends on having willing pupils.'

'Surely the Department of Health wants to learn anything they can . . . about addiction?'

'They know much more than I do – intellectually – on the subject . . . They have researchers and academics. They write papers and produce reports. – And that's all very valuable.'

'So what d'you do now?'

'I'm still a clinician – although nowadays I work as a counsellor, not as a doctor. – I work with people, trying to help them get what they want in life . . . I don't want to spend another 23 years dealing with admin – and quality control and inspections and all that stuff. – It's excellent in theory but it gets in the way of anyone wanting to try out new ideas . . . or spend time with patients rather than on computers.'

'I want to be a counsellor . . . and build my own rehab.'

'I shall discourage you as much as I can.'

'What? . . . Why? . . . Have I done something wrong?'

'No . . . I say that to everybody.'

'Why? – My mother said that you have a reputation for being a maverick . . . but I never expected anything like this!'

'Hang on a bit . . . There are two reasons . . . First it's the hardest thing I've ever done – counselling and creating and running a rehab.'

'Why?'

'Because I try to sell something that people don't want.'

'Huh?'

'If I were to sell alcohol – or drugs – people would beat a path to my door . . . I sell abstinence. – They don't want that. – They want to learn how to drink . . . or use drugs or anything else . . . sensibly.'

'That never worked for me.'

'Nor me . . . People only come to see me when they're in pain – because nothing else has worked and they can't see any way forward.'

'I couldn't see any way forward . . . in the NHS Mental Health Unit.'

'Nor could I – in the private mental nursing home I was sent to – as a patient – many years ago . . . I was in a blank room on my own – no pictures, no mirror, no view from the window except of the brick wall five feet away . . . After three days with nobody coming to see me – not even the psychiatrist who put me in there . . . nobody other than the lady who brought the food – I was going nuts . . . even if I wasn't nuts already.'

'Yes . . . I felt that.'

'In which case you've paid your entrance fee – to the addicts club.'

'Oh . . . umm . . . Thanks.'

'Yes – I get hopping mad when people say, "We're all addicted to something". – It simply isn't true. – Only 15 to 20% of people have addiction problems of any kind . . . I believe they're due to genetically inherited defects in the mood centres of the brain – the limbic system.'

'You've got me there.'

'You don't need to know about all that neurotransmission stuff yet – or about hepatitis or HIV . . . or methadone maintenance . . . or the principles of harm-minimisation.'

'Why not?'

'It's all designed to get you paper qualifications . . . so that universities and employers can't be sued if you make a mistake . . . None of that stuff helps patients to get well . . . They have a feeling illness, a spiritual illness – and they need a feeling treatment, a spiritual treatment.'

'I don't do God.'

'Nor do I. – My "Higher Power" is the Twelve Step programme of AA . . . It's worked for me for the last 30 years so I'm not going to give it up now . . . I don't want to go back to my days of active addiction. – Too painful.'

'So what d'you do now?'

'The same as you were told in Hazelden . . . I still put the basic principles of recovery into practice in my own life – and use them in my outpatient rehab – today.'

'After all those years?'

'One day at a time. – It's easy that way . . . On my anniversaries I only ever pick up a "one day" chip.'

'Why?'

'It's my personal insurance policy . . . If I do relapse, I've thrown away only one day of recovery – so it'll be easy to get back on the programme.'

'Ha! – You make it sound so simple.'

'It is simple . . . Surely you've heard it called, "a simple programme for complicated people"?'

'No – but that sounds good to me . . . umm . . . What was the second reason you wanted to discourage me from being a counsellor?'

'Wait.'

'But how about the training? – What should I do for that?'

'Wait.'

'Is that all?'

'Yes.'

'Oh . . . umm . . . how long?'

'Two years.'

'Two years!'

'Yes. – Your own recovery won't be secure enough before then – and that's only the beginning.'

'Why? . . . umm . . . Why not?'

'Because you won't be tough enough to take the knocks . . . the abuse from patients – and families . . . and doctors and all sorts of people.'

'Why? . . . Why would they be abusive when you're trying to help them?'

'They'll do the same to you as they do to me . . . and as I did to the people who tried to help me. – I took them apart. – They were taking away the things that mattered to me . . . the things that I could rely on to change the way I felt.'

'And your family? Were they abusive to you?"

'No . . . As I often acknowledge, I treated family and friends – the people who really did try to help me – as enemies . . . And I treated my enemies – the people who just wanted to sell me something and get me into even greater difficulty – as friends.'

'Yes. – That's me.'

'Yup . . . If you say so . . . umm . . . As I said, welcome to the addicts' club.'

'So what do I do right now?'

'The basics . . . Work the Steps every day, go to meetings of AA – to counter your denial, the part of your illness that says you haven't got it – get a sponsor . . . someone to guide you in AA in working the Steps . . . read some AA literature every day, stay abstinent from everything that affects you addictively. – And go on as many psychology courses as you can . . .'

'All that?'

'And more . . . You might ask your father – when you're registered as a psychology student of some kind – if he'd pay

Part 4

for you to go to the *Evolution of Psychotherapy* conference in Anaheim, California . . . They hold it once every four years – so they can book the top people in the world on their faculty . . . That's what attracts over 7,000 delegates – like me.'

'You? – I'd have thought you'd be *on* the faculty.'

'I go to learn – and I learn a huge amount . . . four years' worth every time . . . It's sad that so very few people go from the UK.'

Why's that?'

'Why should people want to learn new things if they already work in a system that's the envy of the world?'

'From what I saw in the . . . Oh. – You're being ironic . . . umm . . . All those lectures – in California – the sheer amount of it . . . sounds like brain-washing to me.'

'My brain needs a good wash every so often . . . I'm an addict – by nature . . . born that way . . . always was and always will be – even though I don't do addictive things nowadays . . . Not for 30 years.'

'Umm . . . There's so much to take in.'

'. . . And the rest . . . Basically, I'm suggesting to you that you do the most difficult thing in the world for any addict to do.'

'What's that?'

'I told you. – Wait.'

*   *   *

I'm so lucky – so very very lucky – to have found a man like Precious . . . Integrity – that's it – that's the name of the game . . . God, I do hope I can land him . . . that we can get together . . . He's everything I could ever want in a man.

oOo

'Speaking as your father . . . er . . . James . . . I have to say you've done brilliantly – turning your life around like this.'

'So do I.'

'Thank you both . . . umm . . . I'll try to be worthy of that.'

'Sure you will . . . Your mother and I both started from difficult beginnings.'

'Yes . . . we had to find our own way. – No money in either of our families.'

'We've always been worried about giving you and Phoebe too much . . . Entitlement culture, that sort of thing . . . Seen it at the commercial bar sometimes – in pupils – when they've had it cushy at home . . . No commitment to work or finding their own way forward.'

'Yes . . . umm . . . I'm . . . er . . . sorry I conned you out of so much.'

'Ha! – There you are, Roddy – I told you he'd got your number . . . as the bank of first resort – not the last. – Umm . . . Well, that as well.'

'I'm not proud of myself.'

'Nor should you be.'

'Don't be too hard on the boy, Lizzie . . . He's doing his best.'

'I was told – in the family group – to show a bit of "tough love".'

'I think what they meant, mother, was that you give the love and the toughness – tough for you to give it as well as for me to receive it – not put the boot in.'

'You stay out of this . . . I'm trying to train your father . . . umm . . . money's going to be tight . . . er . . . tighter than it has been . . . for a long time.'

'Oh, I'm sure we can find a way . . .'

'Don't say that! . . . James can hear you . . . He may be an

. . . er . . . addict – Oh, I do so hate that word! – but he's not deaf . . . or stupid.'

'Gosh, mother, that's a real compliment – "not stupid" – umm . . . coming from you.'

'Well I'm certainly not stupid! . . . Just because I . . . umm . . . can't work at the moment.'

'Sorry, mother . . . I said it wrong . . . I meant, "You have every reason to call me stupid" – after all the stupid things I've done.'

'Good for you, James. – That's the spirit . . . umm . . . While you're in a listening mode . . . er . . . I hope it lasts . . .'

'It will, father, it will . . . I promise.'

'James? – What did they tell you in Hazelden? – in the family group . . . when we were there together?'

'Oh . . . oh yes . . . "No promises. – Let action prove your intention." . . . umm . . . something like that.'

'Something very like that.'

'Yes, mother . . . umm . . . I'm listening, father.'

'Yes . . . Good . . . I have to tell you . . . er . . . we don't want Phoebe to know this – with her finals coming up . . . but I've had a spot of bother with me right leg – and me balance is a bit off – and the specialist . . . after all the tests . . . told me I might . . . umm . . . probably . . . have a neurological illness – a nerve problem.'

'Oh you poor man. – How dreadful!'

'Not so bad so far . . . Just a nuisance really . . .'

'It's far more than that, love . . . James can take it. – He's grown up now . . . all of a sudden.'

'Well . . . I . . . er . . . I'm not sure how long I'll be able to do me work . . . umm . . . Can't carry me files too well. Huh! Wonder what'll happen if me other leg goes wonky . . . And the word will soon get round that I'm off me game . . . It's a cruel world at the bar – competitive.'

'Yes . . . like brokering. – And I'm very sorry that this has happened to you – and on top of mother's problems.'

'We'll survive . . . somehow.'

'Anyway, all I would like . . . sometime in the future . . . is a little help to start me off – with a rehab.'

'I'm sure we could find a . . .'

'No.'

* * *

Well that's done – the lectures – for another year . . . Dramatically this time. Ha! – Never expected to fall in love with a student . . . Wonder where that'll lead . . .

* * *

That young girl I saw – months ago – premature menopause at 28 . . . Nothing to be done . . . IVF with a donor egg maybe – but the possibility? – and ethics? – with all her genetic . . . umm . . . defects – no – disorders – no – difficulties – no – differences – yes – phew! – That's better, sounds better . . . such a sensitive issue . . . She deserves all the help she can get . . . Rights? . . . Responsibilities? . . . God, I don't know . . . NHS treatment? . . . Depends on cost, I s'pose . . . Depriving someone else of something . . . Wouldn't give her a university place. – Couldn't use it with an IQ of 65 . . . Why should medical issues be a special case? – considering what would or would not be a beneficial use of expensive resources? – Got to look at costs and benefits . . . to everyone . . . Heavens what a dilemma! . . . Dreadful! . . . And what about Roddy and me? . . . Never really needed the state . . . until now – or pretty soon if something doesn't pick up . . . for either of us . . . Roddy and I paid taxes into it for years – just like we paid the insurance company's premiums . . . What's our entitlement now? . . . Ha! – Nothing definite from our insurance company from now on . . . Making one claim makes future premiums more expensive – or leads to things being excluded from future cover . . . Ah well . . . the State's always there to pick up the pieces . . . Or is it? . . . Worrying, really . . . Either way . . .

* * *

God, oh God oh God! . . . What now? . . . I'm glad James told me about mum and dad. – I need to know . . . for my own reasons . . . Hmm . . . Typical of them not to tell me themselves . . . not wanting to worry me before finals . . . Hmm . . . Phobias are really difficult to treat – and neurological problems impossible – except for slowing down the progression . . . a bit . . . if you're lucky . . . Yeah. – They're both in trouble . . . big trouble . . . And where does that leave me? – in my career? and with Precious? . . . Someone'll have to care for them . . . Me probably . . . Ha! The eternal fate of daughters – looking after the people my mother calls wrinklies . . . and then crumblies . . . and then powderies . . . Oh God, I'm not up to this . . . really not . . . I'm not built for it. – It's been like Hamlet. – So quick. – 'And yet within a month' . . . Well, two or three . . . Our lives are falling apart – all of us . . .

* * *

'Life isn't easy, father.'
    'Who ever said it was?'
    'Nobody . . . I mean I discover what I really want to do in life . . . and there's so many obstacles – time, money, training, bureaucracy . . .'

'Sounds par for the course.'

'But I want to do something useful . . . make a difference.'

'If you want the privilege of working in the private sector – being your own boss and putting your own ideas into practice – you have to pay the price.'

'But I thought the private sector was all about having good working conditions and making your own money – on your own terms . . . with no hassle.'

'It's about providing a service that someone wants . . . and is prepared to pay for. – Ask your mother about it. She'll tell you.'

'Tell me what?'

'The 3 "As" of private practice – in any healthcare business.'

'Go on. – You tell me. – I'm very interested.'

'Oh, all right . . . Number one – Availability . . . When the phone goes – day or night, Christmas Day or whenever – you first say, "Yes" . . . and then you ask, "Where?" and "When?".'

'Yes . . . I've never known mum without her mobile . . . She was making calls – not just to you – when we were in America . . . umm . . . What's the second one?'

'Affability . . . She has to be polite – even to the most God-awful unpleasant idiots.'

'Why?'

'Because they're customers . . . She's in a service industry. – She makes profits from the sick . . . Proud to do so . . . She's not interested in the worried well . . . Like you, she wants to see people who really need help.'

'That's good.'

'And she has to make a profit or go out of business . . . or do nothing and get nothing. – She was telling me recently . . . apropos of nothing in particular . . . about some NHS specialists who try their hand at private practice but can't make it – so they have to crawl back into the NHS.'

'Why?'

'Because they're no good at anything else . . . They've been feather-bedded all their lives in the state system. They've become dependent on it . . . So are some patients . . . umm . . . not all.'

'No. – I meant why couldn't the specialists make it? . . . privately?'

'No head for running a business properly . . . no manners – bloody rude sometimes – heads in the clouds . . . And no real talent . . . just examination certificates . . . That's the third "A". – Ability.'

'That might be true of GPs but surely it can't be true of specialists.'

'Oh yes it can . . . They can't live – for the rest of their professional lives – off a couple of exams they took in their twenties and thirties . . . They might get away with that in the NHS but not in the private sector . . . No guaranteed tenure. Same's true in America. – Got to reapply for their own job every few years over there.'

'Oh.'

'And I can't take things for granted either . . . It's very competitive at the bar. – Like opera singers or conjurers. – You're only as good as your last performance or trick . . . And I've got to stay sharp in my trade – or the supply will dry up . . . Wasn't that true for you? – as a broker?'

'Umm . . . Yes, yes of course – but that's only money.'

'What d'you mean "only money"? . . . You can tell a man by his attitude to money. – Despise money, you despise yourself.'

'Why?'

'Because you don't value the skill, time and effort it took to make it . . . You take yourself for granted – no pride . . . And other people – no respect for them . . . Can't run a business that way . . . or a life.'

'Oh.'

'That's one of the things that goes wrong in the NHS – taking people for granted . . . Doctors, nurses, patients – all as bad as each other in this . . . Can't afford any of that in the private sector . . . It's the sheer arrogance that gets to me – the "holier than thou" attitude behind the behaviour . . .'

'Meaning?'

'Because something's free – no direct charge to the patient at the time of need – it means that it's virtuous . . . regardless of the quality of care given . . . Your mother – or anyone else charging a fee anywhere – can't get away with that . . . Customers leave if they don't feel they're getting good service.'

'Yes. That was certainly true in brokering.'

'But they can't leave the state sector. – Most people . . . the patients . . . They've no other choice . . . It's a monopoly.'

'Wow! – That's the father I know . . . umm . . . addressing the jury!'

'Maybe . . . but y'know, James, if an argument isn't persuasive it doesn't work – and therefore it's a bad argument . . . Same's true for the ideas behind the whole of the Welfare State . . . If the ideas don't work in practice they're bad ideas.'

'Yes . . . umm . . . you can certainly persuade me – but not Joe Public – on that one . . . umm . . . Does that make it a bad argument?'

'No . . . It means that people have been drugged into submission – by the promises of politicians . . . and by the belief that they've really got no alternative.'

'Oh.'

'Marx called religion the opium of the masses . . . He was wrong. – It's the Welfare State that fits that description.'

Part 4

'Ha! . . . That turns Marx on his head.'

'The whole of the Welfare State – with all its ideas – needs turning upside down and given a good shake.'

'But what about those who can't afford to pay?'

'That's the same argument – the same emotional blackmail – as saying, "What about the children?" when proposing a cut in welfare payments. – What sort of life are the children having . . . is anyone having . . . in a state dependency?'

'Not much of one, I imagine . . . umm . . . Definitely not in the Mental Health Unit.'

'Y'see James, a welfare state's no different from a totalitarian state . . . really . . . if you take the trouble to think about it – which people generally don't . . . because they don't want to . . . The state's in charge and that's that.'

'So how can we change that? . . . How can I change it? . . . In my work? . . . In my life?'

'With difficulty. – Like coming off drugs, I s'pose.'

'Don't go there, father. – Just don't go there . . . You wouldn't want to know . . . Oh, by the way, you'd be so proud . . . Mother gave me a speech worthy of you . . . in New York.'

'Why d'you think I married her? . . . umm . . . No. – Don't answer that.'

'Ha! . . . No . . . But you're not answering me. – How do I make a difference?'

'You'll have to find that out for yourself . . . in your own life . . . as you go along. – Everyone who got where he is had to begin where he was . . . umm . . . or she was, of course.'

'You're very politically correct all of a sudden, father.'

'Nothing to do with it . . . Simple good manners – and reality . . . in the West . . . That's the freedom – in an open society . . . Read Hayak.'

'Must I?'

'Yes . . . *The Road to Serfdom* will show you exactly why freedom is so valuable. Freedom of speech . . . say something unpopular, outside the party line . . . Freedom of the press to print or report something that the politicians – or even the editors themselves – disagree with . . . And freedom of action – provided no one else's freedom is jeopardised . . . The only alternative to exercising these freedoms is to stay stuck on the sidelines . . . passively watching while the politicians progressively take more power.'

*   *   *

'The more I think about your final lecture . . . Well done, by the way – you really socked it to us – and the more I reflect on my family's medical problems – and I s'pose the more I look at my own position – the more I realise that you've turned my head . . . umm . . . got through to it.'

'The more I think about our relationship, the more I love your head – whichever way round it is.'

'Umm . . . Dear, dear Precious – I'm not in a good place.'

'Oh . . . Why? . . . umm . . . Anything I've done? . . . umm . . . or said?'

'You've done nothing . . . You've been the kindest and most genuine man I've ever met . . . I struggle with your ideas – particularly now I have to work out all my own and put them into practice.'

'After finals?'

'No . . . Right now.'

'What ideas?'

'Putting the Direct Care Law alongside the Inverse Care Law . . . It's very neat – the way you dig out the inadequacies and inconsistencies in the thinking . . .'

'That's what I do for a living.'

'. . . but I'm still not sure that I can make the jump into seeing altruism as a vice.'

'I didn't say it was.'

'You inferred it.'

'No I didn't . . . I said – more or less – that it could be a political Trojan horse – so that people with totalitarian instincts can pass them off as benevolent.'

'That's all politics . . . I'm interested in real people – like you and me . . . and my family.'

'All life is politics . . . Ideas, values, principles – and how to put them into practice.'

'. . . So that the fittest survive?'

'They do that anyway – in any system.'

'I guess it depends on how you define "fittest".'

'Yes . . . Darwin meant "most suited to the environment" – or something like that . . . Politicians have twisted his words to mean "deliberately at other people's expense".'

'It comes to the same thing in the end. – The weakest, the ones with least capacity to look after themselves, go to the wall.'

'Or the firing squad . . . or the Islamic State knife . . . or even hurt themselves – when people with no power have times of loneliness and despair all on their own . . . They go to the wall just the same as any victim of external force.'

'Tell me.'

'People can be defenceless in many ways.'

'I'm talking about people who are ill or old or . . . or . . . what's it? . . . can't cope.'

'Yes . . . And those are the very people that tyrants – throughout history and in many many ways – say they want to protect and support.'

'Not all people who want to care for the . . . umm . . . less fortunate . . . are tyrants.'

'But some are . . . the ones who want power.'

'We all want power – in some ways.'

'Yes . . . We all want the capacity to influence . . . but not necessarily control.'

'But society has to be controlled to some extent . . . Otherwise we'd have riots – as we've seen all over the world – particularly in hot summers . . . and when people highlight political grievances.'

'People protest – you yourself protest – when there's no clear alternative . . . when the people in power don't want to give it up – and always want more.'

'I protest when things are obviously wrong.'

'And the people you protest against will protest back – because they believe that you're obviously wrong.'

'So what's the solution?'

'The minimum state . . . Make it as small as possible – just sufficient for people not to feel the necessity to carry guns and knives to protect themselves and their families, their personal possessions and their legal contracts.'

'But what about people who have none of those things? Who's going to fight for them?'

'Lots of people – voluntarily and gladly – but not the state.'

'The state's reliable . . . volunteers aren't.'

'That's what statists would like you to believe – but the opposite has been more true in history. – You saw an illustration of that in the London Olympic Games . . . Volunteers made it tick.'

'I'm not interested in history – or the Olympics. – This very minute I'm interested in me and my family.'

'Oh . . . umm . . . Sorry . . . – What's up?'

'Everything's up... James is an addict . . . umm . . . How

many times will he relapse? . . . Mum's had to stop work after suffering an anaesthetic awareness – she got re-traumatised when she went back into an operating theatre . . . hoping she might start work again soon . . . And now dad's been diagnosed with some form of neurological illness. – What that means for the future God alone knows.'

'I had no idea . . . I'm so sorry.'

'It's not you – I love talking with you, discussing ideas – but this is real life . . . What am I – and my family – going to do? . . . The bottom's fallen right out of our world – in every way . . . professionally, financially, socially I expect . . . and you and I talk metaphysics!'

'No . . . For once in my adult life, I don't want to do that. – I want to talk about you and me.'

'So do I.'

'Good.'

'Dear Precious, sweet love, it's not good . . . I can't see how we can make a go of it . . . I'm going to have to look after my family – no one else will – and the state's got nothing signifi-cant to offer . . . I've worked that out already.'

'I'll help . . . I'll be right beside you, girl.'

'. . . "Doctor" very soon – or maybe even that won't be possible now . . .'

'I'm not going anywhere without you . . . I don't fall in love that easily . . . You're my kind of girl . . . umm . . . woman . . . umm . . . doctor. – And I told you that talent and human compassion can both thrive when exposed to market forces . . . And . . . umm . . . I said . . . umm . . . inferred . . . it's more probable – in human nature – that people will be prepared to care for others as well as themselves – rather than instead of themselves . . . umm . . . Please give me credit for wanting to do something altruistic – charitable if you like – just for you.'

'But that's just it . . . I'm prepared to sacrifice my personal life – and maybe my professional life as well – for my family . . . for the time being . . . but I'm not having you sacrificing yours for me. – You hardly know me . . . and I'm tough going at the best of times.'

'Ha! I know that . . . Hell! – I shouldn't have said that.'

'But it's true . . . And, y'see . . . I can behave altruistically toward my family – but I won't have you destroying your life for me and my lot . . . It's too much to ask.'

'It's my choice – and I choose it.'

'Listen to me, Precious . . . You've loved before – and you will again . . . I never have . . . until now. – And I'll prove it to you . . . I want you – in advance – to imagine me sitting on the end of my timeline, twiddling my toes in the infinite . . . and thinking of you – every day for the rest of my life . . .'

'Is this "Goodbye"?'

'Yes.'

'Just like that?'

'Yes.'

'No onions?'

'No.'

oOo

Lightning Source UK Ltd.
Milton Keynes UK
UKOW06n1913280515

252481UK00001B/1/P

9 781871 013962